DEATH SENTENCE

An addictive and heart-pounding crime thriller

BILL KITSON

DI Mike Nash Book 17

JOFFE BOOKS

Joffe Books, London
www.joffebooks.com

First published in Great Britain in 2024

Cover art by Nick Castle

ISBN: 978-1-83526-289-4

For Val, my partner in crime.

CHAPTER ONE

The place was cold. It was dark. It felt damp. Where was he? The last thing he remembered was picking his girl up and taking her back to the flat. They had only recently met, and they both recognized that it was no great romance, merely the chance to satisfy their physical needs. They had done this on several previous occasions.

This time, they had only been inside the apartment for a few minutes, and were in the process of undressing, when the doorbell rang. At that time of night, a caller was all but unheard of. He'd wondered briefly if this was an aggrieved boyfriend, but she'd already assured him there was nobody like that for him to worry about. The persistent ringing caused him to answer it, but apart from a momentary view of the man standing outside, his memory was totally blank. Eventually, as consciousness returned, he realized his hands were tied together, as were his ankles. He had clearly been abducted, but why? And where was this place he'd been brought to?

Then, as his senses attuned themselves to the new reality, he heard breathing nearby. He was not alone, but who was there with him? He was no nearer a solution when there was a sudden, bright beam of light he guessed might be from

1

a torch. He attempted to speak, but the rough woollen gag across his mouth restricted the utterance to a mumble.

A voice spoke, the words making little sense. 'This isn't personal, but you know too much.'

A second, brighter flash of light was followed by a searing pain in his chest. Another flash, then darkness.

The killer turned to his other captive and apologized, 'I'm sorry, you were simply in the wrong place at the wrong time.' He fired two more shots. Both his victims were dead. He turned to leave, confident there was little chance of the remains ever being found, not in this isolated place.

He had only taken a couple of strides when there was an ominous rumbling sound. He glanced round, horrified, as his head torch illuminated the wall of the mine, which was collapsing towards him. He ran as quickly as possible in such a confined space. His only goal was survival, and that entailed getting as far away from the devastation behind, as fast as he could. Seconds later, the rumble became an explosion. Already loosened by prolonged rainfall during the previous winter and spring, a cascade of limestone rocks from the roof descended, almost blocking the tunnel behind him. The killer's victims were all but entombed inside a chamber of death.

The way out was a desperate and dangerous route. But then, he was more than desperate — and he knew of no alternative. As he fled, small rocks bombarded him, hitting his head, his hands and arms, until one of the larger pieces of stone struck his wrist, knocking the gun from his grasp. Eventually, he saw the pale glow of daylight ahead. He reached the edge of the tunnel network, seconds before a gigantic rush of air propelled him like a cork from a bottle. Helpless to avoid the fall, the assassin plunged forward, coming to rest in a small dip covered in rye grass, moss and heather. He had been lying there for several minutes before he raised his head, and having glanced round, got cautiously to his feet.

Satisfied that his undignified exit from the tunnel had gone unwitnessed, the killer began to walk, slowly at first, before picking up speed as he covered the distance to his vehicle. He might not have seen anyone watching the hill-side, but that didn't mean the rockslide would pass unnoticed. The last thing he wanted was to draw attention to this remote location.

* * *

The boy watched in amusement as the dog chased a rabbit across the field. There was little chance of the Labrador catching such a small, agile creature, he thought. Seconds later, his theory was proved correct as the rabbit dived into a tiny hole, obviously one of the entrances to its warren. The teenager whistled, and the dog turned tail, loping gracefully back in answer to the signal.

It was unusual for someone of his age to enjoy walking long distances to exercise a boisterous Labrador, especially this early in the morning, but he wasn't exactly a run-of-the-mill adolescent. After several years at boarding school, he had become accustomed to responding to the rising bell at seven fifteen, and even during the holidays, this habit was hard to break.

The other reason for volunteering was the request from his stepmother, who was in the advanced stages of pregnancy and suffering acute discomfort. 'Of course I'll walk the dog, as long as you're going to be OK on your own,' he'd told her.

Seconds after the Labrador returned to his side, the boy heard a loud bang, closely followed by another. The sounds echoed, as if in an enclosed space, but he was able to recognize them as gunshots. That wasn't right, he thought — nobody would be shooting at this time of year. The grouse season hadn't started yet, so none of the local moors would be entertaining guests. After a few seconds, he heard the noise again, and once more there were two reports. Glancing down, he noticed the dog had also reacted to the sound. She was staring across the field in the direction of the noise. With countless generations of gundogs in her pedigree, her response was an inherited reflex.

He had barely time to absorb these puzzling facts when another, louder, even more ominous sound dwarfed the earlier noises. For a second or two, he thought this was thunder. He glanced up into the clear blue sky — not thunder, that was certain. As his gaze switched to the hillside he noticed the grass and shrubs alongside one of the small apertures in the cliff face swaying, but there wasn't even a zephyr of breeze. This puzzled him. He knew the gap he was looking at was an entrance to a series of disused workings, a lead mine intriguingly named the Hand of Glory.

A sudden gust caused his hair to ruffle, and as he watched, a cloud of dust, accompanied by small particles of debris, was emitted from the adit, propelled by a powerful blast of wind. His apprehension turned to fear as he felt the ground beneath his feet tremble. For a moment, he wondered if this was an earthquake, but then the quivering ceased.

Only one thing could have caused such a disturbance, he reasoned. The limestone forming the hillside opposite where he was standing must have suffered an internal collapse. Recalling what he'd believed to be gunshots, the boy was horrified by the possibility that someone might be trapped inside the abandoned workings.

He turned for home, and began running across the fields, his sprint indicative of panic. The dog bounded alongside him, delighted by this new game. Several minutes later they approached the back garden of their property. As he vaulted the dry stone wall, the teenager shouted, his voice conveying the stress he was under, 'Mum! Mum! I think something awful just happened.'

It was a good few minutes before he had calmed down sufficiently to begin his explanation. As he was telling her, she heard a background noise, but the significance didn't register until much later.

* * *

In his office at Helmsdale police station, DI Mike Nash was reading a report into the latest exploit of an irritating offender they had so far failed to arrest. The man had become a nuisance, exposing himself to women in the street, in car parks, close to town centres, and on one occasion, in a corridor leading to the toilets inside a local café. The offender, nicknamed 'Free Willy' by Detective Constable Viv Pearce, had avoided capture for over a year. Viv, a tall Antiguan, was the only male member of Nash's team, and was known for his bawdy sense of humour. The team was depleted at the moment, with Viv away on a last-minute course and Detective Sergeant Clara Mironova on holiday.

Nash's perusal came to an abrupt end when his mobile rang. One glance at the screen caused him to snatch up the handset. 'Alondra, is everything OK?'

His breathing and heartbeat returned to normal at her response. 'Relax, Mike, everything's fine. I asked Daniel to walk Teal for me this morning because baby's becoming restless, and while he was out, he heard something alarming. It upset him so much he came dashing home. Luckily, I was out in the garden and I heard him shouting, but I'll put him on and let him explain.'

Seconds later, Nash heard his son's voice, 'Hi, Pa, I was watching Teal chase a rabbit in the fields, and I heard what sounded like gunshots. They seemed to have come from the foot of Stark Ghyll, but they were a bit odd. Then there was a big explosion, and a load of sh . . . er . . . rubbish came flying out of one of the old mine entrances. Then the ground began to shake. That frightened me silly. I told Mum, and we didn't know what to do, so we thought we'd leave it to you.'

Nash noticed with a glow of pleasure that Daniel had referred to Alondra as 'Mum', which was something new, but his overriding concern was to ensure the facts were correct. 'Are you sure the sounds you heard were gunshots?'

'Yes, I am. And Teal thought so too. She stopped what she was doing and stared across at the mine entrance.'

'When you said they sounded a bit odd, what did you mean?'

'They echoed, as if they were in an enclosed space, not like out on the moors, or in the woods.'

During the previous winter, Daniel had acted as a beater during several pheasant shoots on the Winfield Estate, so he was well used to the sound of gunfire. This didn't sound like a false alarm. 'I think somebody might have been fooling about inside the mine and got trapped, perhaps by a roof collapse, because I can't think of any other explanation for the sudden blast of wind, and the cloud of stuff flying through the air.'

'Did you see or hear anyone near the mine while you were out with Teal? I mean, before or after the explosions?'

'No, Pa, I didn't see or hear anything.'

Nash heard a mutter of conversation before Alondra came on the phone. 'Mike, while Daniel was telling me what had happened, I heard a car engine. Someone drove along the lane past the front of the house.'

The lane from Wintersett village passing Smelt Mill Cottage was a dead end, used only by occasional twitchers or hill-walkers.

'OK, leave it with me. I'll take it from here.'

CHAPTER TWO

Nash knew this was not something he could deal with. It was all very well for him to believe Daniel's story, and to know his son was not prone to exaggeration, but persuading others would be no easy task. His first obstacle came when he phoned Detective Superintendent Jackie Fleming, his immediate superior. 'Jackie, I think we have an emergency I can't deal with.'

Based at HQ in Netherdale, her reaction was guarded, to put it mildly, and was not exactly what Nash had been hoping to hear. 'You're expecting me to alert all the emergency services on the word of your son? I'll have a word with the chief and see what she thinks.'

Nash needed her to see the urgency of the situation. As she was about to end the call, he issued a warning. 'If you feel you must do so, I can't argue with your decision. I just hope you don't come to regret it, because this could be a disaster in more ways than one.'

'What do you mean by that?' Her tone was angry, and provoked a similar response from Nash.

'There could be people trapped inside the old mine workings. If they're alive, every minute, every second wasted increases the danger they're in. A quick response is vital in situations such as these, because that represents their best, probably only, hope of survival.'

Nash's warning proved effective. Minutes later, Ruth Edwards, the chief constable, phoned, asking him to repeat what Daniel had told him. Moments later she said, 'OK, I'm contacting Cave Rescue and the ambulance service. They'll want guiding to the exact location. I need you to phone Daniel and ensure he's on hand to lead them there.'

Nash had only just finished his call to Alondra when Ruth Edwards phoned again. 'The emergency services are on their way.'

'I know, I heard them leaving,' Nash replied. It was some years since all three services had been merged into a new modern building sharing the same site.

'Of course, I forgot your office overlooks the exit. Cave Rescue are the nearest to Wintersett and should arrive first. I've told the leader of the team, Jack Owen, to call at your house for directions.'

'I've just spoken to Daniel. He'll be waiting for them in the lane.'

'I think I should also try to get a mining engineer on standby, in case he's needed to inspect the site, to assess the potential risk for anyone attempting to enter the old workings. But first, I need to ensure it won't all be an unnecessary waste of time and resources. That isn't to say I don't believe Daniel's account of what he saw and heard, but I'd rather not be alarmist.'

Nash knew this was the best he could get and had to settle for it. Before she rang off, he told her, 'I'm heading home to check if Alondra's OK. She's supposed to be resting — some hope! And I want to know Daniel's got over the shock. I'll also wait and see what transpires at the mine.' He attempted to inject a little humour by adding, 'I just hope there isn't a sudden crime spree during my absence.'

The chief constable laughed. 'We'll try and cope the best we can without you.'

* * *

Nash met with the leader of the Cave Rescue team near the adit Daniel had indicated. 'I've been checking the ground surrounding the entrance,' Owen told him. 'I'm now certain your son wasn't imagining things, with regard to the rock fall at least. There is a considerable amount of scree, more than normal directly outside the opening, plus some grit scattered across the grass. That can only have come from within the mine, and the smaller particles would have been washed away by rain, had it happened a while ago.'

Owen gestured to the lower part of the slope closest to where they were standing. 'If you look directly in front of the entrance, you can see that the foliage is a lighter colour than elsewhere. I think that's caused by limestone dust settling on the leaves, and again, that can only have happened recently.'

He took a deep breath before continuing. 'Our next problem involves gaining access to the interior of the mine. Two of our men have ventured inside, and we're waiting for them to return before we can assess the situation. If the fall your son reported is as bad as it sounds, our route could be completely blocked.'

Nash and Daniel stood a few paces away, where Nash had a brief word with Chief Fire Officer Doug Curran, who had arrived by car.

'What are you doing here, Doug? I didn't think the fire service would be required.'

'I heard the alert on the radio and came to see if our equipment might be needed.' Clearly he saw the potential gravity of the situation. 'I'll need to be certain it's worth sending my men into such a hazardous location, Mike. I'm not prepared to put their lives at risk unless it becomes absolutely necessary. You've provided me with a few headaches over the years, but I think this one caps all the others. The HART team should be here soon. Only problem is, they have to come from Leeds.'

Noticing his son's downcast expression following the fireman's remarks, Nash tried to reassure him. 'These guys are being ultra-cautious, Daniel, and the reason they're being so wary is they believe everything you told them. If there is somebody trapped in that mine, and they are still alive, a further rockslide could endanger both them and the rescuers. The Hazardous Area Response Team are specialists in their field.'

Nash waited while Owen consulted with his colleagues. Five minutes later the rescuers emerged and he wandered over to join them. As he approached, the team leader gestured to something one of them was holding. 'All our guys wear a bodycam when we venture underground. Charlie here—' he gestured to the first man who had exited the mine — 'has something I think you ought to see. Whether you'll want to see it is another matter,' he added cryptically.

He turned to his colleague. 'Charlie, tell Inspector Nash what you found, then show him the footage.'

'We were only able to penetrate about fifty yards into the mine before we had to stop because the roof had caved in.' He paused. 'Sorry, bad pun. Your son was dead right. The fall was very recent, and you can tell because there's still a lot of dust hanging in the air. However, the rocks didn't reach all the way to the ceiling of the old workings. There is sufficient space to climb through, but before we did anything like that I removed my bodycam and recorded the area beyond the fall. I rotated the camera so I could capture images of the full width of the tunnel. The rocks which fell from the roof and walls caused an obstruction no more than three metres long, and on the far side of that, the camera picked up an object lying on the floor, something that definitely isn't standard equipment for somebody working in a nineteenth-century lead mine. When I realized what I was looking at, I decided we should report back. Here, let me show you what my camera picked up.'

Nash watched as the camera's footage moved along the roof, the walls and then the floor of the tunnel. After a few seconds, he said, 'Stop it there, can you? Are you able to enlarge that?' He stared at the enhanced image for a while before nodding. 'OK, we definitely need to get someone inside the old workings, and it's fortunate we're going to be able to get past this obstruction.'

Owen, who had remained silent during the video show, intervened. 'Shouldn't we get a mining engineer to check the stability of the level before we try anything of that sort? I think we ought to get hold of a plan of the mine, providing there is one. See if there's an alternative entrance.'

Nash shook his head. 'We don't have time for that. If there is someone alive inside there, we need to get to them ASAP. We also need to recover what your colleague saw, and that task has to be carried out by a police officer. However, if things turn out badly inside the mine, we might need to consult an old plan of the workings, providing we can lay our hands on one. The problem is, we have absolutely no idea where to look for such a thing.'

Owen thought for a moment before telling Nash, 'I reckon your best option would come via the British Geological Survey. They've been cataloguing a lot of old plans, principally of disused coal mines, but they might also have one for this lead mine.'

He didn't add 'if we're lucky', but Nash had already guessed that.

CHAPTER THREE

Nash's mobile rang. He glanced at the screen before he answered. 'I was about to call you, ma'am. There's been a serious development.' He told her what the camera had recorded, and relayed the new suggestion regarding maps Owen had given him. In return, she informed him that HART would be in charge when they arrived. She understood they were now approaching Wintersett village. She would be at the helm liaising with them, plus Owen, Nash and, if necessary, Doug Curran. She would arrange for any new specialists to be brought in, or the delivery of any equipment required.

She ended by telling Nash, 'Given that the bodycam footage clearly shows an automatic pistol within the mine, and taking into account Daniel's statement about what he heard, we have to act on the assumption that a crime might well have been committed within those workings. I don't for one moment believe someone went in there simply to indulge in a bit of target practice. The pistol could be pivotal during the investigation. As such, providing it is possible to enter the workings, the weapon will have to be retrieved by a firearms-trained officer who will be able to ensure there is no chance of an accidental discharge, and equally important, no risk of contamination of evidence.'

'I'd already thought of that, and I'm about to enter the mine along with a member of the Cave Rescue team. We can't wait for someone to come from another force, and as I'm the only one available with the necessary qualifications, I'll have to do it.'

Nash walked over to his son and told him, 'I've been instructed by the chief constable to pass on her "appreciation for your diligent and accurate summary of what happened here".' He waved two fingers in the air, indicating a quote. 'She says you are to be "commended for your observation and interpretation of everything you saw and heard".'

Daniel grinned at his father.

Nash then told him what the camera footage had revealed. 'On the floor of the passage, beyond where the roof caved in, the image clearly shows an automatic pistol lying on the ground.' Seeing Daniel's look of pride, Nash added, 'I suppose that goes some way to offsetting the awful marks in mathematics on your latest school report.'

If this mild reprimand upset Daniel, it certainly wasn't apparent by the broad grin on his face. 'Oh, come off it, Pa. I might not be a brilliant mathematician, but I always get one hundred per cent in French.'

'I'd have been bitterly disappointed if you hadn't, considering you're half French by birth.' He told Daniel what he intended to do next. Daniel was appalled by the idea and pleaded with him to rethink it. Nash shook his head. 'I'm afraid there's no alternative.'

As he was getting kitted up in protective suit, bodycam and head torch, Nash's mobile rang again. This time it was Jackie Fleming, who called with an update, along with a plea. 'Ruth's obtained a copy of the mine plan, which she's sent to your mobile and Mr Owen's. She also told me you intend to go into the workings to recover that gun. Please don't do that, Mike. Send someone else in.'

'There isn't anyone else with the right qualifications, Jackie.'

'Isn't there anyone in uniform branch?'

'Not that I'm aware of, and even if there is, I'm already on site. If, as we suspect, a crime has been committed within that cave network, there could be more evidence to uncover.'

Nash didn't give voice to his other thought, that the 'evidence' in this situation was highly likely to include bodies. Once again, the statement was unnecessary. Fleming didn't attempt to argue the point — she knew everything Nash had said made sense, and added up to their only option. She was also aware that he had recently completed a firearms refresher course, as had Detective Sergeant Clara Mironova, but she was currently on leave. 'Just be careful, Mike, and if it's too unsafe, give up the attempt and retreat. That's an order.'

* * *

Once Nash and his companion had entered the small opening to the mine, Nash was surprised to find the interior opened out into a wider passageway. Having walked slowly and carefully for a fair distance along the tunnel, Nash's guide pointed ahead to a pile of boulders that blocked further progress. 'We're going to have to get over those. I'll go first, then you can come and collect the pea shooter.'

Nash was mildly surprised that his companion could see humour in their situation, but guessed this was due to a greater familiarity with such conditions. As they walked slowly towards the obstruction he was also startled by his own reaction. His surroundings evoked a schoolboy memory, when he had learned a poem by Samuel Taylor Coleridge, entitled 'Kubla Khan': '*Where Alph, the sacred river, ran. Through caverns measureless to man . . .*'

Nash shook himself mentally — this was neither the time nor the place for daydreaming. A few minutes later, after scrambling carefully over the limestone rocks that barred their way, Nash's head torch picked out something metallic glistening at the base of the tunnel. He put a restraining hand on the caver's arm, before fishing an evidence bag from his pocket.

The rescuer watched as Nash added a second pair of gloves, before stooping to pick up the pistol. Having checked that it was empty, he sniffed it, placed the gun inside the bag and sealed it. His nod, added to the grim expression on his face, told the caver the weapon had been fired recently.

Nash was in the process of placing the evidence bag carefully back inside his pocket when he heard his companion cry out. He glanced to his left, and saw that the caver had scaled another bank of fallen rocks, the boulders reaching just above head height. 'Inspector Nash, over here!' The man's voice was a wail of distress. 'You've got to see this!'

Twenty minutes later, they emerged from the entrance, hurrying as swiftly as safety allowed towards where the HART team leader was standing, along with Owen and several others. Those awaiting their return had been augmented during their absence. The group had been joined by Chief Constable Edwards and Superintendent Fleming, their anxiety obvious. In the lane stood a group of villagers, curious as to the need for the emergency services, mobile phones in hand filming the scene.

Nash spoke to the chief. 'We can stand everyone down for tonight. There are two occupants inside the mine, but the only place they'll be going is the mortuary. I did check for a pulse.'

He handed Jackie Fleming the evidence bag containing the pistol. 'It's quite safe,' he told her, 'the magazine is empty. However, the gun has been fired recently — you can still smell the residue.'

He walked over to his son, slipped his arm around his shoulder, and told him, 'You were absolutely spot on this morning, Daniel, but no matter how quickly anyone got into that mine, they'd have been too late. Both victims were already beyond help. Wait there. I need another word with the chief.'

He found Ruth Edwards in conversation with one of the Cave Rescue team. She nodded, before the man turned and left. She told Nash, 'That was one of our Forensic officers.

He's on rest days at the moment, that's why he's here with Cave Rescue. He has volunteered to stay and assist with the retrieval of the bodies. We will need a Forensic presence. He can photograph the scene and look out for any evidence, and bag anything he finds.'

'That could be helpful.' Then with an attempt to lighten the grim revelations, he added, 'I dread to think what Mexican Pete will say when we tell him the location of this crime scene. With a bit of luck his reply will be in Spanish, and I'm certainly not going to ask Alondra for a translation.'

Reverting to a more serious note, he told Ruth Edwards, 'I think we need a mining engineer on site. We ought to have a professional opinion as to the safety or otherwise of the mine before we send anyone else in or attempt to recover the victims. By the way, one of them is male, the other female, and besides the fact there are what look like bullet wounds in their chests, it was difficult to judge their ages.' He paused and then added a grim footnote. 'With what we've discovered so far, we might also need the rest of the workings checked over, in case there's any other evidence — or more bodies.'

CHAPTER FOUR

With no further action possible that day, the Cave Rescue and HART teams departed, leaving officers protecting the scene from nosy onlookers. Nash invited his colleagues to Smelt Mill Cottage, where, he informed them, a fresh pot of coffee was always available.

'I see you've got your weakness covered,' Ruth Edwards commented.

As they entered the house, she told him, 'I've put a mining engineer on standby. If I give him the green light he'll be here in the morning. I've also thought about your comment regarding retrieval of the corpses. If they're available tomorrow, I've asked the HART team to assist. As medically trained personnel, they are better suited than the Cave Rescue people, who deal mainly with accidents. I know they're good, but we need experts on this.'

Nash understood and approved, but Alondra, who was greeting them, overheard and was puzzled. She enquired about it.

'I know, Mum,' Daniel said proudly. 'Pa told me. HART stands for Hazardous Area Response Team.'

Ruth smiled and explained further. 'They're a highly trained unit of specialists, ranging from doctors and paramedics to fire officers, engineers, both structural and civil, plus members with a host of other abilities such as mountain and maritime rescue. They're the go-to guys for major emergencies and accessing difficult and dangerous locations such as this. They can also be trusted to remove the bodies from the scene without contaminating any evidence.'

Once they had enquired as to Alondra's health and were seated in Nash's lounge, supplied with coffee and cake, Jackie Fleming brought up a topic that had been puzzling her. 'Do you know how that mine came by such a curious name? Having seen it this afternoon, and viewed the images from those cameras, I couldn't see anything remotely glorious about the place, so why did it get called the Hand of Glory?'

'That had me baffled for long enough,' Nash told her, 'but then I did some research, or rather—' he grinned and gestured to his left — 'I got Daniel to do it for me. What he found was rather shocking, in a macabre sort of way. The Hand of Glory has a particularly gruesome origin. Apparently, the title refers to a tool used by burglars in medieval times, and later, into the nineteenth century, or so it's believed. Superstition was rife back in those days, and the burglars believed the hand would render them invisible as they went about their nefarious exploits.'

Nash paused before getting to the gruesome part of his tale. 'The hand was severed from the body of a man who had been hanged. In those days, executions were carried out in public, and the villains cut it from the corpse while it was still on the gibbet. They always took the right hand, then drained it of blood and cured it. Once it was ready, the hand was used as a candle holder. The candle was equally obnoxious, as the tallow was made from the fat of the deceased criminal, who had almost been eviscerated during the process, and the wick was plaited from his hair.'

While his father was talking, Daniel slipped from the room, returning moments later with a sheet of paper.

'You weren't exaggerating when you described it as a gruesome tale,' Ruth commented. 'But how did they believe this revolting thing would help them? I can't imagine they thought it actually made them invisible.'

'In a sense, they did. The burglars believed that once it was lit, the magic powers of the hand would cause the occupants of the house to remain asleep while they stole their possessions, and likewise would keep the thieves awake. They also believed the only way to extinguish the candle was to pour blood or milk over the flame.'

'That has to be one of the most revolting stories I've ever heard,' Jackie stated. 'But is there any truth in it, or is it merely a tale made up to scare naughty children?'

'It is true, and apparently the use of the hand goes back almost a thousand years.'

Daniel interrupted. 'Would you like to hear this? I found it during my research, and I'm going to use it back at school for a project, especially after today. It's an extract from *The Ingoldsby Legends*, 'The Nurse's Tale', by Richard Harris Barham.'

Having received nods from the adults, he began to read.

*For low, yet clear, now fall on the ear, where once pronounced for
    ever they dwell, the unholy words of The Dead Man's Spell!
Open lock to The Dead Man's Knock! Fly bolt, and bar, and
    band!
Nor move, nor swerve, joint, muscle or nerve, at the spell of The
    Dead Man's Hand!
Sleep all who sleep! Wake all who wake! But be as the Dead for
    the Dead Man's sake!
Nor lock, nor bolt, nor bar avails, nor stout oak panel
    thick-studded with nails,
Heavy and harsh the hinges creak though they had been oiled in
    the course of the week.
The door opens wide as wide may be, and there they stand, that
    murderous band, lit by the light of THE GLORIOUS
    HAND,
By one — By two — By three!'*

Daniel grinned. 'I'm not sure how many still exist, but I do know for a fact there is one not too many miles from here. If you're desperately keen to see a Hand of Glory, there's one on display at Whitby Museum.'

Ruth smiled. 'Thank you, Daniel, this is all highly interesting, but I think I'll forego the trip to Whitby.' She turned to Nash. 'Mike, you still haven't explained to Jackie how this hideous article gave its name to the lead mine, or don't you know?'

'I certainly do, largely thanks to Jonas Turner, who is a mine of information on local features.'

Nash waited until the groans at his dreadful pun died away, before explaining what the old man had told him. 'Apparently, much of this is circumstantial, plus gossip which no doubt has been exaggerated with the passage of time. You also have to add into the mix that Jonas had downed a pint or two when he told me. Apparently, the mine belonged to a local farmer, who supplemented his meagre income by burgling the houses of rich landowners. Legend has it that when he was apprehended and hanged, the burglar's son intended to follow the family tradition. He made a Hand of Glory, cutting it from his father's corpse hanging from the gibbet. But before he could carry out his plan, he went searching for treasures his father had stolen and secreted within the mine. However, he was killed by a rock fall, and the hand was buried with him. In later years, miners, who were of a superstitious nature, told of occasions when they heard footsteps in the remote parts of the mine where nobody was working. These were accompanied by a strange light they believed emanated from the Hand of Glory, as the ghost of the dead burglar attempted to find a way out of the workings where he'd been trapped.'

'Who owns the mine nowadays?' Ruth wanted to know.

'I'm not certain, but I believe all the land round there forms part of the Fell Head Manor estate.'

* * *

Later, when their guests had departed, Nash was on the receiving end of a severe dressing-down delivered by Alondra, who was backed up by Daniel. 'Don't even considering doing anything so dangerous again. Ever! Do you hear me, Mike? You had us worried stiff. Not only me, sitting here wondering what you were doing, but Daniel too. You think I don't know what you did? Daniel phoned me, he was so worried. In case you haven't noticed, things have changed around here since the bad old days when you had no responsibilities, nobody else to consider but yourself.' As she was speaking, she subconsciously stroked her bulging abdomen. 'Back then, you could do what you wanted and were free to indulge in all sorts of exploits, whether at work or play. Now you're a family man, with a wife and son who care deeply about you, and another little one who will soon be looking to you for guidance and support as they grow. It is unfair and selfish of you to put Daniel and me through such torment.'

Alondra ran out of breath at that point, but Daniel took up the cudgels on her behalf. 'Mum's absolutely right, Pa, and I hope you realize what agony you put us through. I actually felt sick all the time you were inside that awful place. I've already lost my birth mother, so how do you think I'd have felt if anything bad happened to you? You were almost killed when those men blew up our flat, and we almost lost Mum to those awful men who kidnapped her. Get someone else to volunteer for any other dangerous assignments. I know you've always led by example, Pa, that's one of the reasons I'm so proud of you, but I think it's time you let go. Soldiers are of little use unless they have a commanding officer to lead them.'

Nash stared at them both, totally dumbstruck.

He apologized profusely, the session ending with a group hug involving all three of them, or, as Daniel corrected the equation, three and a half.

With an attempt at humour, Nash told them, 'That felt a bit like being eight years old again, being told off by my mother and father for misbehaving — not that I ever did misbehave, of course.'

The outburst of derisive laughter from his wife and son told Nash his claim of innocence had not been accepted. Once he'd been forgiven, Nash reflected on what had happened. The best thing to emerge from the scolding was the depth of feeling Alondra and Daniel had for him, and the strengthening bond between his wife and son.

CHAPTER FIVE

True to his word, the engineer was on site before eight o'clock the following morning, and having given cautious approval as to the safety of the workings, Ruth Edwards was able to call on the services of HART. Rather than waste fuel on a journey to Helmsdale, Nash remained at home until he saw the specialist recovery vehicles drive past the house.

From the safety of the fields overlooking the site, he watched as they entered the workings along with the Forensic officer. Half an hour later, he phoned Jackie Fleming. 'HART are inside. They've inspected the tunnel as far as they can, and should be able to recover all the bodies by this afternoon.'

There was a long silence before Jackie responded, 'Sorry, did you say *all* the bodies?'

'Yes, I'm afraid so. There are four in total. When I went in yesterday I couldn't see the other two, which were obscured by some of the fallen rocks. Apparently, from what the paramedics reported, one of them is skeletal, the other is in a fairly advanced state of decomposition.'

With nothing further to contribute, at that point Nash returned home, the lure of coffee and his family overwhelming.

One glance at his expression told Alondra the morning hadn't gone well. 'Did the mining engineer say it was unsafe?'

Nash's response shocked her. 'No, he declared it OK, so HART went in. It was what they discovered that got to me. They hope to have the bodies recovered by mid-afternoon. That's all four bodies,' he added. He smiled slightly. 'I didn't even have to phone Professor Ramirez. Jackie's done that. I'll wander back and meet up with him in a while, but first I could do with a caffeine stimulant.'

'You always need a caffeine stimulant.'

'Not always,' Nash protested. 'Sometimes you're the only stimulant I need.'

'Maybe, but not at the moment.' Alondra smiled as she patted her bump.

* * *

An hour later, Nash wandered back to the fields bordering the foot of Stark Ghyll, where he noticed someone had erected incident tape, which he considered somewhat unnecessary. He was joined a while later by the pathologist, who, contrary to Nash's fears, seemed cheerful rather than angry.

'We value your services too highly to allow you to enter the mine, Don Pedro,' Nash greeted him. 'But you'll be able to view proceedings from here via the wireless link set up by the HART team. In this instance, I reckon the term "body cam" is highly appropriate.'

Ramirez disguised his relief by retaliating. 'Does that mean I have to stand here and listen to your appalling jokes, Don Miguel?'

Professor Ramirez, although Spanish by birth, was known as Mexican Pete throughout the force, an oblique reference to the *Ballad of Eskimo Nell*. After Nash married Alondra, who was brought up in Spain, the professor began calling him Don Miguel. In turn, Nash often called him Don Pedro.

They watched the Forensic officer at work, checking the area for footprints and any other evidence, before Ramirez requested photographs of the bodies from different angles, before he gave permission for the retrieval process to begin. Having given his approval to the professional manner of the extraction, Ramirez told Nash, 'I have lectures all day tomorrow, so I'll conduct the PMs the following day.'

'I don't suppose twenty-four hours will make any difference.'

* * *

The post-mortems were as close to a formality as possible. 'Three of the victims were female, one male,' Ramirez told Nash. Cause of death in three of them is definitely the gunshot wounds to the chest. I believe that to be so with the other corpse, but there is an element of doubt. Because those remains are skeletal, there is no entry or exit site visible. However, the diligence of our officer helping to recover the bodies was such that he collected bullets from beneath the remains. I have sent them, plus a number of empty casings he retrieved, for ballistic testing. But I have little doubt they will all prove to have come from the handgun you took from the floor of the mine, and will probably have collected the victim's DNA when they entered the body.'

Ramirez consulted his notes. 'Time of death in the two most recent cases — one female, one male — can be given precisely thanks to your son's intelligent observations. Where he got such skills from, I've no idea.'

Ignoring the insult, Nash asked, 'What about the other victims? Do you know how long they've been down there?'

'One was killed somewhere between three and six months ago, judging by the decomposition and predation. The other was killed much earlier. This is only speculation, but I wouldn't be surprised if she's been in that hellhole for as long as ten years, possibly even more. As to the ages of the victims, the women were all in their twenties or thirties — the male possibly just the wrong side of forty. None of the women had given birth,' the pathologist paused, 'and neither had the man.'

25

Nash groaned and shook his head.

Ramirez continued, 'I checked the two most recent corpses and their fingerprints are not on record. The only piece of good news is I've taken samples for testing. Perhaps one of them scratched the gunman.'

* * *

With nothing else to go on, Nash pinned his hopes on the tests, but three days later, when the results came in, those hopes were dashed. The only positive result came with a couple of huge reservations, as the Forensic officer reported.

'We tested the gun you retrieved from the mine, and can confirm the striations on the bullet cases prove it to be the weapon used to kill all the victims there. However, that weapon has not been used in any other reported offences. There were minute traces of DNA on the gun, but sadly, whoever fired it isn't recorded on our system.'

CHAPTER SIX

Six months earlier at Felling Prison, Frank Watson had been sitting in his cell reading. It wasn't his favourite pastime, nor was he particularly good at it. However, he needed to keep up-to-date with the outside world, and TV news bulletins only gave a sketchy picture.

Frank was looking forward to the day of his release, only six months away. Then he could claim the reward due for his silence. As part of the gang labelled the Country House Bandits by the media, Watson and his colleagues had enjoyed a long and highly successful career — until the law caught up with them.

Like Frank Watson, Joe Lambert, Terry Palmer and Peter Swallow, aka Birdie, had all been incarcerated for identical ten-year terms. Part of the reason for the lengthy sentences handed out was the failure of the police to recover any of the highly valuable stolen items. That, plus their unwillingness to cooperate with the investigation, ensured the burglars received the maximum term of imprisonment. To anyone reading of their escapades it was obvious there were more gang members at large, ones the police had failed to identify.

Admittedly, Frank would have to share the proceeds of their crimes with his co-conspirators, but he would still be very wealthy. He didn't begrudge them their part of the spoils, because they too had been forced to suffer in silence for ten long years. Once he was released, Frank could indulge in the pleasures he'd been denied, many of them only possible once he'd claimed the money due to him. Other pleasures would cost him nothing, but would be even more enjoyable. Principal among these involved keeping company with his long-suffering partner, who had remained loyal over the years. It would be one of his first delights on his release to satisfy the yearning he still had for her.

Better not to dwell on the pleasures of the flesh, not in an institution comprising solely of several hundred men. Putting such thoughts firmly to one side, he returned to the newspaper he was holding. His reading was interrupted by a voice behind him. As he turned, Watson saw one of his fellow inmates standing nearby. 'I have a message for you, Frank.'

He barely heard the follow-up because of the excruciating pain in his side. As Watson lost consciousness, his killer told him, 'The message is "goodbye".'

* * *

It was the first prison visit the woman had made to see her husband since he had caused Frank Watson's death. As she greeted him, the officers watched them, their interest minimal as the couple exchanged loving greetings. Once the inmate was certain their conversation was not being monitored, he asked the all-important question. 'Have you got the second present, and put it in a safe place?'

She knew exactly what he meant. Her voice was little more than a whisper as she replied, 'Yes, although I'm not sure I ought to touch it after what you did to earn it. It's blood money.'

'Don't even think that way. Listen here, that money is for you and the girl. There was no way I could refuse. If it hadn't been me, they'd have got someone else to stick him. There'll come a time when you'll be prepared to do anything to lay your hands on some readies, if only to pay for her treatment. There's no way I'm going to be able to provide for her and you, not while I'm stuck in here for the rest of my natural.'

He attempted to lighten the moment by adding, 'Of course, I could write my autobiography and hope it becomes a bestseller, but that's unlikely. You know how bad I am at spelling.'

She was astonished that he could treat the matter so lightly, given what he'd done and the trauma that was ahead of them as a family.

It took her a moment to summon up the courage to answer his follow-up question. 'Anyway, let's get down to more important things. How is my darling little girl?'

The rest of the visit was spent discussing their daughter. Although they tried to put a brave face on it, they both knew the invasive condition afflicting their ten-year-old child was incurable, and the end was inevitable. It was only a matter of time, and the child had far too little of that.

* * *

As the gates of Preston Prison clanged shut behind him, Joe Lambert glanced round. He hadn't expected there to be anyone waiting for him, so he wasn't disappointed. During his incarceration his wife had divorced him, and was now living in Tenerife with a bar-owner. That didn't bother him. It was good riddance to bad rubbish as far as Joe was concerned. His focus was on finding somewhere to live and locating his share of the reward.

The first part wasn't difficult. His sister, who had been widowed after her husband lost a prolonged fight against cancer, had offered him accommodation for the time being. The second part was going to be a bigger challenge. In order to claim his reward he would have to discover the identity or whereabouts of the little-known leader of the Country House Bandits. The man referred to by senior gang members as 'The Keeper'. He was the one who took care of the loot, disposing of it when most advantageous and laundering the proceeds. The fact that the Keeper was a shadowy figure, unknown to all but one of the gang, didn't unduly worry Joe. That had always been part of the structure. That way, they couldn't reveal his identity, whether they were lured by inducements or unable to keep their mouth shut because of alcohol or other substances.

Now that he was on the outside, Joe could begin to search without having to rely on second-hand information or waiting for the secret to be revealed by his colleague. For the moment, the only money he had was the little he had earned in prison and the discharge grant. His grant application had caused comment among both prisoners and warders regarding his need for this when he reputedly had a hidden fortune.

He used the travel warrant, and having left the train at Netherdale station, he walked to the Carthill estate, where his sister lived. Norma was a few years younger than Joe, but had stood by him throughout his troubles, even in the darkness of her own grief after her husband Don died. Sadly, she and Don hadn't been blessed with children, which Joe knew she regretted, but at least the lack of them meant that he would be able to accustom himself to life on the outside without too many noisy distractions.

Joe reached the small, neat house that Norma and Don had bought from their landlords, Netherdale Council, a few years earlier, before Don became ill. One of the terms of the mortgage had been a joint life insurance policy, so at least Norma hadn't that worry around her neck. Joe strolled up the garden path and knocked on the front door. Light streamed out as Norma opened it. She flung her arms round her older brother and dragged him inside. For the first time in many years, Joe felt the pleasant sensation of unrestrained affection.

Less than forty-eight hours before Lambert became a free man, another former member of the Country House Bandits, Terry Palmer, had also been released from the prison in London that had housed him. He didn't glance back as he walked away from the jail. He'd seen more than enough of the inside, so the outside view held no attraction. As he strode briskly down the street, nearby CCTV cameras recorded his passage. The outdated T-shirt he was wearing, with the colour and logo of a famous football team, presented a striking image.

Palmer's principal objective was to return to Yorkshire. That posed a problem. Unaware he could have applied for a grant, he had very little money. The travel allowance he'd been given was the value of a train ticket, but he decided to try and hitch a ride north, hoping that eventually he would reach Netherdale. Even then, Terry would have to find somewhere to stay. He was a good deal younger than the other gang members, and as an only child, and an orphan, he had nobody close enough to visit him during his imprisonment. At one time, he and Joe's sister had been an item, and Terry had hoped that the arrangement might have become permanent, but that had ended long ago.

Before seeking a ride north, Palmer decided he'd celebrate his release. He reckoned he'd earned a pint — or two.

Palmer's involvement with the robberies had been minimal, or so his counsel had pleaded during the trial. Co-opted as driver and lookout purely because of his connection to Lambert, he had no influence on the others or their criminal activities. Despite the barrister's assessment of his minor role in the gang's operations, Palmer had been given the same term as the others. They had served their sentences hundreds of miles apart. His sense of grievance at what he believed to be the unfairness of his treatment had resulted in years of brooding anger and deep depression.

However, he knew the other members of the gang were also due for release. They too would be eager to find the Keeper and claim their rewards for the past ten years — or to exact retribution, should the recompense not be forthcoming.

It would be a further two days when the final member of the team was at liberty. Peter Swallow, known as Birdie to his friends, would have to travel from Worcester, where he was being held. Frustratingly for the others, Birdie was one of the few who they believed were aware of the Keeper's true identity. Frank Watson was also thought to have known who the Keeper was, but he had carried that secret to his grave. Watson's death, only months earlier, from a stab wound inflicted by a fellow inmate, had shocked the incarcerated gang members when the news had trickled through the prison grapevine.

At approximately the same time as Swallow was preparing to leave his prison cell for the final time, Joe Lambert told his sister, 'I'd like to go to the pub tonight. Will you lend me some cash? I've only got a bit, and I promise I'll pay you back when I find a job, or when we're able to get our hands on what's due to us.'

'Of course I'll lend you some cash, Joe. Don't worry about paying me back, either. I don't want to know about the robbery money, though.' She opened her handbag, took out her purse and passed some notes to him. 'Is that enough?'

Joe glanced down and smiled. There was over £100 in his hand. He held the notes up. 'I'll be late back, and I might be a little under the weather. I've ten years' drinking to catch up on, and I'm out of practice. Apart from the night out, I want to hear all the news and gossip.'

'Just don't go getting into bother, Joe,' Norma cautioned him. 'Remember that even a minor offence could land you back inside.'

'Don't worry, Sis, there's no way they're going to get me back in that place.'

CHAPTER SEVEN

The bar of the Red Bear was crowded, as usual on a night when there was a darts or dominoes match. The pub had been built at the same time as the estate it served, and bore similar signs of neglect. A council official, after inspecting the premises prior to granting a new licence, remarked, 'The Red Bear? "Threadbare" would be a more appropriate name.'

The regulars weren't bothered about the down-at-heel appearance, the peeling paintwork, or the shabby interior. For them, the pub provided what they needed. Good beer at a reasonable price, plus, when the authorities weren't looking, other more potent but less legal stimulants at far higher cost.

Joe wasn't interested in the drugs — he'd seen enough of them and the effect they had on users while he was in jail. All he wanted was beer, plus the chance to catch up with old acquaintances, and possibly acquire some information. He was successful in two out of three items from his wish list. By the time he left he'd certainly taken on board plenty of beer, plus a few shots of whisky when his liquid levels were reaching saturation point. He'd also met up with several people he'd known prior to his incarceration. To them, Joe was something of a folk hero, and they were keen to welcome him back by buying him a drink, thus reducing the cost of the evening dramatically.

Despite the warmth of his welcome, Joe learned nothing of value during his stay in the Red Bear. In one sense that was good, because it meant that the Keeper's anonymity was still secure. But it also meant a frustrating wait for Joe before contact could be re-established.

Joe knew he would have to meet with Terry Palmer and Peter Swallow. The need to talk matters over with Terry and Birdie was too urgent to be ignored. The encounter with Terry would be difficult, a painful reminder of the angry and bitter dispute that had preceded their loss of freedom, but the money they were owed was more important.

It was past midnight when he left the pub and made his way a trifle unevenly back towards Norma's house. Halfway there he took a shortcut, using an alleyway between two of the roads in the estate. He'd almost reached the end, where the street lamps failed to provide more than a modicum of illumination, when he heard his name called. He turned and peered into the gloom. It took a moment for his eyes to adjust, another for him to recognize the shadowy figure standing only a couple of yards behind him. 'You!' he exclaimed in astonishment. 'What are you doing here?'

'I have something for you,' the person standing close to Joe replied.

As he heard this, Joe saw a glint of steel in the dim light and simultaneously felt a burning pain in his chest. Then the darkness closed in around him.

The killer waited for a few seconds to ensure the victim was beyond human aid. Having ascertained that Joe Lambert was dead, the killer calmly put the weapon away before striding over the body and walking slowly out into the street.

* * *

It was still dark when the phone rang. DI Mike Nash switched on the bedside lamp and turned to his wife, who was blinking at the sudden glare. 'Sorry.'

'It's OK, Mike, I was only dozing.' As she spoke, Alondra patted her tummy. 'Junior seems very restless tonight.'

As he picked up the phone, he said, 'I know, he's been using my back as a football.'

Unexpectedly, the caller was Steve Meadows, their uniform sergeant at Helmsdale. After apologizing for disturbing Nash's sleep, he explained he was covering for his counterpart at Netherdale. Meadows then asked, 'Do you remember the Country House Bandits?'

For a moment, Nash thought this was the name of a rock band, and that Meadows had been drinking. It was a few seconds before he made the connection. 'Weren't there a few of them, and didn't they get long prison sentences?'

'That's right, they specialized in burgling stately homes and the like, stealing jewellery, ornaments and other small, or large, high-value items. Four of them got ten years apiece, but the investigators reckoned there were several others who were never identified. None of the loot was recovered. Although two of them lived in or near Netherdale, and one in Leeds, the robberies were all committed elsewhere, so our involvement was minimal.'

'All this is fascinating, Steve, but couldn't it have waited until morning?'

'No, Mike, because two of the gang have been released. Joe Lambert got out three days ago. A bloke staggering home from the pub an hour ago found Lambert's body in a ginnel close to the Carthill estate. He'd been stabbed in the chest. The wound punctured his aorta and he bled out.'

'OK, I'm on my way. Will you round up the troops, or those we have available? By that I mean Lisa Andrews, Mexican Pete and CSI.'

'Already done, Mike.'

'Better tell me the location of the ginnel too.'

After ending the call, Nash turned and kissed Alondra. 'Sorry, I've got to go, but hopefully I'll be back in time for breakfast. Will you be OK walking Teal?'

'No problem, Mike — I'll co-opt Daniel. But before you go, please tell me, what is a ginnel?'

'Sorry, I forget you're not used to the Yorkshire dialect.' He laughed. 'It's a narrow passageway between two buildings. Think about the market square in Helmsdale — you've seen lots of them.'

* * *

Although it was still an hour before daybreak, the approaches to the ginnel were flooded with searing illumination provided by police arc lamps. Nash pulled his Range Rover up behind an ambulance and ducked under the incident tape. He approached a man clad in protective suiting, who was watching the stretcher bearing Lambert's corpse being manoeuvred towards the vehicle. 'Good morning, Professor.'

Ramirez turned and gave Nash a sour glare. 'I might have known you'd be along soon. Why couldn't you have stayed in bed with your lovely wife and sent your delightful sergeant instead? Or is the prospect of drooling over a body too much for you to resist?'

'Clara's on leave until the weekend,' Nash replied tersely. 'What can you tell me about the murder?'

'The victim was stabbed in the chest, and the wound was so severe it was almost a through and through. On its way, the weapon punctured his aorta. Death would have been almost instantaneous. The time of the attack was probably after midnight, and before 2 a.m. I can be reasonably sure because that's when he was found. There is a strong smell of alcohol emanating from the corpse. So possibly the victim died happy. The rest can wait until the post-mortem. That'll be later today. I'll let you know the time.'

With that, Ramirez turned away and signalled to his assistants to complete the loading process. Nash walked over to the CSI team leader and asked for a briefing. It didn't take long, as there was little to report. As they were talking, another car pulled up and DC Lisa Andrews emerged, striding over to join Nash.

'Morning, Lisa. Sorry to drag you out at this hour. Are you OK?'

'I'm on call, and I'm not fragile. And I promise not to throw up over the crime scene,' she added. At three months pregnant, Lisa was determined to continue as normal.

Nash brought her up to date with what little he knew, and together they approached the uniformed officers who were awaiting instructions. Despite the early hour a small knot of spectators had gathered, their curiosity roused by the sirens and lights. 'Might be worth asking around to find out if anyone saw or heard anything,' Nash suggested. 'Take a uniform with you. They're a dubious lot round here.'

He watched as Lisa began questioning the onlookers, and could tell by the body language that she wasn't meeting with much success. She rejoined him after a few minutes. 'Nothing, apart from the guy who phoned it in, and he's too blathered to make much sense. The only good part of what he told me is he recognized Lambert immediately. They'd been drinking together only a while earlier. The rest of the spectators came out when we disturbed them.'

'We need to find out where Lambert had been and where he was heading.'

'I know that already — the drunken body finder told me. Lambert had been in the Red Bear all evening, and was on his way back to his sister's home, where he was lodging, apparently.'

'Has anyone told her about this?' Nash waved a hand towards the crime scene.

'Not yet. Do you want me to ask uniform to go?'

'No, I think we should do it. We'll need to talk to her anyway.' He stared thoughtfully at the ambulance as it pulled away from the kerb, the lights flashing, but the sirens silent. 'I wonder how he knew.'

He hadn't realized he'd spoken aloud until Lisa asked, 'You wonder how who knew what?'

'Sorry, Lisa, I was thinking aloud. I was curious as to how the killer knew that Joe Lambert had been released from prison, and that he'd be walking this route.'

'You think the killer knew him? Couldn't it have been a mugging that went wrong?'

'That's unlikely. I doubt whether he'd have much worth stealing — his wallet and money were still in his pocket. And it still doesn't explain the second part of my question, unless the killer had been watching Joe. And the only way he could have done that is by knowing where he was living, and maybe following him to the pub. This was no random stabbing. Joe Lambert was targeted, and the killer was probably someone he knew. I think it also suggests a motive.'

Lisa was fascinated that Nash seemed to have drawn so many inferences from so few facts. 'Would you like to share all that with me? I've been so busy I've missed my mind-reading classes for the past few weeks.'

Nash smiled slightly. 'If the killer knew Lambert, he'd be more likely to be aware of his release date. Assuming he did know, and that he was familiar with Joe's lifestyle before he was banged up, he would have to assume that even if he wasn't lodging there, at some point Joe would visit his sister. That being the case, he would go to the pub where some of his old acquaintances hang out.'

'I get that, and that you're probably right about the fact that the killer knew him, but what about the motive?'

'Money! Joe's only been out a couple of days, so he's hardly had time to create new enemies. Therefore, it must be connected to the crimes. He and the other gang members were convicted of multiple robberies. According to what Steve Meadows told me, none of the stolen goods were recovered, and there was no indication of the money they'd have got if they'd managed to sell the items on the black market. Either someone is anxious to locate the proceeds, or to prevent Joe from getting them. And that in turn might mean other gang members are in danger.'

'Who are they?'

'I don't know, but let's see if Steve can tell us.'

Nash phoned the sergeant, but after his initial request for information, spent the rest of the call listening. After ringing off, he turned to Lisa, who noted the grave expression on his face. 'Four members of the Country House Bandits were convicted, each of them getting ten years inside. Of the four, Frank Watson was stabbed to death six months ago by another inmate. We've got Joe Lambert here, so that only leaves two others. Terry Palmer was also released this week, and Peter Swallow, aka Birdie, is due to come out today. Both of them could be targeted.'

'Do you think the motive is purely the money? Couldn't it be revenge?'

'I doubt that. There were rumoured to be several other gang members who were never identified. Maybe they're worried that the four who were convicted might come seeking retribution, or back pay. Let's go see Lambert's sister. Apart from breaking the bad news, I've got some questions for her. Do we know her name and address?'

'Mrs Walsh, Norma Walsh. She's a widow. Her husband died of cancer a few years ago. She lives here on Carthill.'

'Why doesn't that surprise me?'

CHAPTER EIGHT

It was clear that someone had beaten them to it, and Lambert's sister was already aware of Joe's death. Her tear-stained face as she glanced at their warrant cards was ample evidence of her grief.

She allowed them inside, and once in the sitting room, sat in silence opposite the detectives as Nash expressed their condolences. He paused and asked, 'I know this is a bad time, Mrs Walsh, but would you mind answering a few questions? They might help catching the person who did this terrible thing.'

She hesitated for a moment before agreeing.

'Do you know of anyone who had reason to kill Joe?'

Norma shook her head.

'Have you noticed anyone watching the house? Anybody acting suspiciously? What about his old friends — had Joe seen any of them since his release? Terry Palmer, for instance?'

That did get a reaction, but it was hardly the one Nash and Lisa were expecting. Norma's head came up, her grief turned instantly to anger. 'Don't mention that bastard. He wouldn't have the nerve to come near me, and certainly wouldn't go within a mile of Joe. Not after the way he behaved. If they had met up, it would likely have been Palmer who was laying dead, not poor Joe.'

'Sorry, Mrs Walsh, you'll have to explain. Why wouldn't Palmer be welcome with you or Joe? What was it he did that was so terrible?'

'I went out with Palmer for a few months just before they were all arrested. I was young and didn't know any better,' she added bitterly. 'And for a while I thought the sun shone out of his . . . er . . . well, you know. Terry was small, no taller than me, and he once told me the best things come in small packages, and for long enough I believed him. I didn't know he and Joe were part of that gang and were going round robbing houses. That wasn't the worst bit. When Joe heard that I'd been sleeping with Terry, he went mad and threatened Palmer. I hoped Terry would stand up to him, would stand by me, but the snivelling coward did nothing of the sort. He gave in and promised Joe he'd stop seeing me. That was how little I meant to him. All he was after was getting his end away. That meeting was the last time Joe and Terry saw each other before they were arrested. Joe blamed Palmer for the arrest.'

'What did Terry say about it?'

'I don't know. The weasel never had the balls to contact me. No phone call, not even a letter.'

Lisa went to make a cup of tea for Norma, while Nash offered to send a victim liaison officer to stay with her. 'In cases like this, the press will probably get involved, and the officer would be here to protect you from them.'

Nash agreed to make the arrangements and they left, promising to keep her updated of anything relevant.

'What's next?' Lisa asked Nash once they were outside.

'Back to Helmsdale and we can make a start on the paperwork. We also need to try and find out where Terry Palmer is.'

'You think he might be the killer? He certainly sounds to have a good motive.'

'Actually, I think it's the other way round. Like Mrs Walsh said, if it had been Palmer who was stabbed to death, Lambert would have had a very strong motive, but I can't see Palmer's betrayal of Norma over ten years ago giving rise to Lambert's murder within days of his being released from jail.'

* * *

Norma Walsh remained seated for a long time after the detectives left, her thoughts on the dreadful events of the previous few hours. It was only after his arrest that she'd learned that Joe had been part of the gang who had pulled of a series of high-value and audacious robberies, for which he had paid the penalty via a long prison sentence. Much good it had done him. He hadn't even been given chance to enjoy his freedom, let alone profit from his crimes. She knew Joe's weakness had made him easy prey for the others, who had used him and taken advantage of his easy-going nature. Her hatred for the other gang members was now absolute. In particular, she blamed and detested Terry Palmer.

Norma, an impressionable teenager, had fallen hard for Terry. He'd seemed so confident and mature — so charming. He'd been a refreshing change from the brash youths she'd encountered before, only interested in getting their leg over. It had come as a terrible shock when she found out he was a liar, a con man, and wasn't even strong enough to stand up for her when confronted by his best mate.

The detectives had implied that Palmer might be a victim. He'd be no loss, but it wouldn't bring Joe back. Norma began to cry, as she hadn't done for a long time. When her husband finally succumbed to cancer, Norma had remained calm. The long months of suffering prepared her for the inevitable. She'd been fond of him in a way, but theirs was no passionate love match. Not like . . .

As she thought again of Terry Palmer, her tears fell faster.

* * *

Shortly before he was due to attend the post-mortem, Nash asked Lisa, 'Are you busy tonight?'

'Not specially. Alan's away on business, so I was going to have a quiet night in.'

'Do you fancy going to the pub?'

Lisa blinked with surprise. Nash wasn't a frequent pub-goer that she knew of, nor did he socialize much with work colleagues. This, it soon turned out, was business, not pleasure.

'Where were you thinking of?'

'I thought we should go to the Red Bear and ask for information about Lambert's last night.'

Lisa whistled with surprise. The arrival of two police officers in a pub such as the Red Bear was likely to be as inflammatory as throwing a lighted match into a pool of petrol. Still, she could hardly let Nash go alone.

'OK, I'm up for it,' she agreed, 'but it would have to be a soft drink for me.' She patted her stomach, where the evidence of her pregnancy was beginning to appear. She paused before asking, 'Should I wear a stab vest, do you think?'

Nash smiled fleetingly. 'I don't think that will be necessary. I'll nip home after the post-mortem and then meet you outside the Red Bear later, say nine o'clock?'

By the time they reached the pub, Nash reasoned, a fair number of the regulars would be in attendance. Shortly before then, Lisa pulled up alongside Nash's Range Rover. Theirs were among the few other vehicles in the pub car park. The bar was a lively hum of chatter and laughter as they entered, but this gradually died down as they were seen, and recognized. There were several angry glares, most of them directed at Nash, who seemed to be the focus of the drinkers' dislike. He had a quiet word with the landlord and waited by the bar. A couple of seconds passed before the publican rang the bell, called for silence and explained that the police officers wanted to say something.

Nash turned to face the sea of scowling faces and smiled slightly. 'I'm sorry for disturbing your evening, but as you're probably aware, Joe Lambert was murdered after he left here last night, stabbed to death in a dark alley. I guess many of you knew Joe, and some of you were his friends, so I'm sure you'll want us to catch the killer. That's why I'm here to ask if any of you saw or heard anything that might be useful, and would share that information with us.'

'How do we know your lot didn't do it? Joe was no friend of the police,' a man near the back of the room shouted.

It was the sort of reaction Lisa had expected, but the way Nash dealt with it had her smiling with admiration.

'That is a ridiculous suggestion,' Nash said calmly. 'Have you any idea how much paperwork we would have to fill in if we stabbed anybody? Even fitting someone up for a job they didn't do is hardly worth the hassle these days.'

There was stunned silence for a moment, and then someone laughed. It was no more than a chuckle, but the humour was enough to cause several others to grin. Nash pressed home his slight advantage. 'Regardless of the crime he went down for, Joe Lambert was well-liked, and wasn't a violent man. So, if anybody can help us it would be much appreciated. You can do so in confidence by phoning Helmsdale nick, or by ringing the number on the cards I'm going to leave behind the bar. You can ask for me or for DC Andrews,' he said, gesturing to Lisa. 'The cards have the CID direct phone number on them, for those who don't already know it.'

There was another ripple of laughter at this comment, but this died away as Nash said, 'Please help us if you can, for Joe's sake, and for his sister. She's had too much tragedy in her life already. If anyone here has reservations about grassing to us, please put them aside. I know that in normal cases it would be frowned on, but the cold-blooded assassination of a defenceless, unarmed man is different. I'm not supposed to reveal how Joe was killed, but I can tell you it was a stabbing so violent the weapon almost went through him.'

He paused, allowing the full weight of that statement to sink in, before adding, 'That suggests it was a professional hit, callous and premeditated. I hope what I've told you tonight will convince you to give any help you can towards putting the killer behind bars. Have a think about it. Something you might have seen or heard and don't believe is relevant could be a clue, which would be one more than we've got now. Thank you for listening, and the landlord has a fund to repay you for lost drinking time.'

Nash turned, thanked the landlord and handed him some cash. As they were walking to their cars, Lisa said, 'That was brilliant, Mike. Getting us out of there without being lynched was the best I could have hoped for before we went in, but you managed to get them on our side. I wouldn't be surprised if we get some calls as a result. By the way, how much did you leave behind the bar?'

'Fifty quid. That way they should all get one drink out of it, and it doesn't appear too blatant a bribe. I'm not sure we'll get any calls, though. At best it's a long shot, because of the time and location of the killing. They were probably all blathered, as you succinctly put it, by then. And unless someone noticed a suspicious character when Lambert was in the pub, there will be nothing to tell us. I wanted to ask about Terry Palmer but I didn't dare to.'

'Why not?'

'It might make it appear as if we think Palmer is the culprit rather than a potential victim. The last thing we need is someone jumping to conclusions and taking the law into their own hands. We're supposed to be preventing crime rather than encouraging it.'

CHAPTER NINE

With few other local news items, certainly with none as sensational as a murder, the *Netherdale Gazette* had been quick to take advantage of the stabbing. After a hasty conference between Nash, Superintendent Fleming and Chief Constable Edwards, it was agreed that the name and history of the victim should not be released. Putting this idea forward, Nash explained his logic.

'Lambert was part of the Country House Bandits, as they were nicknamed at the time. Another of the four, Frank Watson, was killed in prison. Lambert had only been out of jail a couple of days when he was murdered. Another member of the outfit, Terry Palmer, was released at the same time, and the final one who had been locked up, Peter Swallow, is out this week. If Lambert's murder was connected to those crimes, and frankly I can't see any other motive, the killer might want to strike again before we've made sure the others are safe. Apart from the timing of the murder, the method makes it appear like a professional hit, rather than a mugging gone wrong or a crime of passion. Lambert had only been at liberty a couple of days, hardly long enough to go tampering with someone else's woman.'

'I agree about not releasing the victim's name — the press are capable of finding that out for themselves. But assuming there is a connection, what about warning Palmer and Swallow? Have you contacted them?' the chief constable asked.

'We can't find Palmer, and frustratingly, Swallow left prison half an hour before I put a call into the governor, so we're unable to get in touch with either of them, which is why I think we should release as little information to the media as possible. If Lambert's killer believes we've not made the connection, it might give us sufficient breathing space to provide protection for the other two.'

'I agree with Mike,' Fleming added. 'I think we should keep a tight hold on the media. If we can make the connection, they will, and the whole story with be in the local TV and radio bulletins tonight and on tomorrow's front pages.'

'You must do your best to discourage them, Jackie,' the chief constable said. 'And Mike, you should make it your priority to find these two and offer them protection. Put your full team on it.'

Nash smiled. 'My full team is only two,' he reminded her. 'Clara's away until Monday and Viv's on that training course you insisted he attend, so it's just Lisa Andrews and me. Still, we'll do the best we can.'

'I suppose this is a bad time to discuss further possible budget cuts,' the chief constable murmured.

It was only when he noticed Ruth Edwards' smile that Nash realized she was joking.

Fleming got up to leave and Nash went to follow, when the chief held up a hand. 'Don't leave yet, Mike.' She picked up her phone and requested refreshments for them. Minutes later, there was a knock at the office door and Ruth's secretary appeared with a tray of coffee.

Nash took his cup and settled back in his chair, wondering where this conversation was going.

'I have some excellent news for you,' the chief announced, 'regarding both your staffing levels and the introduction of some new technology I think you will find extremely helpful. As you're probably aware, I had a high-level meeting a couple of months ago with senior officials from the Home Office. Because we still don't have a replacement Police and Crime Commissioner, I have to deal with them direct. The subject of that meeting was to discuss the future funding for our area's force. I made my point very strongly, and as a result the restrictions which have impeded our activities in recent years have been lifted — slightly.'

Ruth smiled again as she saw Nash's startled expression. 'I have to admit, I was pleasantly surprised by their reaction, and by the level to which they're prepared to go to increase our funding. This means I have been recruiting more officers. Inspector Grant of Traffic Division will be delighted to hear he is to have two new unmarked cars, all fitted with the latest on-board ANPR systems. So far, I have interviewed two specialist traffic officers. Traffic Constable Peter Starkey, who was keen to come back to North Yorkshire, having been co-opted by Derbyshire. And another returnee, David Hutchinson, who has served with the Teesside force, utilizing his driving skills to maximum advantage. Despite his successful record there, David wanted to return to the area where he spent his childhood.'

Nash was unsure how this would help him.

She continued, 'The Netherdale control room is also taking on new emergency operators. Sadly, the funding does not allow for a specialist police helicopter, but we will have what, in my opinion, is an equally efficient and much more cost-effective alternative. More of that shortly, but for the immediate future, thinking about the CID crew, I'm aware that DC Andrews will be going on maternity leave, and also, once Alondra has given birth, you will be needed for nappy-changing duties. With that in mind, I've persuaded the powers that be to authorize an extra full-time team member.'

Nash sat forward, delighted but concerned. Knowing how well his team worked together it could prove difficult engaging with a new officer.

'The good news gets even better, because the applicant I've selected is an experienced detective. He is *au fait* with IT, and was a specialist drone operator before he transferred to CID. Of course, he still has those skills.'

'We don't have a drone,' Nash pointed out. 'Although, given the terrain we cover, I've often thought one would be extremely useful.'

Her smile widened as she pointed to the corner of her office, where two boxes were stacked. 'Yes, we do. In fact, we have two! The course Viv Pearce is on covers drone operation, so we'll soon have two pieces of equipment, together with the manpower to use them. That was what I meant by an alternative to a police helicopter.'

'OK, so who is this paragon of virtue you've selected to join us?' Nash was trying not to show his concern.

'Someone I understand you met briefly a good few years ago, when he was only a boy. You obviously made a good impression. Don't ask me how, because he said you and the team inspired him to join the force when he grew up.' She shook her head in mock dismay.

She passed Nash a personnel folder and explained, 'His name is Adil Hassan, detective constable. His family once owned a newsagent's that was the subject of a racially motivated arson attack.'

'Yes, I remember. In fact, I think he was instrumental in getting his family to safety during the fire.'

'I believe that's so. At interview, he told me that event changed his life, because he'd never have dreamed of a career in law enforcement until then. It was the action of our team that convinced him. He's been serving in West Yorkshire, and more recently in Greater Manchester, but now he's keen to return home.'

'Does his family still live round here?'

'His mother and sister do, despite having sold the shop a few years ago. Sadly, Adil's father died eighteen months ago. That's part of the reason Adil wants to come back, so he can be near his family. I believe he has a brother who lives and works in London.'

'I thought the shop was destroyed in that fire.'

'It was, but the local community was so appalled by the racist action they organized a crowd-funding event. A benefactor heard of it and gave a six-figure donation, which enabled them to rebuild the premises completely. That's another reason Adil is keen to work here — he believes he and his family owe a debt to the people of Helmsdale. He's arriving on Thursday.'

'Then I'd better see to the reorganisation of the general office in CID to incorporate another work station. Fortunately, there's ample room.'

* * *

Nash decided to visit Norma Walsh again. One glance at the woman's face told him her grief hadn't abated in the slightest.

She followed him into the living room and asked what he wanted, her tone listless and depressed. Nash was surprised the family liaison officer hadn't answered the door, and asked where she was.

Norma sighed. 'You must be joking. This is the Carthill. I don't want police on site constantly.'

Nash nodded his acceptance, telling her she could always change her mind if the press became a problem. He glanced at the mantelpiece, where he saw a photo he guessed was Norma taken at about the age of eighteen. She'd been a lovely young girl, and even now, she was a handsome woman. Focusing on the request he had come to make, he said, 'I know you must feel bitter about Palmer and Swallow, but I need all the help I can get. I must offer them protection, but I can't do that unless I can find them.'

'What makes you think I can help, even if I wanted to? Which I don't — certainly not in Palmer's case.'

Despite the negativity of her reply, her tone of voice betrayed some interest. Nash explained what he wanted her to do. 'The last thing either of them will want is to talk to us. However, after being inside so long they will want to meet up with people they know. If you pass the word along that they might be in danger, someone might warn them before it's too late.'

He left a few minutes later, having obtained Norma's agreement to think about his request, and that, he thought as he drove away, was as much as could be expected.

As she watched the detective depart, Norma thought again about Terry Palmer. It was only when she began to cry that she realized, with something of a shock, the nature of her true feelings for him. Despite the bitterness of their parting, despite everything she'd said and thought about him, Norma finally acknowledged that, deep down, she still loved Terry.

CHAPTER TEN

It was early evening when Peter Swallow stepped off the sprinter train at Netherdale station. Birdie knew the town well, having visited it many times when he'd linked up with Terry Palmer and Joe Lambert, travelling from his home in Leeds with Frank Watson.

The small suitcase he was carrying was his only possession. There was nobody waiting on the platform to greet him, nor had he expected there to be. During the journey he'd reflected on this, remembering his wife, wondering where Cindy was now. She'd vanished shortly after he and the others had been found guilty and sentenced.

At the time the disappearance hadn't seemed suspicious, but the more Peter thought about it, and he'd had plenty of time to do that over the years, the odder it seemed. She'd seemed quite happy, working part-time as a waitress in a Leeds city centre café, and hadn't even been particularly shocked or upset by his arrest. Only a couple of weeks after he was imprisoned, Cindy had written to tell him she'd applied for a visiting permit, but then she'd failed to turn up when scheduled. He'd thought no more about it than perhaps she'd been unable to get time off, or to afford the fare. But when she didn't make contact or request another visit, he asked the prison authorities to get the police to conduct a welfare check to see if she was all right.

That had been difficult, but after prolonged badgering, the local force visited their flat. No trace of his wife was found, and the sparse report he received stated that there was mouldy food in the fridge, the bed was unmade, and it looked as if Cindy had simply walked out on her old life. Birdie had insisted on reporting Cindy as a missing person, but to no effect.

Now he was free, Swallow could begin to look for Cindy in earnest, and hopefully he'd be able to find out what had become of her. And he knew just where to start. That would have to wait, though. First, he needed to see Palmer and Lambert. They would want to help him locate the Keeper, so they could all collect the large amount of money due to them.

Swallow walked from the platform, reflecting that little seemed to have changed. He headed for the toilets. He'd visited the bars in both Leeds station and York, as he'd waited for the trains that would take him to Netherdale. He'd only had four pints, not much by his previous standard, but his bladder was unused to being put under so much stress, and now he needed to relieve the discomfort.

The tiled gents was empty. Swallow set his suitcase down and stood at the urinal. The door opened. He glanced over his shoulder, surprise turning to astonishment and fear, as he recognized the figure standing in the entrance. Shock rendered him speechless. That fear was justified, as into the silence the newcomer spoke — only three words, a short valedictory message that was neither romantic nor amusing.

'Bye, Bye, Birdie.'

A split second later, Swallow fell backwards against the urinal, a pool of blood and urine mixed together as it spread across the tiled floor. Swallow was beyond noticing as he stared sightlessly at the ceiling.

A couple of minutes later, another of the passengers from the late train decided to use the facilities. He opened the restroom door, the procedure hampered by the large suitcase he was hauling. One glance inside caused him to turn abruptly, almost cannoning into another would-be user.

'You can't go in there.'

'Why not? I have to . . .' The man's voice tailed off as he saw the blood-stained corpse on the floor. 'I'll use the ladies,' he muttered as he dashed away.

The passenger set aside his luggage, stared inside the room for a few seconds and then took out his mobile.

* * *

Mike Nash had just reached Smelt Mill Cottage and was in the process of greeting Alondra and their Labrador, Teal, when his mobile rang. He glanced at the screen and grimaced. 'Steve Meadows,' he told Alondra.

He listened and then responded. 'I'm on my way. Let me have the details when I'm en route.'

He glanced at Alondra and shrugged. 'Sorry, darling, but I have to go. A man's body has been found in the toilets at Netherdale station.'

'Oh dear.' She nodded, understanding how Nash's life could be so easily disrupted. 'I'll turn the casserole down after I've fed Daniel. We can eat later.'

'Don't wait for me. Have yours, I don't know how long I'll be.'

'OK, let me know when you're on the way home.' As she watched Nash drive away, Alondra wondered how hungry he would be after what he was about to see.

Nash was halfway to Netherdale when Meadows reported back. 'Apparently the guy who found the body is a police officer, name of Adil Hassan. He asked for you by name, which suggests he knows the area.'

'He certainly does, and that's not a very nice welcome when returning home. You'll get to meet Adil very soon, probably as early as tomorrow. He's a detective constable who will be joining our team.' Nash explained Hassan's background briefly, and said, 'I'll fill you in with all the details later. By the way, why are you in Netherdale Control again?'

'Overtime,' was the simple answer.

When he reached the railway station, the entrance to the toilet block was being guarded by a uniformed officer. Nash flashed his ID.

'Evening, sir. My colleague's in the station master's office with the man who found the stiff,' he told Nash, directing him across the concourse.

'OK, I'll just take a look inside. Then I'll go talk to him before I put fancy dress on.'

The officer smiled at Nash's description of the protective clothing used at crime scenes. Having glanced at the body, Nash went to greet Hassan.

The tall, good-looking young man with designer stubble bore little resemblance to the boy he had met years earlier. To the confusion of the officer caring for a potential witness, or maybe even the culprit, Nash reached out and shook Adil by the hand. 'Adil, good to see you, although this isn't exactly how I thought we'd meet up.'

'Me neither, although I'm quite used to seeing bodies, Inspector Nash.'

Nash dismissed the officer, who was now even more confused. 'I'll take it from here,' he told him.

He turned to Adil. 'It's Mike, not Inspector Nash. We work only on first names in our team — unless we're in public,' he added. 'I was delighted when the chief told me you were joining us, but let's get down to business. Tell me what you saw and heard.'

'I can't be certain, but the dead man might have been on the Leeds train I arrived on. There weren't that many people aboard, and almost all the others headed straight for the car park, so I guess they were commuters. I didn't see anyone else on the platform, so I assume the killer was waiting for the victim.'

'That would suggest a targeted, premeditated crime. Anything else?'

Adil thought for a moment. 'I certainly didn't hear any raised voices or anything like a scream. And from what I saw, there appears to be a stab wound to the victim's chest.'

'Did you see anyone suspicious in the vicinity of the toilets?'

'There was one bloke, who appeared to be quite elderly. He was wearing an overcoat and hat, so I didn't get a good look at him.' He paused, before adding, 'He was using a walking stick. I guess he was bad on his pins, because he seemed to be leaning heavily on it. If I think of anything else, I'll let you know.'

'You must need to get home. One of our guys can give you a lift. I don't imagine you want to spend your first evening here watching Mexican Pete at work.'

Noticing Adil's puzzled expression, Nash told him, 'Professor Ramirez. He's our tame pathologist.'

'I think I'll forego the pleasure, if you don't mind. My sister's coming to collect me, so I won't need a lift.'

'In that case, we can catch up at Helmsdale tomorrow. You can make a statement, then we can get to work solving this murder.'

'Actually, I've been told to report to the chief constable first thing. I believe she's got a package for me.'

'That'll be your drone.' Nash thought for a moment, before suggesting, 'While you're there, it might be a good idea to give your statement about tonight to someone outside the team you'll be working alongside.'

Nash was about to allow Adil to leave when he had another thought. 'Do you like coffee?'

'I do, but why do you ask?'

'We more or less live on it at Helmsdale, so you're going to fit in really well.'

* * *

DC Lisa Andrews was in reception, talking to Steve Meadows, when Nash arrived at Helmsdale next morning. He told them, 'DC Adil Hassan, our new team member and drone pilot, is due to join us today, but he's calling at Netherdale to report to the chief constable and collect his equipment first.

While he's there, he'll also be giving a statement regarding the murder he almost witnessed yesterday evening. I thought it better for him to talk about it to someone he won't be working closely with.'

'Steve was in the middle of telling me about it. So, what exactly happened?'

Nash was about to reply when his mobile rang. Lisa stifled a giggle at the comical grimace on Nash's face as he answered. 'Good morning, Professor. I thought you'd scheduled the post-mortem for this afternoon, has that changed?'

'No, it's still on for after lunch, but first I thought you'd like to know the identity of the victim. In fact, if you'd used one of those fancy hand-held fingerprint gizmos last night, you'd have got it then and there.'

'I take it he's in our system?'

'He certainly is, and he's closely connected to another occupant of my drawers. His name is Peter Swallow, aka Birdie, and he's another member of the Country House Bandit gang. I would call that coincidence, but I understand that word has been excluded from your dictionary.'

'It certainly has, Professor. Thanks for the info. I'll see you this afternoon.'

Nash told Meadows, 'I want you to order up the files on every member of the Country House Bandit gang, with every reference to associates, next of kin and personal history. Plus the files referring to their trials, and the investigations into the robberies they committed.'

'Why is that relevant?' Lisa asked.

'Because Mexican Pete has just revealed the identity of the victim of last night's stabbing. It was Peter Swallow, another member of the gang. Which means three of the four gang members locked up for crimes have now been murdered. One while in prison, the two others within days of their release.'

As the detectives were about to set off for the CID suite, Meadows told them, 'By the way, there was a delivery for you earlier, probably while you were still eating your breakfasts.

By the names on the boxes, I guess it's the additional computer equipment for our new colleague. I got the driver to place it on the spare workstation in the general office. The technician from HQ will be here shortly to set it all up.'

As they were walking upstairs, Lisa remarked, 'Steve gets more and more like Jack Binns every day.'

'That's no bad thing. Jack was a great team member before he retired, and Steve's shaping up to be a good replacement, his weird sense of humour apart. Have you any idea why he's doing so much overtime? Is there a problem?'

'Not that I know of, but leave it to me and I'll find out. Have you given any more thought as to the motive for killing off the gang members?'

'I've barely had chance, but a couple of ideas crossed my mind when Mexican Pete told me about Swallow. It could be a victim of their robberies seeking revenge, but I think that's unlikely. The more probable motive is someone cleaning house.'

'Cleaning house? What do you mean by that?'

'When Steve phoned me about Joe Lambert's murder, I recall him mentioning a note on Lambert's file to the effect that there could possibly be other gang members who were never identified. If that's correct, those people could be afraid one of our victims was about to grass them up. However, until we have a look through those files, all this is idle speculation. We have far greater immediate priorities.'

'Such as?'

'Getting the coffee machine filled and switched on. Despite Steve's slanderous remarks, it's been a long time since breakfast. After that, I'll ask Steve to help me move the furniture round before the tech guy arrives.'

'Don't bother Steve. I can help,' Lisa said.

After rearranging the furniture in the general office, they surveyed the result. There were four desks, which they had placed in pairs so the occupants faced one another. Pearce and Hassan would occupy two, which Nash had designated 'IT corner', while the others belonged to Lisa and DS Mironova.

Once the technician had arrived, he unpacked the equipment and soon had it working. After running a few tests, he was satisfied and left. Lisa was tasked with taking the packaging to the bin. On her return, she went to Nash's office and told him, 'Steve's got some of those files you asked for, ready to download. He's been able to access the personal data of the gang members, plus the transcripts of their trials, and some of the investigations into their burglaries. Unfortunately, because some of the offences took place a long time ago, and were in rural locations similar to here, files relating to them have never been digitalized, so he's had to order paper copies. Do you want me to download and print off those that are available?'

Nash was about to agree, but then told her, 'No, I've had a better idea. Adil should be arriving shortly. In the absence of our computer whiz, Viv, let's put him to work using his IT skills. It'll make a really meaningful first task for the lad, and get him to feel part of the team from day one.'

As Lisa took her seat, she said, 'He's getting married.'

'Adil? How did you find that out?'

'No, not Adil.' Lisa laughed. 'Steve. Steve Meadows. You remember? He came back here — for love,' she said, fluttering her eyelashes dramatically. 'He's working any hours he can get, saving for the wedding. How romantic,' she sighed.

Nash shook his head. 'Lisa.'

She smiled at him. 'Yes, boss?' she giggled.

'Go and make some more coffee.'

CHAPTER ELEVEN

Steve buzzed through to announce Adil Hassan's arrival and Nash went to meet him. On the reception desk, Nash noticed the two boxes he'd last seen in the chief constable's office. 'I'll give you a hand upstairs with them,' he offered. 'We can't afford to leave valuable equipment lying around here.'

'Definitely not,' Meadows commented. 'My officers are totally untrustworthy.'

Nash grinned and shook his head. 'You'll get used to him,' he told Adil.

Having been introduced to Lisa and supplied with coffee, Nash invited Adil into his office and asked how his meeting with the chief constable had gone.

'Actually, I met with both her and Superintendent Fleming.' Hassan smiled, prompting Nash to ask what he found amusing.

'Superintendent Fleming referred to what happened yesterday evening as a baptism of fire for me. I didn't like to tell her we don't do baptism in my religion.'

Nash grinned and listened as Adil continued, 'After that, I met Mr Pratt, who had been designated to take my statement. It was good to see him looking so well, because I remember he was taken seriously ill during the time my family had all that trouble with the fire at the shop. Wasn't he the chief superintendent?'

'Yes, in the days before cutbacks. But Tom couldn't stand retirement, and as a civilian support, he's still a valuable member of our team. He and his colleague Maureen take a lot of the burden of administration from us, leaving us free to pursue investigations. Anyway, now that you're here, let me explain the seating arrangement. You and Viv Pearce will occupy those desks in the far corner. The tech guy has left you a password to access the system, and says you must set up your own. Of course, you're fully aware of all that.' Nash shook his head and laughed. 'Lisa and DS Clara Mironova use the other two. I keep out of the way in here. Unless my door is closed, you don't have to knock before coming in. I told you, we don't do formality round here. Remember, first-name terms — unless we're in public, of course — but never call me "sir". Now, Lisa will show you round, primarily the coffee machine, then I've got a job for you.'

Adil had one question, which he asked Lisa when they were in the kitchen. 'Mike mentioned DC Pearce and DS Mironova, but I don't see any sign of them.'

'That's because Viv's on a drone-handling course, and Clara's on leave. You'll meet both of them on Monday. As a small team, we don't normally have two people off at the same time, but Viv had orders from above.' She laughed.

Adil's memory of past events stirred. 'Is DS Mironova a fair-haired lady?'

'Yes, that sounds like Clara. She's actually Mrs Sutton now, but it's easier to keep to Mironova at work.'

'I remember her now. She was extremely kind to me and my family after the arson attack. It will be nice to meet her again — even nicer to be working alongside her.'

After setting Hassan to work on the computerized files that needed downloading, Nash told him and Lisa, 'I'm off to Netherdale now, to watch Mexican Pete at work in his butcher's shop.'

The remark puzzled Adil, but once Nash was out of ear-shot, Lisa explained, 'That's just Mike's sense of humour. What he meant is, he'll be the attending officer present while Professor Ramirez conducts the post-mortem on the toilet victim.'

* * *

It was late afternoon when Nash returned, but instead of entering his office, he perched on the edge of Pearce's desk whilst he had a word with Adil. 'When we were talking yesterday evening, you mentioned seeing an elderly man using a walking stick near to the place where Swallow was killed. Is that correct?'

'Yes, Mike.'

'Are you certain he was an old man?'

'I thought so, because of the way he was walking, leaning heavily on the stick for support. I couldn't see his face, because he was wearing a hat, and an overcoat with the collar turned up . . .' Hassan's voice trailed off.

Nash had guessed the implication, but wanted his colleague to put the idea forward. 'What is it?'

'Now I've had time to think about it, there was something really odd about that man and the way he was dressed. It was quite a warm evening, and yet he was wearing an overcoat with the collar turned up. Unless he had some disorder that meant he had to keep his body temperature up, the only reason for dressing like that is to avoid someone recognizing him.'

'Why is this so important, Mike?' Lisa interjected.

'It's important because I think Adil's just realized the man he saw had only a few minutes earlier stabbed Peter Swallow to death.'

'If that's correct, what did he do with the weapon? Do you think it was concealed under his coat?'

'No, I believe Adil also saw the weapon, although he couldn't have known that's what it was. Mexican Pete revealed that both Joe Lambert and Peter Swallow were stabbed with a long, extremely sharp blade, either a sword or a rapier. Brandishing something of that nature in an alleyway during the early hours of the morning would carry very little risk, but waving one around in a railway station during daylight hours is a totally different matter. I think the only way the killer could have concealed it is by using a swordstick.'

Establishing the potential murder weapon might have been viewed as a step forward, but as Nash remarked, it brought them no nearer to discovering a motive for the crimes, let alone pointing to the identity of the killer.

'Perhaps your theory was correct, and someone was afraid either Lambert or Swallow would grass them up,' Lisa suggested.

Nash grinned. 'You mean they were worried that Birdie would sing?'

Lisa groaned. 'You have my sympathy, Adil. That's the sort of bad joke you'll have to get used to round here.'

Ignoring Lisa's jibe, Nash told them, 'I suggest we wait for the paper files to arrive before we do anything more. When we have everything, we'll be able to form a more rounded picture of the gang members. By that, I mean their personalities, background, any relationships they were in, plus more detailed knowledge of their MO when they conducted the burglaries. Steve Meadows reckons the files should be here tomorrow, as they're being delivered via an express courier service.' Nash paused. 'Just don't tell the chief constable we're spending money so lavishly.'

'Er, Mike,' Adil said, 'do you want me to check on the station, see if there are any cameras to show us the old man? We could get a facial.'

'Good idea. Use your initiative and do what you can with any case we're working. You don't need permission, as long as you keep me or Clara in the loop. Put in the request and start in the morning. Let me know if you find anything. Before we leave I need to update you as to the current workload. Come into my office. It's more comfortable in there.'

* * *

Nash told Adil of the other cases that were occupying their attention, and showed him the photographs of the scene at the lead mine. The major case, he told him, was the discovery of the four bodies, the victims thus far unidentified. 'The other matter we might have to deal with in the near future is the presence in our area of a major drugs dealer. We believe he has migrated here from Manchester, but thus far we've been unable to find him, let alone pin anything on him.'

Three months earlier, Superintendent Fleming had called a meeting with the team at Helmsdale to inform them of a disturbing development in the area.

Nash relayed the context of that meeting. 'Jackie said she'd got a call from a member of the drugs unit in Greater Manchester. He wasn't able to give precise details, but he told her about a rumour circulating among the criminal fraternity there. The gossip concerned one of their region's biggest drugs dealers. He should have said "suspected" drug dealer, because the man in question has never been arrested, let alone convicted of any criminal offence.'

'I heard about the drugs operation on the station grapevine when I worked in Manchester, but I wasn't involved. Why should that concern us?' Adil asked.

'Because if the rumours are accurate, the suspect has left Greater Manchester with the intention of settling down somewhere near here. That's as much as their informant was either able, or willing, to reveal. But it's a major cause of anxiety on two counts. Number one, if he continues his activities, we'll have to deal with another major influx of narcotics, with the resultant increase in crime. Apart from that, the other worrying factor concerns the reason for him leaving Manchester.

'Jackie said that a couple of months ago, the man, Corey Davies, had his house destroyed in an arson attack, suspected to have been carried out by a rival gang. Luckily for him, Davies and his wife were absent, along with their two-year-old son. A week later, one of the men suspected of being behind the arson was found on waste ground near the outskirts of the city. Someone had tied him up, poured petrol over him, and set him alight. If that turf war continues, we'll not only have to contend with the upsurge in illegal substances, but also the strong possibility of a dramatic increase in violent crime here.'

Adil was thinking. 'Do we have any details about this guy, apart from his name? Things like photos of him and his family. A likely address where he'll be living would be useful.'

'Don't count on him using his real name. From what I was told, Davies more often than not uses one of a number of aliases. We do have some photos, but there's no certainty where he and his family will be. At the time, Lisa pointed out that it was a shame the child wasn't older, because he'd have to be registered with a school in the area. Here are photos of Davies, his wife Brittany, and the boy, whose name we don't know. There's also a list of those aliases Manchester knew, but there could be others we're unaware of.'

'What about known associates?'

Adil's question made Nash smile, but without much evidence of humour. 'There's no indication of anyone following him here. So, Manchester are working on the theory that, far from scaling back operations, Davies is actually using the arson attack as a means to an end — extending the scope of his activities. Jackie had one idea which proved useful. If Davies continued to get supplies from across the Pennines on a regular basis, we could pick up suspect vehicles carrying the drugs, by using our network of ANPR cameras, plus CCTV. That involved close monitoring of the system, but that was a task for Netherdale uniform and traffic branches. I want you to take these files and study them carefully. You might find the Corey Davies file amusing, in an ironic sort of way.'

Nash called through to Lisa, 'I'm still bringing Adil up to speed, but all this talking is making my throat dry.'

* * *

Having outlined all the cases, Nash headed for home. His absence gave Adil chance to ask Lisa about something

Nash had said in passing. 'Is the chief constable really so tight-fisted?'

'No, it's all part of a long-standing joke between Mike and Ruth Edwards. If she was really mean, she wouldn't have fought tooth and nail to get you on board, and persuade the powers that be to invest in the drone equipment, which can't have come cheap. Come on, home time. Steve will lock up.'

'I'm sorry, why would he lock up?'

Lisa began to laugh. 'Hasn't anybody told you? This station operates office hours, nine till five, Monday to Friday, unless we have a big case on. All prisoners go to Netherdale if they're overnighters.'

'Aren't two murders and four dead bodies big cases?'

'Of course, but wait till we're all here on Monday and you'll be lucky to eat regular meals. We could be working late nights and over the weekends.'

CHAPTER TWELVE

Within a couple of weeks of Jackie's original briefing, it seemed as if the surveillance, added to intelligence passed from Greater Manchester, was about to pay dividends.

Corey Davies had settled into his new location and begun trading, although 'continued trading' would have been a more accurate phrase, as he had already been supplying a network of dealers in the area for several months. The success of this sphere of his operations had been one of the reasons for choosing to move to Helmsdale.

Being of a naturally cautious nature, Corey knew he needed to adapt his style of trading to his new surroundings. With a large shipment of class A drugs due, he needed to ensure the goods arrived safely, and also wanted to test out the possibility of his activities being monitored by the local police. Knowing little of how they operated, Corey settled on a scheme he hoped would kill two birds with one stone. This would tell him how vigilant the force in this area was, while at the same time creating a diversion to allow the delivery to be made in safety.

In order to activate his plan, Corey contacted his associates in Manchester and issued a string of detailed instructions, some of which left them dumbfounded, until he explained.

Only then did they realize the cunning behind his strategy. Any reserve they might have entertained in carrying out his order to the letter was negated by the lucrative remuneration he'd added into the mix, as a reward for carrying his wishes to the letter — and by fear of the consequences should they fail to do so. A week later, with all components in place, they activated the scheme.

In Netherdale, Jackie Fleming had received a tip-off relayed via the Manchester force about a suspect vehicle rumoured to be heading in their direction. Only a few hours later, the indication of something brewing came via an ANPR camera on the outskirts of Netherdale. This flagged up a ten-year-old Citroen which showed no current MOT, no registered keeper and was untaxed and uninsured.

Alerted by Inspector Paul Grant, three patrol cars were sent to intercept the small vehicle, adopting a strategy known as TPAC, tactical pursuit and containment. This resulted in them boxing in the target vehicle on a deserted stretch of the Netherdale ring road.

Having detained the young driver, who smelled strongly of cannabis, officers conducted a search of the car, and discovered a large carrier bag bearing the name of a major supermarket chain. The shopping bag contained hundreds of small wraps of white powder, enough for one of the officers to exclaim, 'If that's what I think it is, there must be thousands of pounds' worth in there.'

'Yes,' his colleague replied, 'and I'm a bit surprised, because I didn't know Asda sold cocaine.'

A roadside drugs wipe on the driver confirmed the presence of cannabis, resulting in his arrest for suspected driving under the influence, plus driving an uninsured, untaxed vehicle, and not possessing a licence. A far more serious charge, known in traffic police slang as PWITS, possession with intent to supply, was also added to the youth's list of offences.

At about the same time as the young driver was being shown into his cell in Netherdale police station, Corey Davies took delivery of the drugs he'd been expecting.

Once the traffic officers had dealt with the driver, they adjourned to the station canteen for a well-earned mug of tea, essential in their mid-shift break. One of them commented, 'The weird thing is, that lad didn't seem at all worried by the drugs charge. You'd think someone so young would be wetting themselves if they knew they'd be facing a long stretch inside.'

They weren't to know that the young man they had locked up had been well paid for his services.

Within twenty-four hours, Inspector Grant sought out Superintendent Fleming. He stuck his head round her office door, telling her, 'We've released the driver of that Citroen on bail, and we've dropped the possession with intent to supply charge.'

'What about that huge quantity of wraps found in the car?'

Grant smiled ruefully. 'I think we've been made the butt of a practical joke. We can't make the charge stick, not unless cornflour has been made an illegal substance.'

'What?'

'That's correct. The lab confirmed that every single one of those wraps contained cornflour. So either someone set out to cheat local dealers, or we've been made to look a right set of plonkers.'

Fleming's immediate reaction was to call Nash. Having engaged speakerphone, she asked Grant to repeat what he'd just told her.

After listening to the story of the deception, Nash said, 'I think we can guess who organized that, don't you?'

'You think it was Corey Davies?'

'That would be my first choice. If the intelligence from Manchester is accurate, and Davies has been dealing for several years and escaped arrest, we've got to assume he's a lot smarter than the average drug peddler. Either that, or he's extremely lucky.'

'That may be so, but how do we prove it?'

'What is there to prove? The only crimes that have been committed are the motoring offences. Apart from wasting yet more resources on a wild-goose chase, all we'd achieve is making ourselves a laughing stock.'

Fleming winced at the accuracy of Nash's summary, but asked, 'So what do you recommend? Do we let the whole thing drop?'

'I'm not suggesting that. Let's look at the background to what happened. First of all, do we know where this vehicle the young lad was driving came from? Or for that matter, where the driver lives?'

'The car was previously registered to someone from Altringham in Cheshire, but they part-exchanged it for a new one nine months ago. The dealer stuck the Citroen in an auction, and someone bought it, paying cash. The youth we arrested lives in Wigan, and Paul Grant reckons the vehicle is a pool car.'

A pool car, as Nash knew, described a vehicle used by criminals, usually one without a registered keeper, often untaxed and uninsured. The Citroen fitted that to a T.

'I think the fact that both Altringham and Wigan are in Greater Manchester more or less proves that Corey Davies was behind the scam.' Nash thought for a moment, before adding, 'What I'm about to suggest might be a waste of time, but it might prove useful to discover if Davies used this tactic to divert attention, in order to ensure safe delivery of a drugs supply.'

'And just how do you suggest we do that? Use a crystal ball, or consult a fortune teller?'

Nash grinned at the waspish tone in Jackie's voice. 'Neither of those, but it might give us a clue if we checked ANPR footage around the same time Captain Cornflour was arrested. See if any other vehicles entered our area from Greater Manchester, vehicles which made the return journey a short while later. That would confirm the drugs had been delivered, and might give us an indication as to where Davies is operating from, even if it's only a general area.'

* * *

Two days later, Nash received an update. 'We did as you suggested, and trawled through the CCTV footage,' Jackie told him. 'Your idea was spot on. A silver Audi registered to someone in Wythenshawe, Greater Manchester, passed through cameras on either side of Netherdale, travelling towards Helmsdale. We can't pinpoint the exact address it went to. But less than an hour later, the same vehicle made the return journey. We contacted West Yorkshire and Greater Manchester police, who confirmed it had travelled straight back to the registered keeper's address. Manchester are very grateful, because the person in question hadn't been on their radar before. The registration number is now in the ANPR system. If it hits a camera again, we'll know. So when, as we expect, it returns, we'll be able to follow it to Davies' address, arrest him and the courier, and seize the drugs.'

That was all very well in theory, but the plan failed to take into account the depth of Davies' cunning. Over two months had passed, but the silver Audi had not reappeared.

* * *

After the successful deception and safe delivery of a large quantity of drugs, Corey Davies was still struggling to devise a new, secure method of obtaining supplies on a regular basis, without arousing suspicion. It was during a shopping expedition with his wife and son to Netherdale that he noticed a vehicle whose appearance suggested a possible solution to the problem.

He thought the idea over until he was satisfied the plan would work. A couple of weeks later, after having made a couple of phone calls, Davies had driven to Netherdale, caught a train to Leeds, then changed to another, heading for Manchester, where he was collected by his second-in-command. The strategy was more time-consuming than a road trip, but it would confound anyone following him.

Later that evening, when he'd returned to Helmsdale, Corey had all the elements of his scheme in place. Despite the brilliant subtlety of his plan, he had made one basic error. In hiring the services of a specialist to carry out part of the required work, Corey had failed to take into account a word that was not familiar to the workman. That word was 'dyslexia'.

Although time had passed and there was no evidence of the Audi triggering an alert on the ANPR system again, one of the officers monitoring the street cameras saw something on his screen that captured his attention.

He viewed the image a second and then a third time, before calling Inspector Grant, who immediately came to see what the officer had found so interesting. Grant took a long look and then reported to Superintendent Fleming. She gave specific instructions as to their follow-up actions. Forty-eight hours later, once backup evidence had been obtained, Fleming decided it was time to involve Nash and the detectives at Helmsdale. She ran down the schedule of events Grant had presented and realized this could wait until the following week, when the unit would be augmented with DS Mironova and DC Pearce. Fleming smiled ruefully — the two returnees were in for a rude awakening.

CHAPTER THIRTEEN

Despite the use of an express courier service, it was almost lunchtime on Friday before the paper files on the Country House Bandits' nefarious exploits arrived. After photocopying these, Adil ensured the paperwork was added to the computerized records already downloaded, giving each member of the team a full history of the burglars and their activities.

Nash told them, 'I think we should come in tomorrow to continue looking through these, make notes individually, and compare them. But on Monday, refrain from telling Clara or Viv anything of interest we find. That way, they can start from scratch, with no pre-conceived ideas. I'm not suggesting anything we learn from these files will definitely lead to Lambert or Swallow's killer, but every scrap of information we glean could prove crucial. Don't ignore anything that attracts your attention, no matter how trivial or inconsequential it might appear. And take your time. There's a lot to get through.'

When Nash had gone to his office, Adil asked Lisa, 'If we come in on weekends when the station is closed, how do we get in?'

'Steve will come in sometimes if he has paperwork to finish, but both Mike and Clara have keys.'

Midway through their examination, Nash called a halt. 'Time for a coffee break, and to walk away from the paperwork.'

Adil looked confused.

'It's the way we work, Adil. I once heard a proofreader say unless they pause regularly, they start reading the story, rather than examining the text. The same applies to us. We could miss something vital if our brain has moved onto the next paragraph. For that reason, we should also refrain from discussing what we've found so far.'

It was late when the session ended, but there was still time for them to compare notes. All three had picked up anomalies within the personal histories of the Bandits, which Adil outlined first.

'I found it strange when I noticed Swallow requested a welfare check after his wife failed to arrive for a scheduled prison visit, and he was unable to raise her on the phone. The police officers found the flat empty. Cindy Swallow was gone, having taken few, if any, of her belongings with her. Despite Swallow reporting her as a misper, no trace of her was found. It would be useful if we can discover whether she's resurfaced, either here, or living it up on the Costa Del Crime.'

Lisa smiled at Adil's reference to the section of Spanish coast where career criminals were wont to hang out, but agreed with his comments, adding, 'I also spotted a file note about Frank Watson's widow, which made me wonder. When police visited Lauren Watson to tell her about her husband being murdered, there was nobody at home. The officers noticed some empty milk bottles on the doorstep, so they contacted the local dairy. The roundsman said Mrs Watson had left a note cancelling all deliveries until further notice, citing an extended visit to her sister in Canada. There's nothing in the file to say whether she's returned, or even if she knows her husband is dead. Having read about Cindy Swallow's disappearance, I find it rather sinister. It could be nothing more than a coincidence, but I'm not allowed to use that word round here.'

Nash agreed with both his colleagues. 'What about the robbery files? Did either of you spot anything useful in those?'

Both detective constables confessed they had failed to pick up anything of significance regarding the actual burglaries committed by the Country House Bandits. So Nash told them, 'There were a couple of pieces of information I noticed that suggest earlier speculation about there being more gang members might be correct — ones that have never been identified.'

'What was it your eagle eye discerned?' Lisa asked.

'I was checking the amount of property stolen from each house they burgled, and the descriptions of some of the missing items. To load such a large quantity into a van would have taken a long time. Time they didn't have at their disposal without fear of someone seeing them and raising the alarm. However, if there were two or more additional pairs of hands, that would shorten the timescale, and thereby lessen the risk of detection. That's one facet. The other is the sheer weight of a couple of items — the statues. Moving those without the aid of a forklift truck would have taken more than the four men arrested, unless they wanted to risk a hernia.'

Nash then mentioned another thought that had occurred to him. 'From what I read of their background, none of the four arrested men had much in the way of expertise at opening locked doors or cracking safes. They must have had someone else to do that, and to disable burglar alarms.'

One of the other items Nash had found interesting was the way the four robbers had been caught. They had become victims of their own cunning, albeit due to a lack of local knowledge. Prior to the burglaries, they distracted the police by making false emergency calls. Reporting events supposedly happening several miles away from their target property lessened the chances of attracting unwanted attention.

This tactic, which had worked so well, now failed them. Someone made the hoax call from a public phone box sited close to the house they were about to enter. They were phoning, they said, to report a gas leak to the mains supply in a village fifteen miles away, where excavation work to provide supply to a new housing estate was taking place.

Unfortunately for them, the emergency operator who answered the call lived in the village they named, and was well aware there was no gas supply to the village. The nearest mains gas was five miles away. Her suspicions roused, she traced the origin to the phone box and alerted officers, who arrived in time to spot the van containing Watson, Swallow, Lambert and Palmer, plus an array of stolen valuables, as it was leaving the house they had just robbed. Using the pretext of a random traffic stop, the officers were able to pull the van up and arrest the occupants.

Reading this account, Nash wondered why only four of the gang had been present on that occasion. Or could others have been involved, members who had possibly left via another route, in a different vehicle? When the cargo compartment of a van is filled to capacity, there is only sufficient room for a limited number of passengers.

As he was reading this, another stray idea crossed his mind. He asked Lisa, 'Do you recall when we interviewed Norma, Joe Lambert's sister, she mentioned the row between Joe and Terry Palmer, and said it was that argument that led to them being arrested?'

'That's correct, Mike, but what of it?'

Nash gestured to the stack of files. 'If that's correct, how come there's no mention of anything like that in those? The only reason for their capture I noticed was the lack of local knowledge, causing them to alert the emergency operator to their scam call.'

Having pooled their findings, Nash turned to Hassan. 'Adil, I'd like you to discover all you can about Cindy Swallow and Lauren Watson. I'm talking about their personal details, family and so forth — anything that might help. It would be useful to know if either or both of them have reappeared, or where they went when they vanished so suddenly.'

He was surprised when Hassan reported back shortly before they were due to leave. 'I could find absolutely no trace of either woman following their disappearance. I looked under their married names, and also their birth names. In Cindy Swallow, née Pawson's case, she has one sister, Ellie Pawson. She lives in Skipton, West Yorkshire, where she works in a bookshop. I took the liberty of phoning her, and she confirmed she's neither seen nor spoken to Cindy for over ten years, possibly even longer. I got the impression there's very little love lost between the sisters. I didn't explain the reason for my call, just that it was a routine matter, because I wasn't sure you wanted facts about Peter Swallow's murder revealed at this stage.'

'Is that everything?'

'Far from it. What I discovered about Lauren Watson is even more disturbing. She was born Lauren Firth. If you recall, the milkman said he'd received a note stating Lauren was going to visit her sister in Canada. Either he was telling porkies, and I can't think of a reason for him doing that, or there's something highly suspicious about the woman's disappearance. Lauren Firth was an only child. Following her parents' deaths ten and six years ago respectively, she had no living relatives.'

Adil paused. 'There is one other interesting fact about Lauren Watson. She is in our system, because she was arrested three years ago and convicted of drink-driving. She blew almost twice the limit on the breathalyser, and was fined and disqualified from driving for eighteen months.'

There was no doubt in Nash's mind that Hassan's summary of his report as 'disturbing' was highly accurate, and one element of it triggered a memory of earlier that day. 'You've just reminded me of one other person mentioned in those files, someone we ought to check on.'

Nash reached for one of the folders and flicked through the papers until he reached the relevant section. 'Here it is, in the report from the prison where Peter Swallow was an inmate. He had one visitor, twice, in the last six months. The man's name is George Briggs, and he's listed in the prison records as being Swallow's half-brother. Could you run him through the computer? Oddly, there seems to be no other record of him in Swallow's personal data. With Cindy missing, Briggs is the closest living relative we know of, and as such, should be told about Swallow's death. I'll hang on until you've got the result.'

'I'll get straight on it, Mike.'

* * *

Less than half an hour later, Adil presented his findings. 'The prison records are quite correct. George Briggs is Peter Swallow's younger brother, the son of Swallow's mother and her second husband, both of whom are deceased. There is also a note that Swallow asked Briggs to help in the search for Cindy, but no comment as to the outcome. Briggs is single, lives in Leeds and works as a painter and decorator. I have a landline number for his flat, would you like me to call him?'

Nash shook his head and reached for the note Adil was holding. 'I'll do it,' he grimaced ruefully. 'That's one of the penalties of seniority, I'm afraid, being the bearer of bad news.'

Although he tried the number twice before leaving the office, Nash got no reply. Assuming Briggs to be working, he decided to take the details home and try from there when Briggs might be available.

When he met with no success, either that evening or on Sunday, trying at varying times of the day and evening, he resolved to request a welfare check to be carried out by West Yorkshire Police. It was quite possible Briggs was away on holiday, but Nash wasn't prepared to take the chance.

As he reflected on what had happened during his deputy's short absence, Nash realized they now not only had six unsolved murders, but also two, possibly three, mysterious disappearances to contend with. DS Mironova wouldn't be happy returning to work with so much having surfaced in the meantime. He grinned. No doubt Clara would try and put the blame on him. He could retaliate by telling her it was her fault for swanning off on holiday.

Saturday's postal delivery to Smelt Mill Cottage had brought Nash one item of interest, which he later realized would provide further information — and yet more frustration, coupled with a degree of sadness.

Following another fruitless attempt to contact Briggs, Alondra had brought Nash a copy of the newly arrived *Old Boys' Magazine* from his former school. Nash, his brain filled with questions about the Country House Bandits, suddenly remembered a tragic event which had affected a school friend of his. He made a mental note to get Hassan to dredge up the details first thing on Monday morning.

CHAPTER FOURTEEN

On Monday morning DS Mironova and DC Pearce arrived to see the stacks of files on the desks. Clara looked at Viv. 'What's been going on?'

'Don't look at me. I've been on a course for the past week.'

As Nash had predicted, Clara turned on him, asking how he could have allowed so much to go wrong in so short a time.

Nash glanced round to ensure nobody was in earshot. 'Actually, a lot of it happened earlier, but I thought it better to save it so you and Viv don't get bored.'

'Fat chance of that happening round here, not that I'd put it past you,' Clara replied.

Adil was introduced to Clara and Viv, who knew he was expected to join the team. His first remark, as he shook Clara's hand, was to tell her he already knew how to use the coffee machine. The others suppressed their laughter, knowing Adil had been made aware of her terrible reputation where the drink was concerned.

The newcomers spent much of their first day back being briefed by their colleagues, and began to read the files accumulated by Adil.

Clara stared at the file in front of her and muttered, 'Not more bloody cave victims. I thought we'd seen enough of them when we had that Layton Woods mess to sort out.'

'Technically, these bodies weren't in a cave,' said Nash. 'They were in the tunnels of a lead mine, and there's a vast difference. Caves are natural formations, whilst lead mines are man-made. There are plenty of both in this area, given the predominant limestone. Apart from the lower levels of arable land, pretty much the whole of North Yorkshire is honeycombed with natural caverns and old mine workings. Many of them never attract visitors, so there are lots of places to hide bodies.'

Nash smiled at Clara's pained expression. 'Don't get paranoid about the underground system, though. Apart from them, there are plenty of other places round here that people can use to conceal evidence. We have several fast-flowing rivers that can carry a body all the way to the North Sea, plus a good many deep lakes and mountain tarns, as you are aware, to submerge a corpse in.'

Clara shuddered at the oblique reference to Lamentation Tarn. 'Thanks a lot, Mike, that cheers me up no end,' she told him sarcastically. 'There's nothing like a nice easy day when you return to work, and this will certainly be nothing like a nice easy day.'

She paused before changing the subject. 'I meant to ask, how did Tom's party go?'

As she and Pearce were absent, Nash, Lisa, and their respective partners were the only members of the team available to accept Tom Pratt's invitation to a special celebration. The former chief superintendent had requested the presence of his colleagues at his fortieth wedding anniversary party. The event was held at Helmsdale Golf Club, of which Tom was a long-time member.

'It was a great success,' Nash told her. 'Although I'm not sure how keen Tom's wife was about his speech.'

'Why, what was wrong with it?'

'His opening remark went somewhere along the lines of, "I can't believe forty years have passed since I uttered those magic words, 'You're not, are you?'" Which everyone else thought was hilarious, but Mrs P seemed less than happy about.'

'Yes, I can see that going down badly. I hope Tom didn't suffer for it.'

'I saw him a couple of days later — there were no visible scars or bruises.'

* * *

Having set the team to their tasks, Nash instructed Adil to conduct another piece of research. Later, Nash heard the printer churning out several pages. When Adil presented him with the results, he glanced through them and said, 'I'd like you to do more copies — one for each team member, please.'

He'd read through the information and waited, before presenting it to the others once they'd finished studying the files.

Their interpretations of the contents matched those of their colleagues.

'Whoever selected their targets had obviously done their homework,' Clara suggested after examining the burglary reports. 'The list of their victims reads like an extract from *Who's Who*. As I recall there was a stockbroker, an investment banker, a solicitor, two prominent businessmen who headed up public companies, the manager of a Premier League football team, the director of a famous nationwide retail chain store, plus an international footballer. Any of them would have salaries into at least seven figures a year, giving them ample funds to acquire treasures for the Bandits to steal. That all suggests careful planning and surveillance prior to the robberies.'

'That's true, Clara,' Nash replied. 'And there's another factor the victims had in common, but I didn't twig it until you read that list out.'

'What was that, Mike?' Viv Pearce asked.

'If you think about how the victims earned a living, all their occupations involved spending a good deal of time away from home, making their houses easy targets. Our next task is to try and think of a way to further the investigation. We need to identify any other gang members.' Nash paused and changed the subject slightly, introducing the item Hassan had provided.

'Before we proceed, there's another file I'd like you to read. I asked Adil to research this earlier. It may or may not be connected to the Country House Bandits, but the MO seems very similar. In this instance, the outcome was far more tragic than any of the others.'

Clara flicked through the contents, skim-reading the account of a burglary of expensive items that had taken place some eleven years earlier, on the western edge of the county, close to the market town of Skipton. The homeowner had been away, and the assumption from the evidence was that he had been returning home when he was forced off the drive by the thieves' vehicle, causing him to collide with an oak tree, killing both him and his companion.

'How did you come across this case?' Clara asked. 'It isn't in our area, and hasn't been linked to the Bandits, although I agree much of what's described seems very much like their handiwork.'

'It was a stroke of luck, really. I received a copy of my school's *Old Boys' Magazine* on Saturday, and it reminded me of a pupil who was a few years younger than me. His name is Geoff Lister. He used to be a foreign correspondent, but later he became a crime reporter. Geoff is the nephew of the householder in that Skipton crime — the passenger was Geoff's wife. He was somewhere in Asia when he heard the appalling news that they had been killed. I met Geoff at a school reunion a year or so later and he was a shell of his former self.'

The other detectives were in agreement that this could be another of the Country House Bandits exploits, one which had gone horribly wrong.

* * *

When they arrived at Helmsdale on Tuesday morning, they found Superintendent Fleming already on site, in conversation with Sergeant Meadows. They adjourned to the CID suite, to which Fleming insisted Meadows accompany them. There, having asked Adil how he was settling in, Jackie explained the reason for her early morning visit.

'As you're aware, we've been monitoring CCTV and ANPR cameras for almost three months now, looking for the Audi we suspect was used to deliver drugs to Corey Davies, but without success. Luckily, one of our officers noticed another vehicle he thought looked suspicious. The van in question always travels at night, and during the darker months this enabled it to move to and fro without being noticed. However, now the summer is upon us, the better light enabled our man to spot something he knew wasn't right, and after checking the vehicle we knew this was a sham, albeit a very clever counterfeit.'

Jackie took a photo from her briefcase and passed it to Nash, asking him to hand it on for the others to inspect. 'The vehicle purports to be part of a fleet belonging to a national carrier, but if you examine it carefully, you'll notice an error. Having spotted that, we contacted the firm in question, and they do not have a van with that registration number.'

Clara chuckled as she spotted the fault. '"Next day delevery"? As spelling mistakes go, that's pretty bad.'

'I agree, so we investigated further, and what we discovered confirmed our theory. We traced the van's route, along with colleagues from other forces, and found the vehicle had travelled regularly from Manchester via the M62 to Leeds, and then onwards to North Yorkshire, passing through Netherdale to arrive somewhere in Helmsdale. Less than an hour later, the van made the return trip, and we are now certain it didn't make any stops on either leg of the journey.'

Fleming gestured to Viv and Adil. 'What we don't know is the address in Helmsdale the van went to. All the circumstantial evidence points to it being Corey Davies' drugs delivery vehicle, but we need much more than that. Ideally, we'd catch them making a delivery, but if we're right, the driver would be on the lookout for a police presence. The last thing we want is to spook him. If we can't ensure the drop has been made, there is no way we can implicate Davies. That is where our magnificent men and their flying machines could prove invaluable. Even if we use unmarked cars, they could be sufficient to frighten the driver off. The drones can achieve the same results without fear of detection.'

She turned to face Viv and Adil. 'I want both of you on standby every evening and night. As soon as we're notified the van is en route, you can follow its progress with a live feed back to Control. There's only one route into town from Leeds, so, Viv, will you speak to Paul Grant from Traffic and determine the best locations for you both? He will assign an officer to each of you when the situation arises. In this instance, you may each take the drones home with you. Remember to sign them out, please. Then, if everything goes to plan, we can wrap this up and put Davies where he belongs — behind bars, hopefully for a very long time.'

Jackie turned to Steve. 'I'll make sure Control is aware of the situation. They can provide an entry team to assist where necessary. Mike, I want you and the rest on standby to raid the property as soon as we identify exactly where Davies lives. You'll have an armed response unit, because we have no idea what precautions Davies has put in place or what weapons there will be inside the house.'

CHAPTER FIFTEEN

As they were all about to leave the CID suite the following day and head for home, Fleming phoned Nash. He was surprised when the superintendent asked to speak to DS Mironova. He called her into his office and passed her the receiver.

After listening for a few minutes, Clara replied, 'That's no problem, Jackie. I'll let the others know.' She handed the receiver back to Nash. 'Your turn.'

Jackie told Nash, 'It looks as if it could be all systems go for tonight. ANPR cameras in Manchester have just picked up the target van heading towards the M62. If the track record is anything to go by, it should be nearing our patch in a couple of hours or so. However,' she continued, 'I've had instructions from the chief, and these are non-negotiable. Her orders are that you and DC Andrews are not to take part in the operation. That's because your wife is nearing full term of her pregnancy, and you should be available at home. In Lisa Andrews' case, it's a question of safety, because of her condition. Therefore, DS Mironova, DC Pearce and DC Hassan will be the detectives attending the scene. The operation will be headed by the ARU, supported by uniformed officers. Clara, Viv, and Adil's main task will involve collection of evidence at the house, and booking Davies and the courier in. When they have been processed at Netherdale, your team will conduct the initial interviews. Both Clara and Viv are experienced enough to handle things, and it will give Hassan a feel of how we operate as a small unit.'

Nash attempted to protest, but Jackie would have none of it. 'Think of it this way, Mike. It would be extremely unfortunate if Alondra needed you, and you were ten or more miles away dealing with a drug dealer. That would be a severe case of the occurrence you refer to as "Sod's Law".'

With that, he bowed to the inevitable. But when the call was over, he wandered into the outer office, where Clara was briefing Viv and Adil.

'As Lisa and I have been proscribed from attending tonight's fun and games,' he told Clara, 'I'd appreciate a head's-up as to how things transpire once the dust settles — providing it isn't after midnight,' he added. 'I'm trying to get as much sleep as possible before the house is invaded by a howling banshee.'

* * *

Alondra noticed Nash seemed on edge all evening, and eventually asked what was troubling him. 'I hope it isn't because of me. If that's so, you can relax. Junior seems much more settled — he's hardly bothered me all day.'

'No, that wasn't it, but I'm happy you're not suffering,' he responded. 'The reason I'm a bit nervy is all to do with work. Clara and the team are hopefully about to make a major arrest, but I've been forbidden to take part. I'm anxious to know how things are going — they've involved an armed response unit.'

'Why were you banned? Is the person they're looking for someone you know?'

'No.' Nash smiled. 'The chief constable ordered me to sit this one out because it's going down several miles from here. She thought it unwise for me to be stuck out there for hours when you might need me. She also banned Lisa Andrews.'

'That's extremely thoughtful of Ruth, but it's got you like a cat on hot bricks.' She paused. 'Is that the correct expression?' Alondra's English was good, but she often struggled with idioms. When Nash nodded, she continued, 'When will you know how things turn out?'

'Hopefully, it'll all be over with before bedtime. Clara has promised to phone me as soon as she's able. If it doesn't happen tonight, she'll bring me up to speed first thing in the morning.'

* * *

Shortly before 8 p.m., an ANPR camera on the outskirts of Helmsdale spotted the target vehicle, and Adil Hassan picked it up with the drone from his designated position. Daylight made his task much easier as he followed the van's progress. Stationed alongside him, the accompanying officer watched with interest. Control was advising the ARU constantly, enabling the officers to move nearer the area. Eventually, the van stopped outside a house in the middle of Hillside Crescent.

Moments later, Hassan watched the screen as it displayed the driver and a single passenger emerge from the cab. He shifted the drone position slightly to get a clearer image of the back of the van, and zoomed in. As one of the occupants opened the vehicle's rear door, he saw him remove two large shopping bags and hand one to his mate. Then they headed up the long drive to the house. Control relayed this information to the leader of the armed response unit.

'We're already heading in that direction. We'll wait at the junction with Hillside Avenue until they complete the delivery. I want a patrol car blocking the far end of the crescent. As soon as you give us the nod we'll go in, in stealth mode.'

Pearce and his officer listened on the radio as they headed for the address. While on screen the watchers could clearly see the couriers enter the property. Then Pearce heard, 'Go! Go! Go!'

Hassan continued to film, watching as the ARU and uniforms surrounded the property and forced entry into the house.

Over his earpiece, Hassan heard Mironova tell him to join them. After a few moments, he closed down the equipment and climbed into the patrol car.

* * *

At the address, the ARU leader was updating Mironova, Pearce, and Hassan. 'We met with no resistance. The main suspect has been detained. He doesn't seem too bothered about the trouble he's in. We've arrested the couriers and seized the packages. They contain a large quantity of what looks like narcotics.' He paused. 'And before you ask, no, I don't think it's cornflour.'

Clara scowled. Word had obviously got round the force. 'If he's alone, where are his wife and son?'

'Davies said they've gone to visit her sister and brother-in-law in South Wales. He's asked us to contact his wife and tell her what's happened. He even told us his sister-in-law's phone number is on a pad on a table in the hall, next to his landline. That's a measure of how calm he appears to be.'

Mironova stared at the officer in surprise. 'It's almost sounds as if he was expecting this to happen. I think it's time I had a word with Mr Corey Davies. Viv, you're with me.'

As they walked along the drive, Clara asked, 'Has Davies been cautioned yet?'

'Not yet, just detained for a search of the property. I was about to issue a PWITS caution. It'll do for a start.'

'PWITS — bloody acronyms,' Clara said. 'I can't get the hang of them. It's possession with intent to supply,' she muttered, causing Pearce to grin.

* * *

Clara recognized Corey Davies immediately from the photos in the file from Manchester. He was seated in an armchair and looked completely at ease, almost as if he was about to watch *Eastenders* on the flat-screen TV on the wall opposite him. The air of comfort was only marred by the handcuffs restraining his wrists.

Clara took two paces into the room and stopped in her tracks, astounded by the man's greeting. 'Good evening, Detective Sergeant Mironova and Detective Constable Pearce. I'm sorry I can't get up to shake hands, but that's a bit difficult at the moment.' He raised his arms, displaying the manacles, then gestured to the two ARU officers, their weapons at their sides. 'Where's your boss, Inspector Nash? Is he off on his travels, or doesn't he consider me important enough to turn out at night?'

Clara's brain cleared and she attempted to regain charge of the conversation. 'Never mind all that. Corey Davies, you're under arrest on suspicion of possession with intent to supply class A drugs. You do not have to say anything, but it might harm your defence . . .'

Davies listened as she recited the remaining part of the standard caution, then replied, 'No, I don't think I want to say anything this evening. I'm sure you've all got better things to do with your time, so let's leave it until tomorrow, shall we? I'll happily make a statement then.'

The long silence following Davies' remarks was broken by a uniformed constable, who announced the arrival of a van to convey the suspect to Netherdale police station. As he was being escorted from the house, Davies turned and asked Mironova, 'You won't forget to phone my wife, will you? She's expecting a call, and she'll worry if she doesn't hear anything. She knows how dangerous my job can be.' He paused. 'A bit like yours, I suppose.'

When Davies had been loaded into the van, Pearce asked, 'What do you make of that?'

'I'm not sure what to make of it. For a moment, I thought we'd got the wrong house and walked into a tea party. It was only the presence of the ARU that convinced me I hadn't dreamed it all.'

'Does it worry you that Davies seemed to know all about us?'

'At first, yes. But then I thought about his track record, or rather the lack of one. If he's gone all these years without even an arrest, let alone a conviction, he must be both highly professional and extremely well-organized. That being so, one of the most important aspects of his nefarious occupation is to know as much as possible about anyone who poses a potential threat, be they competitors or police officers.'

'How do we proceed from here?'

'Davies said he's prepared to make a statement tomorrow. My guess is that Mike will want to conduct that interview. He wasn't at all happy about being excluded from tonight's shindig, so he won't be prepared to miss out on round two.' Clara paused and gave a comical grimace. 'Telling him what's happened here is going to be a bundle of fun.'

How much fun, Clara didn't know at that point, but when they reached her car, Adil tried to lighten the mood. 'Before I shut down the drone, I spotted a speeding car along Netherdale Road, with three of our traffic cars in pursuit, hoping to perform a TPAC.'

'What's a TPAC?' Pearce asked.

'Another bloody acronym,' Clara muttered.

Adil grinned at Clara's outburst, and shook his head in mock dismay at Pearce's question. 'Don't you watch *Police Interceptors* on the telly, Viv? It stands for tactical pursuit and containment. It's a way of boxing in suspect vehicles when the driver fails to stop. In this case, because the road is narrow and winding, they were unable to do that, so instead they got an officer to deploy a stinger. That's a bed of nail—'

'I know what a stinger is,' Pearce interjected.

'The result was quite dramatic. The car looked to be travelling at over seventy when it hit the stinger full on. The driver lost control, the vehicle overturned and burst into flames. Fortunately for the driver, our guys managed to pull him clear before the fuel tank exploded.'

* * *

As chance would have it, Nash had gone to the bathroom when his mobile rang, so Alondra answered the call. 'Did everything go OK?' she asked, after explaining his temporary absence and assuring Clara all was well with the baby.

Receiving a reply in the affirmative, she told Clara, 'I'm so glad about that, because Mike's almost worn the lounge carpet out, pacing up and down. Here he is now — he'll be relieved, in more ways than one.'

Nash had to wait a few seconds until Clara stopped laughing, then listened intently to her report. He was predictably surprised when she relayed the extent of Davies' knowledge regarding their personnel, and agreed with her theory as to the reason behind it. He was also intrigued by the detainee's calm manner and apparent willingness to cooperate. 'The interview should be quite interesting.'

As things transpired, Clara thought later, 'quite interesting' could well be classified as the understatement of the year.

CHAPTER SIXTEEN

Although Nash hadn't been allowed to participate in Davies' arrest, he'd spent much of the evening, when not worried about how things were progressing, reading the file on the suspected drugs dealer provided by Greater Manchester Police.

What he discovered about the man's background was more than a little surprising, to put it mildly. Unlike many who indulged in such criminal activities, Corey Davies came from a stable family, with parents who were reasonably affluent, and with sufficient spare income to send their only son to a private boarding school. Reports from his teachers indicated him to be of greater than average intelligence, and promised a bright future for the boy.

All that changed, however, when Davies was eighteen years old. His parents had seized the opportunity afforded by his absence to indulge themselves in a luxury cruise, visiting a host of Mediterranean islands on their itinerary. It was on one such island that disaster struck.

During the vessel's overnight stay, necessary to refuel and restock provisions, they had chosen to go on an unscheduled adventure in a hire car. Their route took them along narrow, winding roads that would eventually lead them to the summit of the highest peak, which afforded breathtaking, spectacular views.

Somewhere along the return journey, Corey's father lost control of the vehicle, which plunged several hundred feet down a ravine. The cruise liner sailed. Aware that two of their passengers were missing, the captain notified the local authorities. Three days later, a shepherd gathering his flock of goats spotted the glint of something metallic at the foot of the gorge. By the time rescuers reached the crushed remains of the hire car, it was far too late for Corey's parents.

The shock of their deaths must have been traumatic, but this was heightened by events that followed. Under normal circumstances, the travel insurance would have covered such a tragic event, but as this was an 'off the book' excursion, they refused to pay out. Likewise, the life insurance policy in Corey's father's name excluded anything that occurred on such a hazardous undertaking.

Along with a large house comes a large mortgage, and without adequate cover, there was little in the way of equity. Similarly, Corey's school fees were not provided for to enable him to further his education. As both his parents were in well-paid jobs, they failed to anticipate the need for such precautions.

With his world turned upside down, the eighteen-year-old had been orphaned and made homeless. Worse still, he had little more to his name than some items of clothing and a few pounds in his pocket.

As Nash concluded reading the file note, he thought there was little wonder Corey Davies had embarked on a life of crime. Desperate needs call for desperate measures, and his case was certainly that. Corey's history might also explain why someone so embittered by life had such little sympathy for those he must have considered weak enough to succumb to narcotic addictions.

* * *

During their briefing of the chief constable next morning, Jackie Fleming expressed her wish to be involved in the interview with Corey Davies, but Ruth Edwards overruled her. 'You and I can watch it remotely, but as Clara made the arrest, she should take part in the next stage of the process. I also believe it would be tactically wrong to have someone of such a high rank as yours involved, as it might either give Davies an inflated idea of his importance, or alternatively cause him to be less forthcoming than we want. Added to that, Mike and Clara have years of experience questioning suspects, and their success rate proves how effective they are as a team.'

Ruth thought for a moment before continuing, 'I think the interview should take place immediately, both because of the twenty-four-hour custody restrictions, and because I'm more than a little curious as to what this cool customer is going to tell us. Unless, of course,' she added, 'what he told Clara last night was a pack of lies, and we're going to be forced to listen to yet another "right to remain silent" comedy routine. Why is it suspects don't realize that when they go through the rigmarole of stating "no comment" it more or less proves to us they're guilty?'

As Nash and Mironova were about to set off for the interview room at Netherdale, Ruth asked, 'Has Davies requested a legal representative?'

'I asked him when he was booked in last night and he refused. We'll ask again once the interview recording has begun,' Clara reassured her.

Nash led the way into the room.

'Good morning, Inspector Nash.'

The greeting from their prisoner didn't surprise him, as he'd been forewarned about the man's seemingly in-depth knowledge of their force. He refused to accept the proffered handshake, but his explanation made Davies chuckle, which Nash did find puzzling.

'I'm afraid I can't shake hands with you. Making contact with someone who is in custody could later be classified as an assault.'

'Rules and regulations, I guess? They've been the bane of my life.'

'Shall we get down to business?' Nash signalled to Mironova, who recited the standard introduction for the benefit of the recordings, both audio and visual. When she'd finished, Nash asked, 'I believe you were offered the services of a legal representative but refused, is that still correct?'

Davies agreed, his voice confident and relaxed, before asking, 'Am I correct in assuming this is also being broadcast on CCTV?'

Nash confirmed this to be accurate, prompting Davies to respond, 'I wish I'd known this was going to happen. If I'd been warned, I'd have worn a suit and tie.'

Nash refused to rise to the bait, wondering if this was a deliberate tactic, designed to rile or unsettle him, or whether it was a way for Davies to try and gain command of the ensuing interview.

'The charges against you are extremely serious, Mr Davies, and could result in a very long prison term, should you be convicted. And yet you seem very relaxed. I hope you appreciate the gravity of the situation you're in?'

'Certainly, Inspector, I know exactly what the penalties for these offences are. However, I've been expecting something along the lines of what happened for quite a while, so I've made suitable preparation.'

Davies leaned forward, his hands resting on the table. 'The reason my reaction isn't quite what I assume you expected, is that I'm a very small cog in an extremely big wheel — a middleman, if you like. Yes, I do anticipate having to endure a term of imprisonment, but knowing that, I've collated irrefutable evidence which will show I've been merely acting on behalf of others, and that I'm the victim of a regime of terror, with me, my wife, and our son in constant danger, fearing for our lives. Prison might well represent my best chance of survival, and once I'm no longer of use to those who are running the show, my family will cease to be of interest to them, and therefore the threat will be lifted.'

'Would you care to explain?'

'The organization has been in operation for a good many years, and when I was coerced into joining it, they made it clear what would happen if I didn't toe the line. There have been several attempts to dispose of me recently, when I became less cooperative than they wanted, refusing to become involved in some of their even more sordid activities. The arson attack on our house in Manchester was the very latest, and possibly the most extreme, of their attempts to dispose of me.'

Despite the gravity of what he'd revealed, Davies smiled ironically as he added, 'Although they were trying to get rid of me, they made sure I continued pushing their drugs for them. They won't allow anything to get in the way of their business activities.'

'Hang on, I thought the arson attack was the work of a rival gang?' Clara interposed.

'That was exactly what you were supposed to think.'

'What about the man who was doused in petrol and set alight? Rumour in Manchester at the time was he belonged to another gang, and had burned your house down. Turning him into a human torch was an act of revenge. That gossip also suggests you were the one who ordered the retaliation.'

'Again, that's exactly what you were expected to believe. The man was a scapegoat, and the attack was designed to either kill me, or bind me more closely to the web I was trapped in. Making me appear to be the instigator of that man's death was merely a bonus — for them, not for me.'

Nash allowed Clara to follow this line of interrogation, preferring instead to concentrate on an earlier remark made by Davies, which became the focus of his next question. 'You claimed you had solid evidence proving you were only a middleman within a large organization. What is that evidence?'

'Soon after I was coerced into becoming part of their operation, I took precautions I hoped would come in useful on a day like today. I realized the only way to prove my claim had merit was by having irrefutable proof. And to show how small my involvement and how meagre my rewards were, in comparison to the overall picture. Therefore, I established a limited liability company to trade under, and kept precise details of each transaction, both income and expenditure. Every penny I received, and every pound I paid out, has been meticulously recorded. The company accounts will also verify the salary I received as a director, which was my only source of income.'

There was a stunned silence, which was broken only when Davies continued, 'In accordance with company law, the annual accounts have been scrupulously audited, forming the basis for my tax returns. I'm more than happy to furnish you with the name and address of my accountants, who are based in Manchester, plus copies of all relevant paperwork, such as bank accounts. The details only cover the past six years.' Davies smiled. 'That's sufficient for the Inland Revenue, so I hope it will be enough for your investigation.'

Clara, who was less than familiar with the ways of commerce, asked, 'I presume if you sold drugs, you would be paid in cash. So how did you persuade your auditor to accept the figures you provided?'

'I think the terminology used is "incomplete records accounting", which I was able to convince the accountants were accurate by providing the commission basis I worked on.'

'What about the people you claim you were acting for? How did you transfer huge amounts of cash without raising suspicions of money laundering?'

'That's a very interesting question, and the answer comes in two parts. During the early days it was all cash, and I insisted on obtaining a receipt before I handed the money over. They didn't like that much, but knew they had no choice. More recently, the bulk of their ninety per cent share of each deal was sent via bank transfer to an overseas company. Their name is also on the trading account. The cash element was still handed over in exchange for a receipt.'

'What about the people you claim ran the operation, the ones behind this offshore company?'

'Actually, I believe you'll find the individuals listed as directors of that company might be figments of someone's imagination. Not mine, I hasten to add, but as to the real honchos, I'm afraid I'm not in a position to reveal their identities. I don't know who they are. As for those I do know, I wouldn't tell you their names because I enjoy breathing, and hope to continue doing so.'

Davies leaned back in his chair. 'Once my stay in prison is over, I want to rejoin my family and watch my son grow up. The visibility is much better aboveground than if you're covered by six feet of earth. Apart from my own safety, I have to consider the welfare of my wife and son, who would be highly vulnerable if I was to reveal the names of those I consider to be a potent threat.'

'You do realize we're going to have to check out everything you've told us,' Nash pointed out. 'We can't simply take your word for it. For the immediate future, we have to consider the fact that your arrest, and that of the two couriers, will have become known to your associates. If the danger those people represent to you and your family is as strong as you make out, you might be safer in custody than out on bail, and if they can't get at you, either directly or indirectly, they'll be stymied.'

Much to the surprise of Edwards and Fleming watching via CCTV, Davies agreed to Nash's proposal, confirming he would not object to an extension of the custody term. He made one proviso, the substance of which lent credence to his earlier remarks. 'I'll happily forfeit the right to be released on bail, and be remanded, as long as you promise to ensure my wife and son are adequately protected. That should be temporary, because once the hierarchy have learned that I've remained silent, the danger to my family will pass when the big wheels no longer consider me to be a threat to their comfortable existence.'

CHAPTER SEVENTEEN

One thing Corey Davies hadn't revealed during the interview formed the basis of Nash's next question. 'How did you get involved with these people in the first place? Were you an addict, or was it simply for the money?'

Davies shook his head. 'It was neither of those. I made a huge mistake when I was in my teens, one which led to me being blackmailed into participation in their racket. Once they had me on board, they knew I wouldn't grass them up. My arrest isn't as unwelcome as you might think. You asked at the beginning of our chat why I was so relaxed. The reason is, the spell in prison might be an inconvenience, but it represents my one and only opportunity to free myself from their shackles. All I have to do is ensure I stay alive to enjoy the freedom.'

'What kind of a mistake was it you made?'

'Again, I'm not prepared to give exact details. Suffice it to say I broke the law, and they had evidence of my wrongdoing. Had they chosen to reveal it to the police, I'd have spent the past ten years in prison. Sometimes, I regret that I didn't call their bluff, but I was young, and scared of being behind bars. It's only later I came to realize there are far worse things than being locked up.'

At Nash's request, Davies supplied the name and address of the Manchester firm of accountants, adding, 'You'll need a password for them to release any information. My instructions to them are not to give out anything unless the person can supply my wife's full name and date of birth.'

Nash watched Mironova scribble the relevant information in her notebook and signalled for her to terminate the interview. Once Davies was certain their conversation was no longer being recorded, he asked if the CCTV had also been deactivated. Clara confirmed that the two were linked.

Knowing his comments could not be overheard or accessed later, Davies told the detectives something that had Nash puzzled for a long while. 'You're going to have far bigger problems than me to contend with soon, if all I hear is correct.'

'What does that enigmatic remark mean?'

'You'll soon find out, if it hasn't already started. Let me put it this way, supply of narcotics is only a small part of their operation, and strange as it might seem, the answers to the questions you'll soon be facing are right under your noses.'

'Would you care to explain that? Because at the moment you're speaking in riddles.'

Davies shook his head. 'You're the detective — you work it out. I'm not paid to do your job for you. However, it would only be fair of me to give you a couple of clues. First of all, I didn't choose to come and live in this neck of the woods by accident, nor was it for the admittedly delightful scenery.'

From being relaxed, his tone suddenly changed, reflecting a level of stress the detectives found surprising. 'The reason I opted for this area is I knew it would make life uncomfortable for the bastards who tried to have me and my family burned alive. That was a step too far. I didn't mind living with the danger, but not when it extended to my wife and child. There had been previous attempts, sparked by the fact I refused to have anything to do with their other, even more unsavoury activities.'

Davies took a deep breath, as if trying to rid himself of the thought pattern he found distressing. When he resumed, his voice was noticeably calmer. 'Going on from there, have you ever asked yourselves how some folk can afford to live in swanky stately houses, driving flash limos that cost well into six figures? Just because a family occupies a grand house doesn't mean they're upright citizens. Quite the opposite, in some cases.'

Davies paused and then revealed the most illuminating fact thus far. It was quite a while before the detectives saw the light, however. 'Earlier, when you asked how I got involved, I told you the organization had many facets. I'm talking large-scale fraud, human trafficking, bringing young women and children to be forced into sex work. Plus widespread prostitution, money laundering and much more I probably don't know about. The whole thing started up via a string of burglaries. I had a hand in some of them, and have lived to regret it ever since. I'm not talking of breaking into a semi-detached on the outskirts of town, either. They used to set their sights much higher, and for that matter, they probably still do. Anyway, that's enough from me. I'd like to return to my luxury accommodation now, please, because I still haven't finished this morning's cryptic crossword.'

* * *

When Davies had been escorted back to his cell, Nash and Mironova met up with Superintendent Fleming and the chief constable.

'I have to say that interview was not in the least what I expected,' the chief began. 'At times I wondered if you were going to get a word in edgeways, and I'm still trying to get my head round what Davies said, and his relaxed attitude, bearing in mind he's facing a long term in jail.'

'To be honest, I thought the whole thing was a fairy tale, a figment of a weird and hyperactive imagination,' Jackie commented. 'Are you absolutely certain Davies isn't under the influence of some of the drugs he's been flogging, especially the hallucinogenic ones?'

Clara shook her head. 'I don't think so, and to make certain, we conducted a drug wipe last night, and that came back clean. I also requested a blood test, but naturally we haven't got those results yet. However, looking at Davies during the interview, his eyes seemed clear and the pupils weren't dilated, as you'd expect them to be if he was under the influence of anything along the lines of what you're suggesting.'

The chief turned to Nash, and asked, 'What did you make of it all, Mike?'

Nash thought for a moment. 'I'm beginning to wonder if Mr Corey Davies might turn out to be far more astute than we've given him credit for, and that may also apply to the people he's associated with. We already have one example of his shrewdness, or cunning, call it what you like. I'm referring to the cornflour incident, which I'm sure he set up to test us, and to get his delivery safely.

'I accept that much of what Davies said might appear far-fetched. But I don't think he would offer up such detailed evidence to support his story, evidence that would be easy to discount, unless it was genuine. There's an extremely simple way to prove or disprove what he told us. All we have to do is phone those accountants, and if they provide hard facts by way of audited figures, that will settle the matter.'

Nash paused. 'I'm far more concerned by what Davies told us when the interview was over. Obviously, with the tape and CCTV switched off, you won't have heard it, but I'll try and remember exactly what he said.'

'You don't have to, Mike,' Clara interrupted. She glanced at the chief constable a trifle anxiously, before explaining. 'When Davies started talking he was looking directly at you, so he didn't notice I'd switched on the recording app on my mobile phone.'

'You do know you have probably broken a whole host of regulations?' the chief constable told her severely. 'You're getting to be as bad as your boss.'

'Yes, I'm sorry, ma'am. I know it was wrong. Do you want me to delete the conversation?'

'Yes, you must certainly do that — immediately after we've heard what Davies said that's got Mike so wound up.'

Edwards and Fleming listened intently to the recording, their expressions twin mirrors, reflecting a mixture of horror and disbelief. When it was over, there was a period of stunned silence until the chief constable managed to give her reaction.

'I'm beginning to hope Jackie was right, and the blood test Clara ordered comes back positive. I also hope that firm of accountants claim they've never heard of anyone called Corey Davies. Because if he isn't on drugs, or suffering some form of mental aberration causing delusional fantasies, there is a chance that everything he told us isn't a figment of his imagination. If that turns out to be so, I dread to think what the message he gave you implies.'

'I agree, so I suggest the first step we take should be verification of that blood test, plus putting in an urgent call to the Manchester auditors.' Nash took a deep breath before adding, 'I hope all that can be dealt with here, because at the moment, our priority must be to continue investigating the six unsolved murders we have on our hands. Actually, I think that figure might be incorrect. If we include the stabbing of Frank Watson in prison, the number is actually seven. I appreciate his death was initially written off as a dispute between inmates that got out of hand, but with the murders of the two other members of the Country House Bandits, I believe we should reopen the investigation into Watson's murder.'

'That makes sense. Do it,' Edwards agreed. 'I'll chivvy our Forensic people into getting that blood test result ASAP, plus analysis of the drugs seized at Davies' house. Jackie can follow up with the accountants, which will free up your team to concentrate on the killings.'

CHAPTER EIGHTEEN

Almost a week passed with little progress, before the results began coming in. When they did, it was a deluge of information rather than a trickle. Nash's phone was ringing when he entered his office the following Monday morning. The caller was Detective Superintendent Fleming, who brought news — and an apology. 'Mike, I'm sorry I doubted your reading of Corey Davies' character. On Saturday I was in town shopping, and I parked at HQ. While I was here, I called in and picked up a parcel that had just been delivered. It contained the accounts for Davies' limited company. The accountants from Manchester sent them through, and because they're accountants, they naturally used second-class post. They also included copies of the paperwork Davies had collated to provide figures for the audit, both monies received and disbursements. I was intrigued enough to take them home and spent Saturday evening studying them.'

'My, what an exciting life you lead,' Nash teased her.

Ignoring this, Jackie told him, 'From my rough calculations, I would say everything Davies told you at interview was correct, and unless my calculator is faulty, he only retained ten per cent of the income from drug sales.'

Jackie paused before adding a chilling postscript. 'And if Davies was being truthful during one aspect of his story, he might also have been accurate when he mentioned the potential difficulties we might be expected to face in our area.'

Less than ten minutes later, as Nash was relaying this news to Clara, his phone rang again. This time it was the chief constable, who had another update for the team to consider. 'I've had the results back from Davies' blood test. They clearly indicate he hasn't been taking any form of illegal substances, which is pretty much what Clara suspected. Forensics also reported on the substances seized from his house. They include cocaine, heroin, cannabis and some amphetamines with a totally unpronounceable name. They put the value of the packages at somewhere in the region of seventy-five thousand pounds, which means we're good to go with the case against Davies. However, from what Jackie's just been telling me, it looks as if we're once again hauling in the small fry, while the big fish swims safely away.'

* * *

There was an hour and a half's respite before the next part of what Nash referred to as 'the information cascade' arrived, and this part was delivered by their pathologist.

Ramirez greeted Nash cheerfully, which rather surprised the detective, but the reason for his upbeat manner soon became clear. 'I'm clearing my desk prior to going on holiday, and some test results came in a few minutes ago which I am certain you'll want to know about immediately. I'm referring to DNA extracted from the victims found in the lead mine with such a curious name.'

Nash heard the sound of paper rustling before Ramirez continued, 'The DNA tests have yielded positive results in respect of two of the victims. Sadly, the other remains are as yet unidentified. Having stated that we know the identities of two victims, this is only partly correct. The one we can definitely put a name to is the female whose remains were partly decomposed. She is, or was, Mrs Lauren Watson, wife, or widow, of the man stabbed to death in prison. I'm unable to say if she predeceased her husband or outlived him. As for the other positive indicator, that's where it gets a little trickier.'

Ramirez paused — possibly, Nash guessed, to marshal his thoughts. 'The man who died most recently, when your son heard the gunshots, has strong DNA similarities to another recent murder victim. Results show that he is closely related to Peter Swallow, and it's highly likely he was Swallow's half-sibling. The young woman is still unidentified, and more than that, I cannot say, except to confirm that should you have any luck identifying potential matches, we now have DNA from all four, including the skeletal remains. Now I must go, otherwise I'll miss my plane.'

Nash put the receiver down and sat for a few minutes pondering this development, before calling Clara into his office.

'What is it?' she asked, in a world-weary tone. 'Not more coffee already?'

'Not yet, but it's a kind thought. I have more news. Mexican Pete's just rung in a mad panic because he's jetting off on holiday, and he wanted to update us before he catches his flight. He's got DNA confirmation back on two of the lead mine corpses. One of them, is, or rather was, George Briggs, Peter Swallow's half-brother.' He paused before the final revelation. 'The other identifiable victim is Lauren Watson, Frank Watson's wife. That means at least two of the four victims found within the mine are connected, either directly or indirectly, to the Country House Bandits.'

Clara's reaction was immediate, and mirrored Nash's thinking exactly. 'Do you think the other two might also be linked to the gang in some way?'

'There's a strong possibility that at least one of them is, and I think we can almost put a name to her. The skeletal remains, I believe, will prove to be those of Cindy Swallow, Peter Swallow's wife. If you recall, she went missing soon after he was imprisoned, and has never been heard of since. By my reckoning, that timescale more or less matches the period Mexican Pete believes the skeleton has been in the mine.'

'How do we prove it, one way or the other?'

'I haven't had chance to read through Swallow's file again as yet, certainly not the section referring to his background. If memory serves, Cindy Swallow has a sister living somewhere in West Yorkshire. We should get onto the local force and request a sample from the sister for testing. If that yields a positive result, it will mean the death toll of those connected to the Country House Bandits has now risen to eight.'

Nash passed the relevant file to Clara and asked, 'Please phone West Yorkshire Police and organize the DNA test, will you? I'll update the chief and Jackie.'

* * *

When Nash had spoken to the chief constable and Fleming, he went in search of coffee, but was stopped en route by Clara. Nash held his hand out for her mug, a reflex action, but as she handed it to him, she said, 'Coffee wasn't the reason I stopped you. I've been looking through the Peter Swallow file you gave me. Although it lists Cindy Swallow, her sister Ellie Pawson and Swallow's half-brother, George Briggs, there is no mention of whether Briggs was married, in a relationship, or if he had any other relatives.'

Clara hesitated before putting forward her idea. 'Bearing in mind what happened to Briggs, would it not be sensible to ask the local force to conduct a welfare visit to Briggs' home address, in case there's a wife and children wondering what's happened to Daddy?'

'Excellent idea, Clara. Organize it, will you? I'll go and wrestle with the coffee machine.'

'I'll certainly do that, Mike, but I also had another idea.'

'Wow, two in one morning? Go on, then, what is it?'

'If Briggs lived alone, might he have been abducted from there and taken to the mine, where he was killed? If that's so, with no other family members to contaminate what is potentially a crime scene, would it not make sense to ask the force there to do a forensic sweep of the property?'

Nash peered at his deputy suspiciously. 'That's two brilliant ideas in as many minutes. Have you been taking some of Corey Davies' products?' He smiled at the distinctly unladylike gesture Clara gave him in response.

* * *

The team had plenty of work to occupy their time. Principal among these was preparation of backup paperwork for submission to the Crown Prosecution Service in respect of the Corey Davies case, but soon, they had other events to concern them.

The first of these came via a call made to Netherdale control room on Friday evening. The operator took the message, and promised the caller someone would attend to the matter immediately. DS Mironova was the CID officer on duty, so she took the call, listening with growing surprise to what Control told her.

'A woman who has been away visiting family in South Wales returned home this evening. She arrived at the house only a few minutes ago to find there had been a break-in. She told me the place had been ransacked.'

'That sounds awful. Where did this take place?'

'Number twenty-eight, Hillside Crescent. The woman who reported the burglary gave her name as Mrs Brittany Davies.'

'Brittany Davies, as in Corey Davies' wife?'

'I believe so. I thought, rather than getting a patrol involved, you should know immediately, then you can decide what action you want to take.'

'There was a search of that property. Is she sure it isn't just the after-effect of that she's seeing?'

'Not with cupboard doors wide open, drawers removed from cabinets, and the contents strewn everywhere, even the fridge-freezer. Our lads don't leave a place in that state.'

'OK, I'll let Inspector Nash know, and then I'll set off for the address. Will you organize a CSI team, please?'

Clara rang off and pressed the short code on her mobile. Seconds later, Mike answered, and was equally surprised when Clara explained the reason for the call.

'You'll have to treat this as you would any other break-in. When the forensic sweep's done, ask Mrs Davies to begin compiling an inventory of missing items as she sorts through what sounds to be a real mess. The usual routine. You cannot allow the fact that we have Corey Davies in custody to influence your actions, or what you say to his wife. On a separate note, I find it curious that his house, among all the others on the Hillside estate, was chosen as a target for burglary. The timing of the intrusion could also be highly significant. However, that cannot cloud our judgement.'

'The arrest created a lot of interest from the neighbours. Someone could have put it on social media, so the house was known to be empty,' Clara suggested.

'Maybe you're right.' Nash was about to end the call when he had an idea. 'It might be worth paying special attention to the method of entry. By that I mean, was it brute force, or something more sophisticated?'

'I'll look into it. There's another point of potential interest. From memory, I believe Davies had a burglar alarm fitted.'

'Keep me informed, but it can wait until tomorrow, unless it becomes urgent. I'm still taking the weekend off. Alondra needs to rest, and I'm determined to make sure she does.'

CHAPTER NINETEEN

Clara arrived to find Brittany Davies being comforted by a neighbour. She was seated on the step outside the front door, tears running down her cheeks, as she cuddled a small boy.

'Mrs Davies? I'm Detective Sergeant Mironova from Helmsdale. Can you tell me exactly what happened?'

'I've been staying with my sister, and when one of your officers phoned to say Corey had been arrested, I thought I'd better come home. I didn't want the house standing empty. It's bad enough that I'll have to manage without my husband, but to find all this.' She gestured at the house. 'I opened the door and put our bags into the hall and went back to the car for Thomas. He'd slept most of the way, and I intended to take him straight to bed.'

She began to sob. 'But he woke up, so I took him to the kitchen for a drink. It was then that I saw the mess. I glanced into the lounge . . .'

The neighbour, an older woman, put her arm around her shoulder, patting her gently, saying she would go home and make some tea. 'Would you like a cup, officer?' she asked, politely.

'Er, no thank you, I need to get on. Did you enter any of the rooms, or touch anything at all, Mrs Davies?'

'No, I came straight outside and dialled 999.'

At that moment the CSI van arrived. The officers took their equipment from the vehicle and headed up the drive.

'All right, Clara?' the lead officer asked.

'Fine, thank you. I've not been inside yet, so I don't know what you're facing.'

'Leave it to us.' He and his partner headed indoors, to return a moment later, tossing a pair of overshoes to Clara. 'I think you should see this.'

'Won't be a minute,' she replied. 'Mrs Davies, can you go and sit with your neighbours? We seem to be gathering an audience, and I wouldn't want little Thomas being more upset by them.'

Brittany agreed, picked up her son and headed next door.

Clara donned the footwear and went to look at the scene.

* * *

It was almost midday on Saturday when Clara made the promised phone call to Nash. She rang to report progress — or lack of it. 'That burglar was a class above anything we've encountered, at least since Jimmy Johnson returned to the straight and narrow.'

Nash smiled at her reference to the retired burglar, now a respected locksmith.

Clara continued, 'I've spent all morning going through CCTV footage supplied by some neighbours covering the street, but the range is limited, because the field of vision is restricted by the position of the house, which is right in the middle of the crescent. There's certainly no images of anyone approaching the door of the property, at least not since the postman delivered yesterday morning.'

'So how did the burglar gain entry, if not from the front of the house?'

'We were baffled, because there was no sign of forced entry at either the front or the rear, and the neighbour's

CCTV showed nothing more sinister than a cat prowling across the back lawn. We might still have been stumped, but then we got lucky. One of the CSI team noticed a first-floor window at the rear of the house was unlocked. I checked with Brittany Davies, and she confirmed she had definitely secured every window before setting off to Wales. But her husband might have left it unlocked.'

'I assured her that we would have left the house secure after our search.'

'So, how did our master criminal gain entry?'

'The window has one of those metal sliding latches. One of the CSI men told me it's possible to move the latch with a really strong magnet. So I borrowed one from Jimmy Johnson to check out the theory, and wonder of wonders, it worked a treat. We got confirmation too, via a couple of small fragments of soil on the windowsill. Plus, there are indentations in the flower bed where a ladder had been propped. The ladder had been borrowed from alongside the greenhouse. The thief couldn't even be charged with going equipped.'

Nash smiled at Clara's joke. 'How much did our talented thief get away with? It must have been a lot to make all that effort worthwhile. Apart from everything else, it's getting to sound more like a professional job, not the work of a gifted amateur.'

'Now that's the weirdest part of the whole business, Mike. I've had Brittany Davies sifting through the contents of cupboards and drawers that were strewn all over the place, but there doesn't appear to be anything missing. What is even stranger is her jewellery box is still on the dressing table, and having looked at the contents, I'd say they were worth well into five figures, possibly even six.'

'As you said, this is getting to sound really weird. I don't suppose you've had any luck with prints or DNA, have you?'

'It's too early for DNA, but from what our CSI men said, I wouldn't hold your breath. As for fingerprints, the only ones we found, apart from those that should be in the house, belong to the drugs couriers we arrested inside the house.'

'If nothing of value was stolen, the fact that drawers and cupboards were gone through so rigorously suggests the intruder was searching. Looking for something specific Davies might have secreted there. It might be worth having a word with him, to see if he's prepared to tell us what that might be. Even if he won't say, his reaction might be revealing.'

In the event, both Corey Davies and his wife were as mystified as the detectives as to what the intruder might have been looking for. None of them, neither the occupants nor the police, gave any thought to the notion that the burglar might have entered the house to remove items the Davies family were unaware of. Nor, from a technical point of view, was the offence of robbery merely trespass, as the intruder was merely retrieving their own property.

* * *

Over several months, a spate of farm thefts had left both uniformed officers and CID puzzled. They were all executed overnight with no forensic evidence, and were no nearer being solved. The most recent, a month ago, had been at Aldwick Farm, which was in two parts, the combined property bisected by the main road from Netherdale to Helmsdale. Here, in the lower reaches of the dale, the land was mostly arable, the richer soil giving excellent potential for growing cereal crops.

The amalgamation of the two properties which formed the farm had been brought about by the current owner, who had married his neighbour's daughter. When the wife inherited her family's farm, the couple had set about maximizing the financial reward from the combination. With two sets of living accommodation deemed excessive, they had chosen to occupy one, turning the other into a holiday let.

Nor was this by any means their only deviation from traditional farming practices. The land to the rear of the letting property commanded spectacular views of the countryside, an ideal location for glamping.

This still left a large area of surplus land. Utilizing this, they had fenced a section off and converted it into a small but flourishing market garden, adding substantially to their income.

It had been early morning when the farmer-cum-horticulturalist had discovered all was not as it should be. His task for the day ahead was to prepare a section of land for planting, involving the use of a rotavator. When he'd reached his equipment shed, he'd realized his plans for the day were in ruins. He'd turned abruptly, and dashed back to the house for his phone.

'I want to report a robbery.'

In response to the operator's request for further information, he'd told her, 'My name's Ted Calvert, from Aldwick Farm on the Helmsdale road. Some light-fingered swine's broken into my tool shed and nicked everything inside, including my trailer.'

Viv Pearce was on call, but was unavailable, so DC Lisa Andrews had responded. As with the previous cases, she was puzzled as to why someone had gone to such trouble for so relatively little reward.

Later, when she had relayed details of the robbery to Nash and Clara, Lisa repeated her opinion. 'The thieves took a small open trailer, one the farmer used to move things round the farm. I think the robbers loaded all the stolen gear into the trailer and simply drove off with it in tow. Apart from the trailer, they took a hedge trimmer, a ditching tool, a rotavator, two power strimmers, a scarifier, plus three electric drills and a jigsaw. All told, I reckon the items stolen would be worth little more than three or four thousand pounds. That, by the way, is the brand new, retail price.'

Nash had asked why she had taken the call. 'Viv was already out on a shout, so Control phoned me.'

Viv hadn't arrived yet. When he did, he explained that shortly after daybreak, the emergency operator had taken a call from another irate farmer reporting the loss of equipment. The two uniformed officers attending the scene assessed the situation and called CID.

Nash was dumbfounded, and told Viv that Lisa had just returned from a similar incident. 'They're getting bolder, two in one night.'

The first point of interest Pearce highlighted, which Nash had picked up on immediately, was again the remote location. Scartoft Farm was near to the summit of Stark Ghyll, on the slopes overlooking Riven Scar. If someone wanted to access the outbuilding, which Pearce described as being almost one hundred metres away from the farmhouse, that would be difficult enough. Removing the stolen tools and carrying them away would be even harder.

The farmer had told Viv it was his elderly father's hobby that had attracted the thieves. The old man's pastime had turned into a lucrative vocation, and used the outbuilding as his carpentry workshop. Inside, the retired farmer had honed his woodworking skills to become a respected crafts-man, producing a wide range of furniture and decorative pieces. The list of stolen property covered a number of power tools, including drills, planes, saws and even a lathe. This had Nash and the team somewhat puzzled. They were at a loss to understand how the miscreants had been able to remove them without attracting the attention of the occupants of the farmhouse.

There was only one access route to the property, a track Pearce had described as a boneshaker, which stretched for the best part of a mile from the main road, which in itself was nothing more than a country lane.

Entry into the workshop had been easy for the thieves, as the farmer told Pearce. 'Father never locks the door — never seen the need. I never thought, even in my wildest dreams, we'd be robbed out here. In fact, I'm not right sure where the key is, but I'm bloody well going to find it now.'

One conclusion Pearce had arrived at, and recorded, was straightforward, and one moreover that Nash had completely agreed with. These were no opportunist thieves. The robberies had been carefully planned and executed. That factor in itself was puzzling, because for someone to take so much time and trouble, let alone the risks involved, to steal items with such a relatively low resale value seemed completely illogical. That situation had remained until further robberies came to light, ones which proved equally baffling.

Meanwhile the files sat in a tray on Lisa's desk.

CHAPTER TWENTY

The detectives were awaiting further information from other sources. The first item came via West Yorkshire Police, who had visited George Briggs' apartment in Leeds. Clara, who had instigated this, reported to Nash and the team.

'The officers found nobody at the property, the door to which was unlocked. There were signs of a struggle. They spoke with neighbours, who confirmed Briggs was single. One of them, who they categorized as the local nosey parker, told officers Briggs had a succession of lady visitors. But in the past few months, only one woman came to the flat on a regular basis. In the circumstances, they called in a Forensics team. Fingerprints belonged to Briggs, plus one other set, which tallied with those of the most recent female victim from the lead mine.'

Nash noticed Clara smile as she mentioned the second prints and asked what she found amusing. 'The guys from West Yorkshire took great delight in explaining where they retrieved those prints. Apparently, they were on the head-board of Briggs' bed. They also retrieved semen and vaginal fluid from the sheets and mattress, which have been sent for analysis.'

Final confirmation came when the laboratory confirmed the samples from the bedding belonged to Briggs and the as yet unidentified female found with him in the mine.

Twenty-four hours later, Nash received further news and told the team, 'I've just heard from the lab, and the skeleton from the mine is definitely that of Cindy Swallow. They've checked her sister's DNA.'

Nash summed up their findings. 'We can now say for certain that all four victims found in the lead mine are connected, either directly or indirectly, to the Country House Bandits. Tie into that the murders of the three convicted gang members, and we now have a total of seven murders to investigate, all linked.'

'What about the unidentified female?' Adil asked.

'I think her connection could be classed as collateral damage, merely because she might have been present during his abduction, in which case she would have seen the killer and would have to be eliminated. That's purely speculation, but I wouldn't bet against it.'

Although the knowledge they'd acquired was useful, it didn't carry their inquiry forward, which was frustrating. Clara asked, 'Have you given any thought as to how we proceed from here?'

'The only routes open to us are to look deeper into the Frank Watson murder, and to try and locate Terry Palmer, the other gang member recently released. In the Watson case, we know the identity of his assailant. Although the inmate claimed it was a dispute that got out of hand, with the new information at our disposal, I think we can safely discount his version of events. The chief's agreed to have that investigation reopened. But before we start interviewing anyone, a bit of background might help throw some light onto the circumstances behind the attack.'

'What do you mean by that, Mike?'

In answer to Viv's question, Nash suggested they begin by examining the assailant's personal life. 'If, as I now suspect, someone is cleaning house, in Watson's case they must have been doing so from the outside. So how did they persuade the attacker to stab him? Was the inmate being blackmailed, or did they offer him a bribe too substantial for him to resist? If so, what was that incentive? I am not discounting blackmail, but the inmate's situation would tend to argue against it being the motive. He was already serving a life sentence, so he had little, or nothing, to lose, even if someone threatened to expose him for another misdemeanour. Therefore, I think we should follow the bribe theory, and find out what would be a big enough inducement. It must be substantial, given what was expected of him in return. As he's going to be behind bars for a number of years, it's perhaps a pension fund for his family.'

* * *

Nash called up the files on Frank Watson, while the team spent the rest of the day re-examining the Country House Bandits files. Although this didn't throw up any new ideas at the time, as Nash was driving home that evening, his route took him past the end of Hillside Avenue, the road leading to where Corey Davies lived.

He pulled into the kerb and parked, pondering what might be a wild theory, or possibly a brainwave. He decided to put it to the test, knowing he would be certain to get an honest opinion. He picked up his mobile.

'What is it now, Mike? Aren't you supposed to be at home taking care of your lovely wife?'

Nash grinned at Clara's long-suffering tone, but told her, 'I was on my way, but something I saw triggered an idea, and I wanted to run it past you.'

'Go on then. After a wasted day like we've had, I could do with a laugh.'

'I want you to cast your mind back to our interview with Corey Davies, and in particular what he told us off the record. If you remember, when he was trying to explain how he got involved in criminal activity, he said he'd broken the law and was being blackmailed by some people into working for them as a drug dealer.'

'Yes, I do recall that, but why is it important now?'

'It might be, if my theory is accurate. Davies told us something else. If I remember correctly, he said something along the lines of "the whole thing kicked off with a string of burglaries", and he admitted he'd been involved in at least one of them.'

'I'm still waiting for the punchline to this joke.'

'He also said the burglaries weren't run-of-the-mill sub-urban houses, but properties with a far greater potential for rich pickings, or something like that.'

'Yes, I remember.'

'Now for the connection. Cast your mind back to how we've spent today, checking files on the Country House Bandits. Davies told us he'd made the mistake when he was in his teens. Wasn't that around the same time the gang commenced their nefarious career? So, what if the burglary was one of their operations? In other words, what if Davies was originally a member of that gang?'

There was a long silence as Clara mulled over Nash's suggestion. She was still considering the implications of it, when he added a telling rider. 'If Corey Davies had been involved with the gang, given what's been happening to the other members and those associated with them, might that provide the real explanation for the recent repeated attempts on his life? It might have nothing to do with Davies refusing to become involved in the sordid side of their trade, more an attempt to silence him — as they've done to all the others.'

As he was speaking, Nash had another illuminating idea. 'If I'm right, Corey Davies might be totally wrong in believing he'll be safe by keeping quiet and being locked away. Given what happened to Watson, Davies might be in more danger inside prison than out. And the threat does not end there. His wife and little Thomas might be in equal danger. They've committed no crimes, and are probably unaware of anything that would prevent them walking the streets in safety.'

Silence followed his remarks, but eventually Clara responded. 'You know what, that actually isn't the weirdest idea you've ever had.' She qualified the masked compliment by adding, 'Of course, there's a heck of a lot of competition for that title. But I agree it does seem a little too convenient for the Bandits to have begun operating at the same time as Davies admitted he took part in high-end burglaries. You will notice how carefully I avoided using the word "coincidence"? My question is, how do we go about discovering if your theory is correct? Or has another famous Mike Nash flight of fancy just taken off? And if you are accurate in your line of thought, where do we take it from here?'

'I'm not sure yet. I'm still coming to terms with the idea, so I haven't considered the ramifications. I suggest we both think about it overnight. Perhaps by morning we'll have come up with something.'

* * *

Next morning, when Clara entered the CID suite, Nash signalled her to join him in his office. 'Have you had any bright ideas overnight?'

'No, Mike, I leave that sort of thing to you.'

'OK, here's what I thought. The only way to test the accuracy, or otherwise, of my theory, is to ask Corey Davies outright. If he admits to having taken part in one or more of the Country House Bandits' earlier exploits, we then tell him what's happened to the other gang members and those close to them. If he was involved, that will really spook him, particularly regarding the risk to his wife and son. In order to protect Brittany and Thomas, Davies might change his mind about his vow of silence. If we point out that someone is cleaning house, Davies is intelligent enough to realize his best option to safeguard his family and himself is by telling us all he knows.'

'It might be difficult getting that point across to him, don't you think?'

'Actually, no, especially if we emphasize the fact there was nothing to suggest the Bandits who have been killed, or the people connected to them, were about to reveal anything damaging. That might be sufficient for Davies to recognize that cooperation with us is his best, probably his only, option.'

Nash's first task was to persuade Jackie Fleming to arrange a visit. She was reluctant to begin with, citing there being little likelihood of mileage in what she termed 'a rank outsider of an idea'.

Ruth Edwards overruled her, however. 'At the moment, we are saddled with seven murders to investigate, all seemingly connected to this gang. The inquiry is going nowhere up to press, so it would be extremely irresponsible for us not to follow up any avenue, no matter how many dead ends we hit. We need to identify, and bring to justice, a serial killer who has been operating within our area for ten years, without arousing even a whiff of suspicion until now.'

She thought for a second. 'I accept that this might be an extremely long shot, and Corey Davies might never have been connected with this gang. Therefore, he will know absolutely nothing of use to us. But, if he was, there is a chance he might provide some evidence. We must do our utmost to prise any information we can from him.'

'I've just received something that might help persuade Davies to cooperate,' Nash told them. 'It comes via some research done at my request by our new recruit. Adil looked into the background of the man who stabbed Frank Watson. Apparently, the inmate has a daughter who is extremely ill. The illness is incurable, and by what Adil could discover, she's entering the terminal stages of the disorder. Treatment and palliative care are highly expensive. As the inmate was already serving a life sentence, my guess is he regarded this as a win–win situation. Maybe not for Watson, but for those the killer cared about.'

CHAPTER TWENTY-ONE

Nash and Mironova revealed their plans to the team, before they began discussing tactics for how the interview should be conducted. Nash's opening suggestion puzzled Clara, but once he explained, she was able to see the logic behind his proposal.

'I think you should take the lead. When you talk to Davies, I want you to sympathize with him over his situation, being sure to mention how difficult it must be for him, knowing he's facing the prospect of long-term separation from his wife and son. Take every opportunity to mention them by name, thereby keeping Brittany and Thomas in the forefront of his mind. That makes it far more personal, and adds an air of poignancy to his dilemma. Going on from there, you need to stress at every opportunity that our only objective is to protect him, and to ensure the ongoing safety of his family.'

Nash allowed Clara to digest this before continuing, 'That will be the point where I step in, telling him about the murders, and asking him point blank if he was involved with the gang. At that stage we can emphasize yet again the need to keep him and his family out of harm's way.'

* * *

In the remand wing at Felling Prison, Davies took his seat across the table and waited for Mironova to complete the opening announcement for the recording, before reiterating his wish to waive the right to legal representation. He then demanded to know the reason for the meeting. 'I've already told you all I'm prepared to say about the drugs operation, and I've also provided the necessary evidence to back up my story, via my accountants. So, what else do you think I might know, or be prepared to share with you?'

Davies concentrated his gaze on Nash, who he believed would be the prime mover in the ensuing conversation, but Clara began to speak. It took a few seconds for him to switch his attention to what she was saying.

'Let me stress from the outset that our only concern in seeking this interview is for your welfare, and for that of Brittany and little Thomas. That's the reason we needed to speak with you as a matter of urgency. We have a duty of care to ensure all measures are put in place to keep you safe, and also to provide adequate protection for your family.'

As she continued, following the script she'd agreed with Nash, it was clear her remarks were beginning to catch his interest. Davies was clearly moved by her frequent references to his family, but also puzzled as to why they seemed to be the focus of her attention. Eventually, after Clara mentioned the possibility of long-term separation from Brittany and Thomas, and the subsequent inability to be on hand to protect them, her comments provoked the reaction Nash had been hoping for.

'I've already said I'll do everything in my power to keep them safe. That's the reason I won't tell you about the people who are behind the drugs operation. If word got out that I was even considering spilling the beans, it would be tantamount to signing my own death warrant.'

Davies leaned back in his chair, clearly under the impression he had delivered the *coup de grâce*, and that the interview was as good as over. He was shocked out of his satisfied state, however, when Nash spoke for the first time.

'When we met previously, you mentioned having taken part in one or more burglaries when you were a teenager. Were those crimes committed along with the members of the gang labelled by the media as the "Country House Bandits"?'

Davies remained silent, but his startled expression spoke volumes.

Nash leaned forward, staring directly at Davies. 'If that is correct, you will no doubt have read or heard that one of the gang members, Frank Watson, was stabbed to death in prison. Initially, this was thought to be a personal dispute, but we now believe it to have been a contract killing, carried out by a fellow convict desperate for money to support his terminally ill daughter.'

There was no noticeable change in Davies' expression, nothing to show Nash had said anything of concern, but this changed after Nash's next snippet of news.

'More recently, three more members of the Country House Bandits were released from prison, having served their ten-year sentences. I am referring to Joe Lambert, Peter Swallow and Terry Palmer. Of those three, Joe Lambert and Peter Swallow were both stabbed to death within days of their release. Terry Palmer is currently unaccounted for. Palmer has not been seen since the day he left prison.'

Davies sat bolt upright in his chair. 'Joe's dead, and Birdie too?'

His question more or less confirmed his involvement with the gang, Clara thought. She listened as Nash drove the point home.

'Yes, neither of them got much chance to enjoy their freedom. But that's not all. Far from it. We are also investigating the murders of four other people whose bodies were found in an abandoned lead mine.'

Davies' expression was now one of total confusion. Clearly, he was unable to see the relevance of this information.

'Three of those victims have been identified. One, nothing more than a skeleton, was Cindy Swallow, Birdie's wife. She had been in that mine, rotting away, since she disappeared ten years ago, soon after her husband was incarcerated. The second victim was Lauren Watson, Frank Watson's wife, or widow.' Nash shrugged. 'We can't be totally certain which, because we're not sure if she predeceased Frank, or outlived him, but either way, she's equally dead. The male victim in the mine was George Briggs, Swallow's half-brother. The other, an unidentified young woman, we believe was George's girlfriend. We think the unfortunate girl was simply in the wrong place at the wrong time. All four of these people were shot to death. So there we have it, seven murder victims, all with either a direct or indirect connection to the Country House Bandits. As far as we're aware, none of the people who were slaughtered were about to reveal damaging information about the gang, but that didn't stop them from being killed.'

Nash paused, as Davies was clearly shocked. Eventually, he continued, 'You mentioned at your previous interview there have been several attempts on your life recently. You believed the reason for them was your reluctance to become involved in people trafficking and the like. I think it was more likely an attempt to silence you. Someone is cleaning house, Corey, and you are a stain on the carpet that must be removed. Are you prepared to do nothing and meekly accept your fate? Are you prepared to wait for news that Brittany and Thomas have vanished, or been found dead in suspicious circumstances? There are a fair number of other disused lead mines in North Yorkshire, plus endless other places to conceal bodies. Places where corpses would remain undiscovered, while the rats and other predators feast on their decomposing bodies, until they have eaten their fill, and the corpses end up as skeletal as Cindy Swallow.'

Nash's dramatic prophecy finally provoked a reaction from Davies. He glared at Nash, clenching his fists. 'How do I know you haven't made this work of fiction up to try and get me to squeal? Because if so, it won't work!'

Nash smiled at Davies. 'I thought that might be your reaction. And because I anticipated you going down that route, I brought some evidence to back my story up. One thing we have in common, Corey, is a distinct lack of trust in what people do, or say, without something concrete to confirm it.'

As he was speaking, Nash opened the folder that had been lying on the desk and spread out a collection of photos. These comprised the corpses of Joe Lambert and Peter Swallow, plus the four victims from the Hand of Glory mine. Davies looked at each of them in turn, lingering over the skeleton that had once been Cindy Swallow. As Davies was attempting to absorb the horror of those images, Nash glanced sideways at Clara, a clear invitation for her to resume her questioning.

Clara's voice was sombre as she began, 'The gang members were murdered because someone feared they might tell someone close to them about the other Country House Bandits. Therefore, they had to be silenced. Not content with that, concerned they might have already passed such information on, the killer disposed of anyone close to the Bandits. I believe that's commonly referred to as "belt and braces" thinking. To my mind, remaining silent was as good a way of signing their death warrants — plus condemning anyone close to them.'

Clara shook her head slowly. 'Looking at it from your perspective, Corey, how could you live with the knowledge that Brittany and Thomas, your beautiful little boy, had perished, simply because of your stubborn refusal to speak out?'

Clara paused, possibly for breath, or because the scenario she'd conjured up was so terrible, but then returned to the fray. 'For that matter, what sort of existence would yours be, wondering, for every waking minute of every day, whether there was someone behind you, someone ready to wield the knife they were carrying? And how tormented would your dreams be, if in fact you were able to sleep, while listening out for every rustle of movement, every creaking floorboard that would signal the approach of your nemesis? Frank Watson must have felt secure within his prison cell, but that didn't stop it becoming his final resting place.'

There was a long silence. When Davies eventually spoke, his voice was little more than a muted croak, the emotion apparent, so quiet Nash was uncertain whether the microphone would pick it up. 'Can I have a break? I need to think about it. I can't take everything in right now.'

Nash nodded in agreement, telling Davies, 'Why don't we give you a few hours' thinking time, and reconvene this afternoon?'

As Clara was about to make the closing announcement, Nash watched Davies, who was still staring at the photos on the table, his expression reflecting obvious distress. In an attempt to divert the man's attention, Nash signalled Clara to wait and changed the subject slightly.

'You've more or less admitted taking part in one or more of the earlier Country House Bandits' robberies. Why were you dropped from the team?'

To the detectives' astonishment, Davies laughed, which, in the circumstances, they found baffling until he gave his reasons. The explanation, while it wasn't without humour, left them even more convinced of the ruthlessness of the people they were hunting.

'You asked why I was dropped. That's a highly appropriate word. We were taking goods out of a house in Cheshire, when I slipped on a patch of ice and lost my grip on a piece of Chinese porcelain I was carrying. I wasn't to know, but apparently it was worth well into six figures. Or it was, while it was in one piece. They made me sweep up the debris. Unknown to me, one of them was filming, and the video clearly showed me holding highly identifiable chunks of broken porcelain. They threatened to post the clip to the police, along with my name and address. They made it clear that if I failed to cooperate with what they had in mind, I'd have been en route to the nearest prison within days. Along with this threat, they told me because I'd cost them so much profit I was banned from further raids. They had other uses for me. Handling goods that even someone as clumsy as me couldn't harm if I dropped them.'

CHAPTER TWENTY-TWO

Nash used the interval to update the chief constable and Fleming, using speakerphone for the benefit of Clara. It was Ruth Edwards who came up with a piece of strategy designed to persuade Davies to cooperate.

Even Nash was surprised by her proposal. 'Do you think that's viable? We'd have to know before we even suggest something of that nature.'

'There's only one way to find out, and that's by asking the people concerned. It might mean delaying the resumption of your interview with Davies until I get their reaction, and knowing them, I can't see that happening until tomorrow at the earliest.'

'What we could do is tell Davies we're prepared to give him twenty-four hours to consider his options, and if we haven't got a reply by then, fob him off a bit longer. Someone can tell him we've been called to another incident.'

Nash paused and then asked, 'Do you think it would be in order to tell Davies what we're trying for, or might that be jumping the gun?'

The chief thought this over for a few seconds before delivering her verdict. 'I don't see any harm in letting it slip. As long as you stress that there's no guarantee, and that the decision is totally out of our hands. At the least, it might colour his judgement in favour of a possible outcome. If we can't deliver, it might turn him the other way, but that's a chance we'll have to take. Call into my office on your way back to Helmsdale, and let me know how it goes.'

When the detectives returned to the interview room, Davies was already there, staring at the victims' photos Nash had deliberately left on the table. Rather than pressing for an answer, Nash told Davies, 'I suggest we leave things as they stand until tomorrow. There are a couple of reasons for this. First off, I recognize what a huge decision you have to make, and the importance of getting it right — for you, and for Brittany and Thomas. In addition to that, having talked your situation over with our boss, she has come up with an idea you might find appeals to you, and might help you decide on the right course of action. Let me stress that I am not making any promises, because that would not be fair. In order for the plan to work, we have to consult with other parties, so I hope you will go along with the delay.'

Nash waited for Davies to nod agreement, although he was clearly somewhat baffled by the vague reference to *other parties*, so he listened intently as Nash explained. 'As we speak, our chief constable is in the process of contacting the Crown Prosecution Service. She is pitching the idea to them that in return for your full cooperation — by which I mean total disclosure, including all names, addresses, events and other ancillary information in respect of people involved in the drugs trade, human trafficking and the Country House Bandits gang — you will be offered a much lesser charge, thereby incurring a far lighter prison sentence. Moreover, you would be allotted special privileges, which basically means a higher level of protection than that afforded to other inmates.'

Nash allowed Davies to digest this, before continuing, 'This will be beneficial to all parties concerned, in many different ways. It will aid our investigation into at least seven murders, possibly more, by providing information we desperately need. It will assist other forces to arrest people involved in far worse crimes than those you committed. And by pleading guilty to those lesser offences, you will save the state the expense of a long and costly trial. The only people not to gain from this arrangement will be the barristers, and my heart does not bleed for them. Above all — and I guess pivotal to your interest — it will enable you to be reunited with Brittany and Thomas, many years earlier than you might have envisaged after your arrest.'

Nash ended by emphasizing once more, 'I must reiterate this is only a proposal, and at this stage no promises can be made, but I believe it is something you should consider carefully before making any decision.'

* * *

When Nash and Mironova reached Netherdale, they updated the chief, and as they were leaving, were surprised to find DC Andrews waiting in the corridor.

'What brings you to Netherdale, Lisa?' Nash asked.

'There's been a sighting of Free Willy here in town. One of the women he exposed himself to in one of the earlier cases spotted him a couple of hours ago, and recognized him immediately.'

'How did she recognize him?' Clara asked, then hurriedly added, 'No, don't tell me. I'm not sure I want to know.'

Lisa smiled. 'It was the very distinctive colour of the polo shirt he was wearing. The same as when he flashed at her.'

'He didn't expose himself to the same woman again, did he?' Nash was astounded at the possibility.

'No, but it's obvious he's active again, and now we have a better description.'

'OK, I suggest we alert uniform division, and then we should have a concerted evening hunting for him. I'll alert Steve Meadows and his counterpart here, and get any available officer on the streets. We'll need any female officers in plain clothes. We also need a code word.'

'How about "whopper"?' Clara grinned.

* * *

An hour and a half later, as the local takeaway was beginning to get busy with the early evening trade, two women were standing, idly chatting, at the corner of the building. They stopped speaking as a stranger approached them and then unzipped his trousers.

'Well, I certainly wouldn't call that a Big Mac, would you?' one of the women said.

'Not likely,' her companion replied. 'It's certainly not a whopper either,' she said, pointedly. 'I doubt it would fill a bap — let alone a hotdog roll.'

Unnerved, the flasher turned to make a bolt for it, but was instantly detained by two men in uniform who emerged from the shadows.

The women watched the arrested man being placed into a police van. As Lisa removed her earpiece and microphone, she told Clara, 'There's a bonus to this, because it's going to put an end to Viv's lousy Free Willy jokes — and not a minute too soon.' She grinned. 'Fancy a burger? My treat.'

* * *

Nash had arranged to meet Clara the following morning at headquarters, for the onward journey to Felling Prison. Clara was already waiting, clearly keen to talk to him.

'I've just been speaking to Viv. He got a call a few minutes ago from Alan, Lisa's partner. Apparently, she's unwell and he's insisted on taking her to the doctor, says she won't be on duty today. I'm surprised they can get to see a doctor at such short notice, unless it's far more of an emergency than Alan made out,' she added.

'That might be right for those of us who have to rely on the NHS. But with Alan's position as a director of a major public company, they'll have private health insurance. They aren't bound by the restrictions we lesser mortals have to endure.'

'I'd forgotten about that.'

'Phone Viv back, tell him to get Lisa's notes on Free Willy, get over here and deal with him before we run out of detention time. Adil can mind the shop, and keep familiarizing himself with all those files. We might be busy in the immediate future, if Davies can be persuaded to reveal all he knows. That will increase the workload dramatically, so Adil's presence will be a great boost. Let's go find out if the chief's had any reaction from CPS yet, or whether we've had a wasted journey. Then we might be able to drag Corey Davies away from his morning crossword.'

Ruth Edwards was clearly expecting them, because she emerged from her office as they approached, and greeted them with good news. 'CPS has already come back to me and, by the sound of it, they're keen for us to put the deal to Davies. The proviso is that he pleads guilty to the lesser offences, and provides us with all the information he knows.' In her hand she held the email.

'I'm surprised they've acted so quickly,' Clara responded.

The chief laughed. 'I think there are two reasons for that. They see this as a golden opportunity to put a big number of major offenders behind bars for a long period, which will give them great kudos. Added to which, saving the expense of a long trial is also attractive. Just keep me posted.'

There was a minor hiccup when the detectives met with Davies. As Clara was about to begin recital of the opening announcement, Davies stopped her. 'I don't want any of our conversation on the record yet. I realize it might be against protocol, and at some stage it will be necessary for this to go public, but I'm concerned that if anything leaks out, it could be dangerous.'

Nash could see the sense in his request, but disagreed. 'Look, we've had an offer from the Crown Prosecution

Service.' He passed the document to Davies. 'That is confirmation from CPS of their willingness to minimise the charges you will face, and also for you to enter a plea for clemency, in exchange for your full cooperation. From you, they require full details of everyone connected to the drugs cartel, in addition to what you can tell us about the Country House Bandits. But we have to have a record of the conversation, or the CPS won't believe you've fulfilled your side of the deal.'

Davies examined the paperwork, before nodding his agreement for Clara to start the recording.

'I suggest we leave the drugs and human trafficking operations out of the equation for now, and concentrate on the Country House Bandits. As I see it, their former activities pose the most imminent threat to your safety and that of your family. We know there are some gang members who were never identified, let alone arrested, so we could perhaps make a start with them.'

Nash's comment aroused Davies' curiosity sufficiently for him to ask, 'How do you know there were other gang members?'

'Because of the volume of goods stolen, plus the bulk and weight of some of the items. Also the professional method of entry, which the four men we know of weren't capable of performing.'

'I'd never have thought of it like that,' Davies admitted. 'I suppose it's a bit of an insight into detective work.' He hesitated for a second, then, as if he'd decided to commit himself all the way, told them, 'I'll tell you what I know about the Country House Bandits, which isn't much, to put it mildly.'

CHAPTER TWENTY-THREE

As she listened to Davies, Clara acknowledged that whatever his faults, he could not be accused of exaggeration. What he was able to reveal might be vague and indistinct, but at least it was more than they already knew. Mind you, she thought, anything had to be an improvement on nothing.

'Naturally, I followed the court case ten years ago when the four men were convicted, and parts of what was reported made me smile. Let me explain . . .' Davies leaned forward as if to emphasize the importance of what he was telling them. 'I have to say, the barrister who represented Terry Palmer got it dead right. He made Terry out to be nothing more than small fry, more or less a delivery boy, who was charged with taking stolen goods to the buyer.

'In fact, I reckon he was even less than that. I'm only going on what little I saw while I was on a job, but to me, he seemed nothing more than a bit of a kid who was along for the ride. I thought so little of him it was only when I saw the photos in the press, following their convictions, that I was able to put a name to him. There is one way I suppose Palmer might have been useful to them, though.'

'What way is that?'

'Palmer was small, no more than five feet four inches tall, and slender, making him very handy for getting through small spaces. I reckon even a toilet window wouldn't have posed much of a problem for him.'

Nash switched the direction of his questions. 'Where were the goods taken?'

'I'm not certain, because my involvement was so limited. From what I overheard, they were sent to a warehouse, before being distributed elsewhere once they had buyers for them.'

'So you don't believe any of the arrested men were the gang's leader?'

'Certainly not. The hierarchy was far more convoluted than that.'

'Do you know the names of those at the top of the ladder? Did you ever get to meet them?'

'Joe Lambert only mentioned someone called the Keeper, whoever he was. I never met the bosses, although I did see them once. Apparently, from something Joe told me, they didn't always make an appearance. It was only when they had targeted something of extra value they already had a client for, that they graced the gang with their presence. That way, they stayed clear of the limelight and reduced their chance of getting nicked. I know very little about them, and certainly not their names.'

'OK, accepting that they are at best shadowy figures, is there anything you can tell us that might help identify them, even after all this time?'

'There were two of them, and they stuck together like Siamese twins. They came and went in the same car, a flashy German limo.'

'You mean a Porsche?'

'No, not quite as easily recognizable as that, but close to it. Their vehicle of choice was a high-end Mercedes. Whoever said crime doesn't pay obviously got that wrong, unless they bought it on the never-never.'

'Can you describe these men?'

'That's where it gets tricky. Most times, they stayed in the limo. But when they did emerge, they were both wearing overcoats and flat caps. Added to which, the driver had a beard, so whether he was sixteen or sixty, I couldn't tell.'

'What about the passenger?'

'He was even harder to spot. In addition to the coat and cap, he was wearing a big pair of sunglasses.' Davies frowned. 'I've never thought of this before, but the fact he was wearing sunglasses is really odd, because it was just after midnight, and there wasn't even a moon.'

'Were there any distinguishing features about them? Height, body shape, that sort of thing?'

'Not that I can recall. They were both medium height, and slim rather than fat, but that's about it.'

'When we spoke before, you suggested they came from around this area. But that puzzles me. If you only saw them on one occasion, and know so little about them, what makes you believe they were from this neck of the woods?'

'It was a fluke. They'd got out of the limo, and were talking to one of the gang. I walked past the car on my way to the van with an oil painting they wanted. Back then, all vehicles had to display a tax disc in the windscreen.' Davies paused and grinned. 'But I guess you already knew that. As I passed the front of the Merc, I glanced at the screen. The tax had just been renewed and the disc was stamped by Netherdale post office. I had to look Netherdale up in a road atlas, because I'd never heard of the place before then. Of course, this all happened nearly fifteen years ago, so for all I know they could be in Los Angeles or Montevideo now.'

'You don't actually believe that, do you?'

Davies stared at Nash, who followed up his question by reminding him, 'You told us you moved to this area to put the frighteners on them. You would only do that if you believed they were still hanging around here.'

'Yes, I'm fairly sure they'd want to stay and keep a close watch on their operations.'

Nash changed tack again, realizing Davies had revealed all he knew about the gang leaders. 'What about the other foot soldiers? Is there anything you can tell us about them that might interest us?'

Davies was about to say no, but then had a flash of memory. 'One of them was the locksmith — that's what Joe and Birdie called him. They said he could pick any lock, disable any alarm, and crack any safe that had ever been invented. He was a good deal older than the rest of us, but he certainly wouldn't interest you, because he's pushing up daisies now, has been for a long time. I read about his death in the paper, and although I'd only seen him once, I recognized him from his photo. I put two and two together from the description of the offence he'd served time for.'

'Can you recall his name, or perhaps when and how he died?'

'I think his name was Arthur something, because the paper used his nickname, "Artful Artie", and he was killed about seven years . . .' Davies' voice trailed off.

'What is it, what have you just thought of?'

'Artful Artie was stabbed to death. His body was found in an alleyway somewhere in Harrogate, as I recall. The police's theory was it had been a mugging that got out of hand. I didn't think anything different, and I don't believe anyone was ever charged with Artie's murder, but with everything you've told me about, I'm beginning to wonder.'

'You think we should increase the Country House Bandit victims by one?'

'I could be wrong. It might be nothing more than sheer coincidence.' He paused and changed topic. 'I've already compiled a list of everyone involved in the drug operation, but you need to bring Brittany to see me. She's the only person who will be allowed access to where the information is stored.'

Seeing the detectives' puzzled expressions, he explained, 'I placed everything you need in a safety deposit box. Brittany and I are the only two people permitted to withdraw anything from there. She'll want me to give the OK before she collects it.'

'Unfortunately, we can't bring her here — I'm thinking of her safety. But we can arrange a phone call.'

* * *

'Even if the man we're seeking still owns a Mercedes, trying to identify the right one round here would be like looking for a needle in a haystack. They're about as common as Range Rovers,' Clara said, as they drove back to Netherdale.

Their briefing of Ruth Edwards and Jackie didn't take long, and left all four officers somewhat deflated.

'It's to be hoped what Davies can reveal about the drugs and trafficking operations is more useful than what he told us about the Bandits,' Nash remarked. 'About the only positive thing to come from our conversation is the revelation about Artful Artie, and that wasn't exactly good news. Apart from what we learned about the locksmith, the only other interesting information came when he revealed that Terry Palmer was nothing more than a bit player.'

'I'm more concerned with the gang leaders, and what he could tell us about them. Apart from the car being from round here, was there anything else?' Jackie asked.

'Not really, although he implied the two top men seemed desperately keen to avoid anyone recognizing them. Apart from that, what he told us could mean we're looking for someone suffering from photophobia.'

'Photophobia, that's having an adverse reaction to bright lights, isn't it?'

Nash nodded. 'That, plus the anonymity thing, might explain why he wore sunglasses, even at night. That's all we have to go on, unless you want us to try and track down every Mercedes from this area between ten and fifteen years ago?'

'What does that cryptic remark mean?'

Nash explained about Davies spotting the tax disc, and was less than surprised when the chief categorized the information as being another dead end. 'What do you plan to do next?' she asked.

'I think our priority must be to escort Mrs Davies to the bank, after Corey gives her the go-ahead. We collect the documentation and begin dealing with the drug runners. Once we've got that sorted, then we can return to dealing with the Country House Bandits.'

'How did you know that about photophobia?' Clara asked, as they were leaving the headquarters building.

'I knew someone a long time ago who suffered from a form of it,' Nash replied. During the journey to Helmsdale, he thought more about this and wondered if the information Davies had revealed, albeit almost accidentally, might be more useful than they had initially believed.

As soon as they entered the CID suite, Nash turned to their new recruit and told him, 'Adil, I want you to try and find out anything you can about a man believed to be a leading member of the Country House Bandits. He was a locksmith. I don't know his surname, but he was known as Artful Artie. I believe he originally hailed from Manchester, and he was stabbed to death in Harrogate around seven years ago.'

As they were about to leave Nash's office, Pearce turned and told him, 'Sorry, I almost forgot, Alan Marshall rang again, and wants you to call him back.'

Nash's concern was mirrored by that of Clara. The ensuing conversation did little to allay that feeling. Having asked Marshall to pass on his kind regards, and those of the rest of the team, to Lisa, Nash told Clara, 'Lisa's in hospital with a threatened miscarriage. I didn't ask for details.'

Clara nodded. She understood, aware of the terrible situation Nash and Alondra had gone through a few years earlier, causing her to leave him and return to Spain.

'Alan's hopeful it's early enough to save the pregnancy. She's on complete bed rest, and has a sick note covering the next two weeks. The doctor said he'll need to ensure everything's OK before signing her off to come back to work, if at all.' He sighed, sat down at his desk, and looked at Clara.

'If she does return, I think it would be best to confine her to desk duties.' He paused, before adding, 'And making coffee, of course. Will you tell Viv and Adil, while I pass the news to the top brass?'

* * *

Having secured the documentation from the bank with Brittany Davies, Nash suggested she return to Wales with her son to be safe. He was then able to pass the details to Superintendent Fleming. 'Fortunately for us, none of the people listed here lives or operates within our area,' he told her. 'Which is a huge relief — we've more than enough on our plates at present.'

'OK, Mike, I'll ensure these get sent to the relevant forces. If everything Davies intimated is correct, there should be a string of major arrests before long. At least this will free you up to continue investigating the murders.'

That was true, but as they had no new facts to work with, the team were at an impasse, until Viv sought Nash out and gave him a slender file. 'Adil found some interesting background info. Artful Artie's real name was Arthur James Fawcett. There's quite a bit in there about his death. What Davies told you is quite correct. Fawcett's body was found in an alleyway near to where he lived in Harrogate. He'd been stabbed. That much is fact — the rest is hearsay. Fawcett was rumoured to have had a long and successful criminal career, but despite that, he was only convicted once, when he was in his early twenties. He was sentenced to four years for burglary.'

'Did Fawcett have any family?'

'Yes, he was married, and had a stepdaughter named Joanne. Sadly, Fawcett's wife died when the little girl was only six years old. After that, Fawcett became Joanne's legal guardian. She'll be an adult now.'

'Have you been able to find out what happened to the daughter?'

'Not yet, but Adil's working on it.'

'OK, thanks, Viv.'

Later, as he studied the details of the Arthur Fawcett case, Nash realized there was little or no new information to be gleaned from it. He spent a few moments studying the photo of Fawcett's daughter Joanne, which had appeared in the local newspaper at the time. Despite the grainy image, there was no doubt she was a stunningly attractive young woman. Nash grinned. If he'd expressed that thought, Clara would have doubtless come up with an immediate insult.

* * *

The following day, Adil gave Nash, Mironova and Pearce an update, which left them more than a little confused. 'I've been trying to discover what happened to Artful Artie's step-daughter, but there's a problem,' he told them.

'What sort of a problem?' Nash asked.

'Joanne Fawcett disappeared only weeks after her step-father's murder.'

'When you say she disappeared, might she also have been killed?'

'I suppose it's possible, but I don't think so. Her vanishing act is more than a bit mysterious, and from what little I've been able to glean, I believe she planned her disappearance.'

'Have you any evidence to support your theory, Adil?' Clara asked. 'Because you should have been told that Mike's the only one in these offices permitted to speculate without an ounce of proof.'

'The evidence I do have is meagre, and a bit negative, but it does seem to indicate Joanne Fawcett deliberately set out to make herself invisible.' Adil looked at his notes. 'Arthur Fawcett lived in rented accommodation, a house owned by a private landlord. For some reason, possibly because of his criminal record, the tenancy was in Joanne's name. After her stepfather's death, Joanne gave notice to quit, but when the landlord tried to contact her, she had already upped sticks and vanished.'

'Why did the landlord need to contact her?' Viv was curious.

'The rent was up to date and the property was in good condition. They simply wanted to return the bond. But when they attempted to transfer the money to Joanne's bank, they were told the account had been closed a couple of weeks earlier, so the money still hasn't been claimed, seven years later.'

'Have you checked things such as voters' rolls to see if Joanne Fawcett is registered at another address?'

'I have, and there's no record of a Joanne Fawcett matching her age living anywhere in the UK. I also checked with DVLA and the Passport Office. According to their systems, no passport or driving licence has been applied for, or granted. It's almost as if Joanne Fawcett has ceased to exist — or never existed in the first place.'

'OK, let's call it a day. Daniel's playing cricket this evening, and I've to get him there. Alondra isn't comfortable driving anymore.'

'Is your son a cricketer?' Adil asked, as he was donning his jacket.

'Yes, he plays for Netherdale Juniors during the school holidays. He was lucky to be selected, but he's doing well.'

'Yes,' Clara added, 'Daniel is cricket mad. He picked their home in Wintersett because the back garden is large enough for a pitch.'

'I've seen him play,' Viv said. 'And he is good.'

Nash laughed. 'Says the man named after the famous Antiguan cricketer. See you all tomorrow.'

CHAPTER TWENTY-FOUR

From early beginnings as a convenience store-cum-off-licence, Stop 2 Shop, based in Bishopton, had expanded, opening branches in Netherdale, Helmsdale and beyond. They had also broadened their product range significantly, stocking clothing, footwear, DIY, and gardening products in addition to the food and drinks on which their business had thrived.

Their growing success attracted a lot of attention, not all of which was welcome. In their haste to expand, they had left themselves exposed to such interest. Their policy had been to maximise profit. This was pleasing when viewing their balance sheet, but it did not reflect their lack of precautionary measures deemed essential by other, larger retailers.

CCTV cameras in and around their stores were few, and security tags on the more valuable stock lines were non-existent. The company's executives ignored such precautions, deeming them to be of low priority. Trained security staff was a measure deemed essential by many of their counterparts, but again, Stop 2 Shop's decision makers opted to delay implementing this policy.

There was a degree of logic behind management's reasoning. The location of their outlets had been carefully chosen.

Opting to base their stores solely in small towns, within primarily rural areas with less competition, was a shrewd business strategy. What they failed to take into account was the determination of those intending to acquire goods without the inconvenience of having to pay for them, and the risk of incursion by such wrongdoers from outside the area.

The manager of Stop 2 Shop's Helmsdale branch was walking along the footwear aisle and noticed all was not as it should be. He summoned the stock supervisor and expressed his displeasure. 'I thought I gave strict instructions for all shelves to be replenished on a daily basis, so how come this one is empty?'

'They were all full this morning. I checked them myself.'

Either there had been a sudden upsurge in demand, or the store had been targeted by shoplifters with a taste for expensive footwear. Having checked with sales on the computer, they accepted the less savoury alternative.

'We'd better check the rest of the stock.'

Missing items included pairs of jeans, jogging trousers, T-shirts, and polo shirts. The retail value of the stolen goods was well into four figures.

An alert was put out to all their stores. By early afternoon, it was clear the Helmsdale incident was only part of the robbers' handiwork. Both the Netherdale and Bishopton stores reported similar losses, and soon the operator in the Netherdale control room had dispatched uniformed officers to all three sites.

* * *

It was overconfidence that proved to be the shoplifters' undoing. Having assessed the Stop 2 Shop outlets and realized their vulnerability, they had assumed a similar lack of technological sophistication would apply to the law enforcement system covering such a rural area.

It was late afternoon when two traffic officers in an unmarked car were en route from Bishopton to Helmsdale.

They had just passed through the village of Bishop's Cross when they received a hit on their on-board ANPR camera.

Hutchinson told Starkey, 'That grey Ford Focus we just passed has been flagged up as having no insurance. The car's registered to an address in Hartlepool, which is knocking on for eighty miles away. It also begs the question as to what they're doing in this neck of the woods.'

'OK, I'll turn round and we can give it a stop. We've nothing else to do at the moment. It's been a downright boring shift so far.'

'Don't tempt fate.'

Once they were in range of the Ford, Hutch reported their intention to the control room. He then activated their lights and siren, to persuade the driver of the vehicle in front to pull over. It failed to achieve the desired result, causing Hutchinson to update Control. 'Vehicle failed to stop. We're in pursuit. Speed is seventy-five in a sixty zone, approaching the village of Bishop's Cross.'

A combination of unfamiliarity with local roads, allied to their desperation to escape, proved to be the Ford's occupants' undoing. It could be argued that a local farmer's carelessness was also a contributory factor to the spectacular crash. The trailer being used to transport manure had not been closed properly, and had deposited a thick smear of viscous animal waste across a section of the road surface.

The Ford began to skid. The driver yanked on the steering wheel to correct this, sending the car out of control. As it spun, the pursuing officers watched in horror as the vehicle hit the banking and rolled, coming to rest on its roof.

'Crash, crash, crash!' Hutchinson shouted to Control. 'Vehicle on its roof.' The officers approached the stricken vehicle and found the driver trapped behind the steering wheel, hanging by his seatbelt. The rear seat passenger was similarly held captive. Both occupants were male, and both appeared to be unconscious — or worse.

The windows were smashed, which enabled the officers to check for signs of life. To their relief, both occupants were breathing. The front seat passenger had not been so lucky. Ignoring the legal requirement, he had failed to put his seat belt on. During one of the car's revolutions, the passenger door had been torn off, and he had been ejected from the vehicle.

Starkey scrambled up the steep bank at the opposite side of the road, where the passenger, whom he guessed was only in his teens, had ended his involuntary flight. There was blood seeping from several cuts to his head, and his legs were at an awkward angle, suggesting both limbs might be broken. It came as mild relief when he noticed the boy's chest moving slightly. At least he was alive.

After Hutchinson updated the control room, Starkey told him, 'If you put out the warning signs and block the road, I'll grab a thermal blanket from our car to cover this poor kid. It isn't much, but by the look of him, this youngster's going to need all the help he can get.'

There seemed little they could do while they waited for the other emergency services. Hutchinson made a suggestion. 'If we can get the car boot open, we might be able to reach the men inside. Waiting for the water fairies to cut the doors off could take a long while, time these guys might not have.'

'Water fairies?'

'Sorry, local slang for fire officers.'

With the assistance of a crowbar, more often employed to gain access to houses, they forced the car boot open. It was filled with boxed shoes and clothing, many items still on hangers. 'Well at least we now know why they travelled all the way from Hartlepool, and why they were so anxious not to chat to us,' Starkey said. 'I think we've found the shoplifting gang. We'd better shift this lot into our car, to make easier access for your water fairies.'

They could hear sirens getting nearer, and Traffic Inspector Paul Grant arrived, followed by two fire engines and two ambulances, to the sound of a helicopter. Grant took immediate charge of the situation, liaising with Chief Fire Officer Doug Curran.

The supervising paramedic from Helimed sought out Inspector Grant and gave him an update. 'The young lad has serious head and spinal injuries, plus two broken legs. He's coming with us. We'll need help to get him round to the cricket pitch where we landed the helicopter. I'm afraid we interrupted a game — there wasn't much choice with these narrow lanes. Both the kids in the car have regained consciousness. I don't believe they've suffered life-threatening injuries. Sadly, neither of them has damaged their mouths.'

'Why do you say that?'

'Because the language they're coming out with is appalling. According to what I overheard, the driver is blaming your colleagues for causing the crash. That, I hasten to add, is a rigorously edited version of what he said. The rest is unrepeatable. Whatever ails these two, apart from foul mouth syndrome, we'll know soon enough, because the fire crew is almost through chopping the doors off.'

* * *

Daniel was enjoying the match. Netherdale batted first and he had scored thirty-seven runs. Play had been suspended suddenly when a helicopter circled the pitch, obviously looking for somewhere to land. The players cleared the field and watched in amazement as a Helimed landed in the outfield. Daniel sat watching the action with his father for a while, before joining his teammates. It was some time before the paramedics returned and loaded their patient into the helicopter and play resumed. Daniel waved to his father before he began to bowl. He had taken his second wicket and looked to the crowd of parents for Mike's usual thumbs-up, but couldn't see him. When the game was over, he headed for the pavilion, to find David Sutton, Clara's husband, waiting for him.

'Where's Pa?' Daniel asked. 'He's not been called out again, has he?'

'In one respect, yes.' David chuckled, and ruffled Daniel's hair. 'Get your kit. I'm afraid you're staying with us tonight. Right now, your father's probably pacing the floor at the hospital.'

'Is Mum OK?'

'She's fine. The baby's coming.'

'Wow,' was all Daniel could say.

* * *

The next morning at Helmsdale station, the team were waiting for news. Every time the phone rang there was an air of expectancy, until eventually, Clara's mobile rang.

Viv and Adil looked at her as her face brightened, and they listened to the one-sided conversation. 'That's wonderful news, Mike. And the weight? How's Alondra? Really? So soon? Yes, of course. I'll tell David. We can bring him home later after we've fed him, give things chance to settle. I will. Congratulations to you both. Yes, I'll tell everyone.'

Clara put her mobile down and looked at the other two. 'What?'

'Come on, Clara, spill the beans,' Viv demanded.

'Eight pound five, Alondra's fine but tired, they're letting her home later this afternoon, and we're taking Daniel home this evening. Mike is now on paternity leave. OK?'

Viv glared at her. 'Clara, other than it being a baby, what is it?'

'Oh, sorry, didn't I say?' Clara was enjoying this. 'It's a girl! Lucy Nash!'

CHAPTER TWENTY-FIVE

Two days later, Mironova was using Mike's office as she usually did during his absence. That meant someone was always
available to answer his phone. She called to Viv as soon as he
arrived and told him, 'I've just heard that both men from the
shoplifters' car have been cleared for release from hospital.
Jackie has arranged for them to be transferred to custody at
HQ. IOPC have been informed as a formality. I'll conduct
the interviews, and take Adil along. That way he can get to
grips with our technique, which could vary from those he's
used to. It also means you'll be in charge here.'

'Have you heard how the passenger who was thrown
clear of the vehicle is?' Viv asked.

'No, I haven't. You might want to try for an update for
me before we leave.'

'Any specific reason?'

She picked up a trio of folders. 'The driver is twenty-one
years old. The car belongs to his mother. The rear passenger
is the driver's nineteen-year-old cousin. The lad who suffered
such horrific injuries is the driver's sixteen-year-old brother.'

Mironova told Adil, 'You're with me. We're off to
Netherdale to talk to our would-be Lewis Hamilton and his
friend, aka the shoplifting duo.'

Turning to Pearce, Clara told him, 'If anything traumatic happens, liaise with Superintendent Fleming.' Clara ended by asking, 'By the way, did you oil the thumbscrews after the last interview you conducted?'

Pearce was still chuckling when his colleagues drove out of the car park.

* * *

On the journey to HQ, Clara briefed Adil as to how she wanted to conduct the interview. 'You'll be in charge of the recording and making the opening announcement. After that, your role will be primarily that of an observer.'

She noticed the slightly disappointed expression on Hassan's face. 'That doesn't mean you've been sidelined, far from it. What you have to do is watch the suspect like a hawk, taking careful note of every facial expression, especially the eyes, which can speak volumes. It's also important to see where the suspect is looking, whether they're trying to avoid eye contact. And also their body language — posture, hand gestures, leg movements. All these can be indicative of guilt — or innocence.' She smiled fleetingly as she added, 'Basically, that means you'll be occupying my seat, doing what I normally do, while, today, I take Mike's part. It's a system we've developed over a good number of years, and it works pretty well.'

'OK,' he said.

Clara added, 'I will do everything in my power to get answers from the suspects, provoking a response in any way I can. I'm particularly keen to get the driver talking. We're not strong on "no comment" interviews, so be prepared for some shock tactics. Don't allow what I'm saying to distract your attention from the suspect.'

If Hassan had any doubts as to Clara's technique, or how far she would go to get a response, they soon vanished. Although the opening question she asked the driver had him puzzled for a while. Clara asked, 'Do you love your brother?'

The driver looked up, clearly startled by the question. It was a few seconds before he muttered, 'No comment.'

'Oh, come off it. It's a perfectly simple question, not one designed to trap you. Do you love your brother, yes or no?'

Grudgingly, he replied, 'Yes.'

'That's nice to hear, don't you agree, Detective Constable?' Without waiting for Hassan to reply, she continued, her tone still friendly, 'And because you love your brother, I suppose you'll want to know how he is, won't you?'

'Yes.' The monosyllabic answer was almost inaudible.

'Well, you'll be pleased to know I can give you an update, because I spoke to the head of the intensive care unit only an hour ago. He told me your brother, who I understand is only sixteen years old, suffered severe head injuries, plus two broken legs, a broken arm, a dislocated shoulder and two broken ribs.'

Clara paused, and Hassan noticed the distress on the driver's face before she continued remorselessly, 'The surgeon is unable to say at this stage whether the brain injuries will impair him, or whether he will regain his full mental faculties. However, he was able to give a definitive diagnosis in respect of the other major traumas. I dread to think what your mother will say, once she knows exactly what you've done to her younger son.'

The driver, who had been staring fixedly at the table separating him from his tormentor, looked up in horror as Mironova told him, 'The surgeon also informed me that as a result of your selfish, reckless stupidity in trying to escape our officers, who only wanted to talk to you about a lack of insurance on the vehicle, your sixteen-year-old brother suffered such traumatic spinal injuries that he will be confined to a wheelchair for the rest of his life.'

The interview had to be suspended at that point, as the suspect was almost in hysterics. Once he had recovered his composure to a degree, they resumed, and the driver's confession became nothing more than a formality.

Having received a similar admission of guilt from the driver's cousin, Mironova and Hassan returned to Helmsdale.

On the journey, Clara noticed Hassan seemed very subdued. 'Is something wrong?' she asked.

'Not really,' Adil told her. 'I was just thinking that if I ever upset you, I'd like forty-eight hours' notice, so I can get as far away from Helmsdale as possible.'

Before the interview, Mironova and Hassan had ensured their mobiles were switched off. The downside of this precautionary measure only became apparent when they reached Helmsdale and discovered neither of them had reactivated their phones. As they walked across the car park, they rectified this omission, and Clara's mobile bleeped, signalling an incoming message. 'It looks as if we're on our own. That was from Viv. He's been called out to another burglary, this time at Thornhill Farm, near Drover's Halt. By the sound of it, a load more equipment's been taken. I hope you realize the serious implications in this for you.'

Hassan was puzzled. 'What implications?'

'It means for the first time you'll be placed in sole charge of the coffee machine.'

* * *

Pairing the new traffic officers together was a natural step. But that had one minor disadvantage as far as the duo were concerned via the ribbing they took from their colleagues. Traffic Constables Starkey and Hutchinson soon became known as Starsky and Hutch.

Thornhill Farm was situated just beyond the village of Drover's Halt and was accessed by a track stretching almost a mile from the main road, although the tarmac surface meandering through this part of the dale was more of a country lane than a traffic highway.

The alert came just as their patrol reached the Netherdale ring road at the start of their morning shift. They were on the lookout for a driver said to be under the influence of narcotics, but they abandoned this in favour of the robbery.

Having informed Control of their intention, they lit up the blues and twos and headed towards the crime scene.

It didn't take long for them to assess the situation. 'I think we need the sleuths and boffins here,' Hutchinson told his colleague. 'This is similar to those other farm jobs we read about in the updates a month or so ago.'

DC Pearce arrived to find the officers parked by a five-bar gate.

'We thought we should let you know about this, especially with the access problem.' They indicated the locked gate, smiled, and drove away.

Before reaching the site of the break-in, Pearce had to wait for the farmer to arrive on his quad bike and unlock the gate. As he watched the padlock being removed and the sturdy chain unwrapped from between the metal bars, Viv asked if the gate was always secured that way.

'Aye, it is. We've had a load of bother over the years with folk treating it as a public footpath. We even stuck some warning signs up, but they seemed to think that was a challenge. Some bastard actually tore one of the signs down and trampled on it. We put up with it for ages, but then one of them let their dog off its lead and it got into yon field.'

He pointed to his right. 'At the time, there were a flock of pregnant ewes in there, grazing away, peaceful-like. Then this dog got to them and chased them. They got spooked, stampeded, and some aborted. We lost a few lambs. That was when I decided enough was enough. I had this gate fitted, and got that sign made and erected out of reach.'

Viv followed the direction of the farmer's pointing finger and chuckled. 'I bet that's as good a deterrent as the locked gate,' he said, after reading the notice. *Private Property. Trespassers will be shot. Survivors will be prosecuted.*

'Aye, but now I'm baffled as how the thieving sods got up to the farm, into the barn, nicked that gear, and got away.'

Pearce drove up to the farm. He inspected the outbuilding, which was a good distance away from the main house.

As with the previous incursions, the equipment taken was reasonably light and portable.

'Have you checked the boundary, see if they got in anywhere?' he asked.

'It didn't occur to me,' the farmer replied.

'Can we take a look while I'm here?'

The farmer chuckled. 'You don't know how big the farm is, do you?'

Pearce shook his head.

'Get on the back of here and we'll take a look.' The farmer indicated the quad bike. 'You'll be quite safe,' he added.

* * *

An hour later, back at Helmsdale, Pearce told DS Mironova about the incident. 'Solved it,' he said.

'Solved what?'

'How the thieves get onto the farms and carry the stolen property away.'

'Go on then, brainbox. Enlighten me.'

'Quad bikes. They get onto the land at the furthest point, through a hedge or fencing, far enough not to be noticed. Ride across the farm and commit the theft, carrying the stolen goods away on the bike. They load up a van, including the quad bike, and drive away without arousing suspicion.'

'And how did you come to this conclusion?'

'I've spent half an hour on the back of a quad, being driven round Thornhill Farm. We found a break in the fencing where the wire had been cut, and tracks leading to the barn. There are tyre tracks, so I've requested CSI go to take some castings. Case solved.'

As Adil watched the interplay, he realized what a good team he had joined.

'Solved? And who actually committed the crime?' Clara asked.

'I have no idea. I've only solved the access issue.'

'In that case, I think you should try and discover if any quad bikes have been stolen lately, shouldn't you?'

Adil was trying not to laugh. 'Need any help, Viv?'

'No, thank you.'

* * *

It was only the following day that Clara came up with a suggestion, having received input from one of their absent colleagues.

'I phoned Lisa yesterday evening to see how she is, and apparently she's bored rigid. The doctors have discharged her, but won't permit her to do anything but the lightest chores. Alan's watching her like a hawk. I told her about Viv's solution to the robberies, and she said she should have realized.'

'Realized what?' Viv asked.

'Alan has a quad he uses for the tracks he can't get the Land Rover down. She thinks she should have worked it out.'

'There's nothing as good as hindsight,' Adil stated.

'Yes, but Alan's quad has a tracker. If we have a stolen bike on our patch, we might be able to track it. Well, the new guys in their hi-tech car might. I also wondered if we should check any CCTV footage from cameras closest to the burglary sites. I admit these could be several miles away, given their remote location, but if they throw up images of the same van travelling along roads leading to and from those crime scenes at approximately the date and time of each robbery, it might yield us some valuable clues. I admit it's a long shot, with no guarantee. We could be wasting our time, but I reckon it's worth giving it a go. Viv, will you and Adil start trawling through footage from any relevant CCTV cameras, please? I'll concentrate on the Country House Bandits.'

Moments later, Viv said, 'I've just noticed something.'

'Well, enlighten us, O Great One.'

'The dates of the burglaries, they're all when it's a full moon.'

'Why would that matter?' Clara was confused.

'Moonlight! They can see where they're going over the farmland.'

* * *

It took many hours of painstaking work before the detective constables were in a position to share the results of their efforts with Mironova. The outcome was not in the least what she expected to hear, and for a while, it appeared to have been a wasted effort.

'These sites are rural, with few cameras, so we examined footage from as close as we could get to all the burglaries,' Pearce began. 'In each set of images the cameras had picked up a grey Sprinter van going to, and coming away from, the general area where those farms were situated. At first, we thought we were onto a winner, but when we examined the images more closely, we discovered the vans all had different registration numbers.'

'Who do they belong to, someone with a vehicle hire fleet?' Clara asked.

'No, and it was only when we ran the plates we found we might be onto a winner after all.' Pearce grinned, seeing the hopeful expression on Clara's face. 'The vehicle descriptions differ widely from what we saw on CCTV.'

'Would you care to explain that?' Clara asked waspishly.

'Cloned plates! The registration numbers belong to various vehicles, from wagons to private cars, all from Leeds and surrounding areas. In fact, the Sprinters we saw are probably all the same vehicle, with the plates swapped every time the owner went burgling.'

'Oh, brilliant, just when I thought we were making progress,' Clara muttered.

'When we realized this, we looked at images from more cameras, and a couple of these showed the sides of the vehicles. At some time there had been a company logo and this had been removed — badly. In a certain light we could see the outline of some letters.' He glanced down at his notes.

'The letters were N, D, M, R, and L, but they were spread across different areas of the panels. We only picked up part of them, so we're a bit stuck, unless we can find an individual or company with those letters in their name. Otherwise, we're almost back to square one.'

'I'm assuming you downloaded those images?'

'Yes, Clara, do you want them?'

'If you wouldn't mind making a copy. I'm going to Mike's tonight. I'll show them to Alondra and see if she has any thoughts that might help us.'

Seeing Adil's puzzled expression, Clara told him, 'Mike's wife Alondra is a bit of a dab hand with a paintbrush.'

Adil now looked completely bewildered. Viv explained, 'Alondra, whose name in artistic circles is Catwoman, is one of the most talented landscape painters around. Her paintings regularly fetch six or seven figures.'

CHAPTER TWENTY-SIX

Next morning, Viv and Adil were surprised to find Nash in his office.

'What are you doing here?' Viv asked. 'You're supposed to be on leave.'

'I know, I'll take the time later. We've too much on our plates at the moment.'

'But what about Alondra? I remember how difficult it was for Leanne when Brian first arrived.'

'It's all taken care of. We have a house guest — Lisa is staying. Alan has been called away on business unexpectedly, and he didn't want her on her own. So she's keeping an eye on things for me. And Daniel is keeping an eye on them both.'

When Clara arrived, Nash had news for the team. 'Alondra spent a lot of time examining those photos. What you failed to mention is that not all the letters are capitals. Therefore, we must assume the capitals are the first letter in a new word. N, M and S.'

The others nodded their agreement.

'Before I explain, let me stress this is purely theoretical — in fact, little more than guesswork.'

'There's a lot of that goes on at Mike's house,' Clara told Hassan and Pearce.

Ignoring the interruption, Nash continued, 'She used a ruler to work out the dimensions of those letters visible on the images, then asked me to find out the size of the side panel of a Sprinter van. Once I'd got that, she was able to determine the approximate size of each letter, and from there, going by the space between them, the possible number of other characters within those gaps.

'As I said earlier, this is all very much speculation, but she believes the text of the logo is split between three words.'

* * *

A week later, after more checking, the CCTV images of the van yielded some more characters from the logo. Having examined these closely the previous afternoon, DC Hassan was travelling back to Helmsdale from headquarters, where he had been attending a review with Jackie Fleming, following his change of police force.

The afternoon traffic was heavy, and he decided to take an alternative route using minor roads. His attention was caught when he noticed a business with lawnmowers stacked outside. Seeing an empty parking space, Adil pulled in and stared at the facade on the large double-fronted building for several minutes, before using his mobile to take several photos. Now, his priority was to get to Helmsdale and share what he had seen with his colleagues, and also to present them with the idea it had spawned.

Having explained his theory, Adil showed the others the images from the shop, and asked if they, like him, thought the company name matched letters on the thieves' van's logo.

Nash stared at them, before asking Clara her opinion.

'Adil could well be right, and now we have a bit more to work with,' Clara agreed.

Nash turned to Adil. 'Would you mind printing the photos from your phone and ensuring their scale matches the ones from the CCTV cameras?'

When he reported back, the team thought they were a possible match.

'Hang on a minute, Adil,' Viv said. 'Email them to me, would you?'

Moments later, he called them over to his computer. 'Look at that,' Viv said.

On screen was the photo of the van from CCTV, overlaid with the image of the shop signage taken by Adil, an almost perfect match.

'I should have thought of doing that,' Adil said.

'It doesn't matter who thought of it, you spotted the sign. But this outfit, Netherdale Machinery Sales, is a strong contender for the role of prime suspect. Before we rush headlong into following this lead, we should check to see if they own a Sprinter van, whatever its registration number is today. If that proves to be so, we could try to persuade Jackie to apply for a search warrant. One way or another, it was a good piece of detective work, so well done, Adil.'

A DVLA check revealed that Netherdale Machinery Sales did own a Sprinter van, so Nash collected the sparse information at their disposal and prepared to meet Superintendent Fleming. For a while, it appeared his attempt was going to prove unsuccessful, until he put forward a thought that clinched his argument.

'These burglaries are proving to be an extremely irritating distraction. As things stand, we've seven unsolved murders on our books, and who knows what next week will bring and add to our workload. We have no clues as to who committed those far more serious crimes. If we could rid ourselves of this nuisance, we might be able to concentrate our energies on pursuing whoever killed those people.'

It was a valid point, and his argument persuaded Fleming to go ahead with their plan. Achieving the desired result, however, would be nowhere near as straightforward as they hoped.

* * *

The proprietor of Netherdale Machinery Sales, Ron Priestley, was hardly your archetypal burglar, Clara thought. His appearance suggested he was pulling sixty years old rather than pushing it, and his arthritic gait indicated he was extremely unlikely to have handled some of the heavier equipment that had been stolen.

After explaining the reason for their visit and handing over the search warrant, Nash waited for Priestley's reaction. It wasn't long in coming, and comprised an emphatic denial of any wrongdoing.

'I've heard tell about stuff being nicked. Some of my customers were complaining bitterly that you lot were doing nothing about catching them as were responsible. If you've come here thinking I was involved, you're barking up the wrong tree. You'll not find any stolen gear in my shop.'

'Nevertheless, we'll have to conduct the search, if only to verify your claim,' Nash told him.

An hour later, the detectives regrouped at the shop counter and confirmed Priestley's apparent innocence.

'There were several items similar to the stolen goods, but these were brand new, so we were able to rule them out,' Pearce told his colleagues.

That left only two possibilities in Nash's mind. He began by tackling the more obvious of these. 'Do you have a warehouse or premises elsewhere, such as outbuildings at your house?'

'There's no warehouse. Never been a need for one. Most of the stuff I sell is too expensive to keep extra stock. I only replace them after I've sold one. I don't have a house, with or without outbuildings, anymore. I live in the flat upstairs. That's all I can afford after my wife scarpered and left me with a crippling mortgage. I had to sell up to afford the lawyers' fees in the divorce case. I finished up all but skint, and with nowhere to live.'

'OK, the only other thing we need to search is your van. I assume that's the vehicle you use for deliveries?'

Priestley glared angrily at Nash. 'More than deliveries. These days I use the van for everything. If I can't afford a mortgage, I'm damned sure I can't fork out for a car and a van. And even that's on the never-never. You'll not find any stolen goods in it.' Priestley delved into his pocket and handed Nash a bunch of keys, which he in turn passed to Pearce.

Minutes later, the DC returned, shaking his head to indicate a lack of success, and drew Nash to one side. 'Did you see the van when we arrived?'

'No, why do you ask?'

'The company name and logo is written clearly on both sides.'

'It is?' Nash asked.

Pearce nodded. 'I think Mr Priestley's telling the truth. The van has a GPS tracker fitted, so the journeys to and from the crime scenes would have been recorded. With Mr Priestley's permission, I'd like to examine the journey logs, just to make sure.'

Having been given the go-ahead, Pearce went back to the van, accompanied by DC Hassan. While they were absent, Priestley told Nash and Mironova, 'I was a bit doubtful about having GPS fitted, because of the expense, but it looks as if it's just paid for itself. I didn't have it on the old one.'

'The old one?' Nash asked.

'Yes, I traded-in my old Sprinter months ago. It was getting a bit long in the tooth.'

Nash glanced at Clara.

She nodded, understanding where Nash's thoughts were heading.

'Did it still have your logo on the side?'

Priestley nodded. 'I tried to remove it, but I made a right mess of it.'

'Can you tell us the name of the dealership where you traded in the vehicle?' Nash asked.

Priestley offered a business card.

'I'll take that,' Clara said. She wandered away, returning a few minutes earlier, and nodded at Nash. 'They sent it to auction.' She sighed and shook her head.

'Then perhaps we should look at this from a different angle,' Nash suggested. 'Did anyone know you planned to change the van?'

Priestley's response was instant — and filled with rancour. 'The only one who knew was Dick. That's Richard Holdsworth. Dick by name and dick by nature.'

'Who is Dick Holdsworth?'

'Used to work for me. He was my right-hand man, and he was very good with machinery. He looked after the shop several times when I was busy elsewhere. I thought the business was in safe hands, but then I found out those hands were sticky whenever they came in contact with money. The only way he could handle it was to stuff it in his back pocket, rather than putting it in the till. I couldn't prove it, otherwise I'd have come to you lot. All I was able to do was sack him. He wasn't happy, especially when I refused to provide him with a reference. He swore all sorts of revenge. At the time, I thought it was just a load of hot air. Now I'm beginning to wonder if he's trying to set me up.' Priestley thought for a moment. 'You know, I nearly had a break-in, but I saw them off before they got in. It's handy living upstairs.'

'When was this?'

Having realized the date matched that of the latest burglary, Clara took Nash to one side and asked, 'Do you think it might have been someone trying to plant stolen property, rather than steal it? If Mr Priestley is right about being set up, then that would tally.'

Nash thought for a moment. 'Maybe they were trying to kill two birds with one stone. Making easy money from the stolen farm machinery, *and* getting revenge on Mr Priestley.'

Pearce and Hassan returned and gave the all-clear. 'The van didn't travel anywhere on the nights of the last two burglaries,' Pearce confirmed.

'OK, that's us done. Our apologies for the inconvenience, Mr Priestley. Before we go, could you provide an address for this man Holdsworth?'

'That will be a pleasure, Inspector.'

* * *

When the detectives returned to Helmsdale, they discussed their next move, having hit a dead end with Priestley. 'This Holdsworth character now looks to be a prime suspect,' Clara said, 'but whoever the perpetrator is, it would be ideal to catch them in the act.'

'I agree. Now we have a potential target, I've an idea how to go about achieving what you suggested, but first I need to elicit Paul Grant's cooperation. Now he's got extra men and vehicles at his disposal, I'm hoping to persuade Paul to detail a couple of his officers in an unmarked car to set up surveillance on Holdsworth. With luck, they might be able to follow him at a discreet distance, and nab him at a crime scene.'

'Can I make a suggestion, Mike?' Adil asked.

Nash nodded. 'Go on.'

'Before going down that route, might it be a good idea to run a check on Holdsworth to see if he owns a Sprinter van,' adding with a smile, 'whatever the actual registration number is?'

'One thing still puzzles me,' Clara said. 'What does the thief do with all the goods he's stolen? I admit some of the tools are quite valuable, but they're hardly the sort of thing you can sell in the bar of the Rose and Crown on a Saturday night, so what's the point of the robberies?'

'That's something we should start thinking about, but first let's establish if Holdsworth owns a van.'

The afternoon brought confirmation that Richard Holdsworth was the registered keeper of a four-year-old Mercedes Sprinter — the previous owner being Mr Priestley. 'And also,' Adil pointed out excitedly, 'a CF Moto ATV.' He grinned. 'That's an All-Terrain Vehicle, Clara. With luck, we should be able to stop all this criminality.'

Nash was headed for his office, but stopped and turned abruptly to face Adil. 'You're settling in well, Adil, and being very constructive. But there's one basic thing you've forgotten since your training. That is, criminals commit *crimes*, not *criminality*. In this office, we stick to facts.' He paused, smiled, and then added, 'And rather than upset Clara, we do not use acronyms either. Just call it a quad bike, OK?'

'Er, yes, Mike. I understand.' Adil looked at Pearce, who was nodding, as if to reassure him.

Clara's earlier question also provoked an idea from Pearce as to why the tools and equipment were being stolen. 'I wouldn't be surprised if this thief, whether it's Holdsworth or someone else, has a website and sells the stuff online. That way, he can keep his name and location secret, and the buyers are far less likely to check things, like previous owners or serial numbers.'

'That sounds logical,' Nash agreed. 'Maybe you and Adil can check that out?'

Pearce glanced at his colleague apologetically. 'Sorry, Adil, I think I've just landed us more work.'

Nash retorted, 'You don't need to apologize, Viv. In case you've forgotten, it's what we pay you for.'

CHAPTER TWENTY-SEVEN

Securing the assistance of Traffic Division, as they soon discovered, was the easy part, but what followed was a period of frustration, waiting for the next full moon. For the detectives and the officers assigned to the task of watching Holdsworth, the job could entail hour after hour of bored inactivity.

Using a drone, they had already conducted an aerial survey of the suspect's premises. As Nash watched the drone sweeping high over the Victorian semi-detached, two-storey house at the end of a cul-de-sac on the outskirts of Netherdale, he noticed a row of outbuildings to the rear, ones he guessed might have originally been stables, and which would provide excellent storage facilities. The location also provided one cause for concern, which was how the officers could keep watch without giving their presence away, especially when the action kicked off.

Nash ran his idea past Clara first. 'I think we ought to have Adil or Viv out with the traffic officers. That way, they can launch a drone when Holdsworth's van is on the move. We don't want him to know he's being followed, and it would lessen the chance of our guys losing him if they're hanging back and he suddenly changes direction or possibly switches his lights off. The other advantage is the drone will operate where the traffic guys can't reach — off-road and over the farm. The footage of the offence being carried out will be cast-iron evidence in court.' Nash kept his face straight as he added, 'It will be like having an eyewitness to the crime — or in this case, an eye-in-the-sky witness.'

Clara groaned. 'I wish I could report you for the crime of committing appalling jokes.'

Pearce and Hassan spent hours poring over their computers, looking for a website where the stolen goods might be offered for sale. They reported their findings to Nash and Mironova. 'We did identify a few UK-based sites that advertise used tools and equipment. A lot of which would tally with items taken during the farm robberies, but we can't be certain this is nothing more than coincidence.' Pearce stopped abruptly. 'Sorry for using that word, but in this case, I couldn't think of another. We were able to discount sites in America, New Zealand, and South Africa. But there are at least four prime candidates for the possible dodgy one. There are no details for the people running the sites, and the only way to be certain if Holdsworth is connected to them would be by examining his computer, or finding a bank account that he's channelling the funds into.'

* * *

It was a full moon, and Starsky and Hutch were on night shift in an unmarked BMW, taking part in the covert operation. Adil Hassan was assigned to them, to pilot the drone. Once they saw the headlights of the Sprinter spring to life, they radioed the news via Control, following its progress with the use of ANPR. As they left the built-up area and began heading into the open countryside where there were fewer cameras, they dropped Adil off. Control sent a patrol car to join him, and after launching the drone, he established direct contact with the traffic officers. Hassan was soon able to inform them he had latched onto the suspect vehicle, enabling them to draw back to a safe distance.

The wisdom of the decision to use the drone became more apparent, as there was little traffic on the meandering country lanes. The 'convoy', as Hutch described it, headed towards the northern end of the dale, and Hassan was concerned they might go beyond the drone's operable range. But as they approached the outskirts of Gorton village, the van slowed and came to a halt.

Hassan reported the development, updating the traffic officers, who had maintained a discreet distance. They parked across a farm gateway, over a mile from their target, thereby ensuring they could not be detected. 'I hope nobody drives past and mistakes us for a courting couple,' Starsky commented.

'Fat chance of that,' Hutch retorted. 'I'm not keen on blokes with beards.' He paused, before adding, 'Come to think of it, I'm not that keen on girls with beards either.'

They had forgotten their link to Hassan was still open, until they heard him comment, 'I suppose that means I'll have to buy a razor.'

Seconds later, all frivolity was dismissed as Hassan reported the development they'd been waiting, and hoping, for. 'Two people have exited the van and are opening the rear doors. They appear to be sliding something out. Yes, it's a ramp, and they've just manhandled a quad bike down it. Wait a second . . . they've climbed on the bike. One of them has opened a gate and now they're riding across the field. Time to call in the cavalry. For all we know, these guys could be armed and dangerous. I'll let you know when they're far enough away for you to drive up to the Sprinter, so you can welcome them back.'

Assistance was summoned, but as it transpired, the precaution was unnecessary. Such was the overconfidence of the robbers, quickly identified as Richard Holdsworth and a local man with previous convictions for burglary, that they were detained without a struggle.

It was almost 4 a.m. by the time the Sprinter van and the quad bike had been recovered and taken to the police compound for forensic examination. The arrested men were placed in the custody cells at Netherdale. Other tasks involved informing the farmer of the theft from his outbuildings and promising the return of his equipment, once it had been logged and photographed for evidential purposes.

Out of consideration for his colleagues — in particular Nash, whose personal circumstances ruled out contact at such an hour — Hassan decided to wait until a less antisocial time before informing the others of the success.

Shortly prior to leaving home, Mike Nash switched on his mobile, and the device buzzed immediately to signal an unread text. He opened it and read the message from his newest team member. '*Operation Night Hawk Success. H + one, caught red-handed @ farm near Gorton. Drone captured all.*'

* * *

At Helmsdale, Adil arrived later than the others. Clara couldn't decide who looked more exhausted — Adil from the overnight work or Nash from a sleepless night with the baby.

Adil gave his report, adding, 'I checked the sides of the Sprinter. It was clear that someone had tried to remove more of the signage on the side panels and failed.'

'That might be when they got the idea to set up Mr Priestley,' Pearce commented.

As the others nodded in agreement, Nash told the team, 'Our main priority has to be securing Holdsworth's premises and checking for stolen goods. We must do this before word of his arrest gets out. If we don't, a load of valuable evidence could vanish mysteriously and ruin our prosecution. We should head straight to Holdsworth's address, and pray someone hasn't beaten us to it.'

'They can't have done that, Mike,' Adil told him. 'I arranged for a patrol car to be parked outside his house overnight. I also got a set of keys from his van, so we can access the property without having to use our big red key.'

Nash smiled at Hassan's reference to the door enforcer. 'That's good thinking, Adil. OK, let's get moving. Viv, don't forget to bring the list of purloined goods along, so we can check serial numbers. I'll ask Steve Meadows to lend us some officers to speed the search up. Meanwhile, Clara, will you update Jackie Fleming, mind the fort, and check those files again? I've got a niggle I can't quite grasp from Corey Davies' statement, something to do with the Keeper.'

There were no surprises at the suspect's property, and when they opened the door to the first of the outbuildings, Pearce stared at the equipment inside, neatly arranged in a semi-circle. 'That looks exactly like the photo on the home-page of one of the websites we looked at, don't you agree, Adil?'

Hassan concurred, and when they began checking the serial numbers, all of the items tallied exactly. It was a long, tedious task, but when the bulk of the work had been completed, Nash left the others to finish up.

Before setting off, Nash explained, 'I'm taking Clara to Netherdale to interview the suspects. We need Forensics to take photos of all the machinery in situ, then wait for our van to arrive. I'll organize that en route. They'll probably need help loading all this gear. I just hope there's enough room for it in the evidence store. Make sure they get Holdsworth's laptop. Ten to one it will be password-protected. There's one thing I want you to do before leaving here: see if you can find any cash or bank details. You know what you're looking for. Above all, well done. This has been a really good result.'

* * *

As the team assembled the following Monday, Nash sum-marized the situation. 'We've had a measure of success in apprehending the shoplifting gang, but that was almost accidental.' He saw Mironova wince and apologized. 'Sorry, bad pun, but not deliberate. Apart from that, the arrest of Corey Davies and the break-up of his ring, the capture of Free Willy, and finally, solving the farm burglaries have all been major achievements. However, we've made frustratingly little progress on the far more important case we currently have on our unsolved crimes list. I'm referring to the string of murders connected to the Country House Bandits. We need to concentrate our efforts in making progress on these. Clara, did you find any reference to the Keeper?'

'No, sorry, Mike. Nothing.'

This deadlock was broken two days later, by what appeared at first to be an unconnected incident. As he entered Helmsdale station that morning, Nash noticed that Steve Meadows appeared tired and more than a little harassed. 'Is there a problem, Steve?'

'Not really, but I had to spend a fair chunk of last night dealing with what we thought was a major RTA, but which turned out to be nothing of the sort — in fact, nothing at all.'

'What do you mean by that?' Nash asked.

'An emergency call came in just before midnight, from a phone box in Bishop's Cross, reporting a farm tractor and trailer had overturned on the road at the far side of Stark Ghyll. The caller claimed the driver was trapped inside the cab, and appeared to be unconscious and seriously injured. Control called me, and simultaneously raised the fire brigade and ambulance to attend. It was only after three of our cars, plus an ambulance and fire engine, spent half an hour combing every lane in the area that the search was called off. We determined it was some form of malicious hoax. Now I have to deal with the aftermath, via reams of paperwork.'

Ten minutes later, Clara entered the CID suite and greeted Nash. 'Steve doesn't seem very happy this morning. Has he had a row with his girlfriend?'

'Worse than that.' Nash explained everything, adding, 'Enough of his problems, we've plenty of our own to deal with.'

He was still speaking when his office phone rang. He listened to the caller, making notes on his pad, before putting the receiver down. 'What was I saying about us having plenty to deal with? That was Steve. He's just had word from Control. Come on, we've work to do.'

He picked up his keys and gestured to the door, explaining as they went, 'We're going to Wintersett Grange. The new owners were staying in Manchester overnight having attended a gig at the Arena. They returned home only a few minutes ago to discover the house had been broken into.'

As they walked to Nash's car, Mironova recalled the recent history of Wintersett Grange. 'That place must be cursed. I wasn't aware anyone lived there. I remember it being unoccupied for a long time, following the murder of the previous owners.'

'It was empty until late last year, when a couple from near Leeds bought it. I suppose, because they weren't from this area, they probably didn't read the gory details about those killings. Therefore, they weren't as deterred as locals might have been.'

'They must be pretty well-heeled to be able to afford a place like that. Even smaller properties in that area cost a bomb.'

Nash grinned at Clara's oblique reference to his house, but told her, 'They're loaded, I believe. He's an insurance broker, and anyone connected to the insurance industry is like a rhinoceros.'

'What?'

'They know how to charge.'

Clara groaned, but listened as he told her more. 'The guy's wife owns a high-end jewellery store, with branches in Leeds, York, Manchester, and Newcastle.'

'Do we know what was stolen?'

'Not precisely, but the operator said there were lots of items of jewellery missing, plus a couple of watches.'

CHAPTER TWENTY-EIGHT

When the detectives arrived at Wintersett Grange, they noticed that in addition to the police car, there was a CSI van parked alongside the entrance.

'The Forensic guys got here pretty quickly,' Clara commented.

'Yes, Steve told me the emergency operator at Netherdale alerted them before she spoke to him, giving them a head start.'

Acknowledging the uniformed officer guarding the door, Nash and Clara entered the hallway. Ralph Whittaker and his wife Suzanne were a charming, middle-aged couple, who invited the detectives into the kitchen, offering them tea or coffee, more like guests than investigators.

Clara followed Nash's lead by accepting a drink, and as his wife was dispensing this, Ralph explained why they were closeted in this room, when there were more luxurious places to sit. 'We've been issued with strict instructions by your colleagues in blue not to allow anyone — and they stressed *anyone* — to enter the rest of the house until the Forensic team has completed their work. By that, I assume you are included in the ban?'

Nash detected a hint of humour in Whittaker's voice. It was obvious the couple were relaxed enough to regard the burglary as nothing more than an inconvenience. 'Do you know how the intruders gained access?'

Whitaker gave a half-smile, half-grimace, before replying. 'They smashed a pane of glass next to the handle of the French windows to the rear of the sitting room, and simply walked inside. We only moved here a few months ago and we were due to have a new alarm system fitted next week.'

'Do you know exactly what the burglars took?'

It was Suzanne Whitaker who replied, as she was placing mugs of coffee on the kitchen island. 'Not yet. Like everyone else, we've been proscribed entry to the crime scene. As soon as Ralph spotted the broken window, I went straight to my office. I saw the ornate cabinet where I keep my jewellery had been taken, plus my briefcase, which houses samples for work. The rest of the room is a mess, the thieves ransacked it. I didn't go inside, and apart from the door handle, I didn't touch anything. I came straight downstairs, by which time Ralph was already on the phone reporting the incident.'

'Suzanne's forever watching TV programmes like *CSI* and *NCIS*, plus any true crime shows she can find,' Ralph told them. 'She probably knows as much about forensics as your chaps do.'

Ignoring her husband's flippant remark, Suzanne told them, 'If, as I suspect, they've taken everything from that room, we could be talking a value well into six figures. And that's without my Omega wristwatch, plus the tatty thing Ralph wears. Luckily, we had them on last night.'

'The "tatty thing" she's referring to is a Longines watch,' Ralph explained.

'I appreciate that you don't have an alarm system yet, but is there any CCTV coverage of the property?'

Whittaker shook his head. 'No, that was due to be installed along with the rest of the system.'

Half an hour and two mugs of coffee later, the detectives watched as Ralph and Suzanne Whittaker were fingerprinted and had their mouths swabbed for DNA. 'We only need these for comparison with any we take from elsewhere in the house,' the Forensic team leader told them. 'They will be destroyed once they are no longer required.'

'Does that mean Ralph will get away with the multitude of crimes he's committed?' Suzanne asked.

The man looked startled, until he saw the smile on her face. Wisely, he refused to rise to the bait, or enter the domestic squabble he could see brewing. It was further evidence, Nash thought, of the couple's refusal to be daunted by the intrusion and loss they had suffered.

Once they had been given the all-clear to enter the rest of the mansion, Nash and Mironova followed the couple as they checked out the rest of the ground floor, where they were able to report everything was intact. They then climbed the broad staircase to the first floor. Having made detailed examination of every other part of the house, they turned their attention to the master bedroom. Here it was a different story. Nash wondered briefly why the burglar had ignored several oil paintings, china, and other items which many would have seen as prime targets, concentrating only on the, admittedly valuable, personal adornments.

'We're going to need a detailed list of the missing jewellery, Mrs Whittaker. I appreciate that might be difficult for you.'

Suzanne just smiled, opened her mobile phone and found the detailed list of her jewellery enterprise. The printer in the office whirled into action, supplying the precise details of each and every item of jewellery. The descriptions were full, including the carat and hallmark, where appropriate, plus the approximate market value. Ralph listened intently to the conversation before he turned and looked out of the window. The detectives couldn't see him smile as he assessed the true value.

* * *

After sympathizing with them, and assuring them they would do everything possible to apprehend the thieves and retrieve the stolen property, the detectives took their leave.

As they set off on the return journey to Helmsdale, Clara stared at the list, before commenting on the precision with which Suzanne had listed each item. 'I'm surprised anyone, even if they're involved in the jewellery trade like Suzanne, would note every piece so exactly, right down to the value. I can understand it for things like a diamond-and-gold pendant, but she gave similar attention to far more mundane items, some of them barely worth three figures.'

'You've obviously forgotten what her husband does for a living. Although they haven't had a burglar alarm fitted, which is admittedly careless, I'm willing to bet every other valuable item in that house is insured to the hilt. I would also be less than surprised if Whittaker is on the phone to the insurance company right now. Did you hear what asked me as they were showing us out?'

'No, I was talking to his wife at the time.'

'He asked me to supply an incident number ASAP. The insurance company will require that to check if it's a genuine claim. There are far too many bogus ones, and until they've got the incident report, they'll be unable to begin the process. By the way,' Nash asked as a rider, 'have you totted up the figures Suzanne supplied?'

'No, not yet, I'll do it now.' Clara looked down at the list and made a brief calculation. 'It comes to somewhere around one hundred and thirty-five thousand pounds, I think, unless I've added it up wrong.'

'Judging by the description of the jewellery, that comes as a relief.'

'Why is it a relief?'

'It means Mr and Mrs Whittaker have been honest with us, and aren't trying to make a profit out of their loss by claiming a higher value than the stuff is actually worth.'

* * *

Back in the CID suite, Clara brought Pearce and Hassan up to date with what had occurred, before opening a file on the

Wintersett Grange burglary. Meanwhile, Nash phoned Jackie Fleming and told her of the robbery, and then obtained an incident number for the file to pass to Whittaker. After that, he instructed the detective constables, 'There is one way you cyber-sleuths can make yourself useful. Try and discover anyone lurking on, or near, our patch who has form and an MO that fits this robbery.'

Nash was about to add, 'You can discount the Country House Bandits,' but in light of the murders, changed his mind, deeming it to be in bad taste.

Although he dismissed it, the thought did have one positive outcome, however, for it enabled him to recall something which had been troubling him for quite a while. 'Have we heard any news of Terry Palmer, our missing bandit?'

'Nobody's seen hide or hair of him since he walked through the prison gates,' Clara responded. 'It's as if he's vanished off the face of the earth.'

'Maybe that's true. Perhaps he's been abducted by aliens,' Adil suggested.

Nash stared at the young detective constable. 'I think it was a mistake putting you next to Viv. Your jokes are almost as bad as his.'

'Why are you asking about Palmer?' Pearce asked. 'Is this in connection with the Wintersett Grange burglary? Do you think *Palmer* might have had a *hand* in it?'

'You see what I mean?' Nash told Clara. 'The pair of them are as bad as each other.'

Clara stared at him. 'You've no room to talk.'

* * *

Inside prison, he hadn't been the sole occupant of the cell, but here, wherever *here* was, he was alone . . . day in, day out, morning, noon, and night. The room was similar in size and shape to the one he'd occupied for the past ten years, but there the similarity ended. Nor was that by any means the only variant. In his prison cell there had been a window, albeit a small one with bars, giving a limited view of the yard that served as a recreation area when weather permitted. That had the added advantage of allowing a modicum of natural light into the cell. Here, there was nothing to alleviate the darkness, save for a naked light bulb set into the high ceiling, far out of reach.

The biggest difference was in his captors. Inside prison he'd known the warders, could recognize their faces, know which of the officers was approaching his cell by their foot-steps, and even knew several of them by name.

In his new accommodation, those holding him prisoner were faceless, their heads covered by a cowl, features obscured behind a mask. He wasn't even sure how many of them there were. For all he knew, there might only have been one person holding him captive. It was all too baffling, and he was far too weary to think about it for long.

It had taken him a long time to assimilate these facts. It didn't help that he was always so tired. He spent hour after hour asleep on the rough metal cot that formed the only item of furniture in the cell, apart from a washbasin and a chemical toilet. Despite these long periods of slumber, the weariness didn't abate. If anything, it got worse. The notion that every meal thrust through the narrow slit in the door, plus every drink, delivered at intervals by the same method, might contain sedatives never occurred to him.

Even the vague flashes of memory he did retain puzzled him. He wasn't certain if what he remembered was real or a figment of his imagination. He had a vague recollection of leaving prison and going for a few beers to celebrate his release. Had that been real or wishful thinking? If it was true, why was he back in a cell? Terry did know that he had served his full sentence, so why he had been brought to this place? What was the room he was being held captive in? And what purpose did keeping him there achieve?

He seemed to vaguely remember hearing someone ask that very question. But again, he was uncertain whether the conversation had been real. It didn't help that the answer he thought he'd heard was too confusing to understand. Now, he'd come to believe everything in his memory bank was nothing more than a dream or some kind of weird hallucination. Why else would he have heard — or believe he'd heard — his captor reply that he'd been brought here because they needed to find an escaped goat?

None of it made any sense whatsoever, but then, Terry Palmer wasn't to know how heavily he had been drugged, or the nature of the substances used to keep him under control.

CHAPTER TWENTY-NINE

Helmwater Hall, as the name suggests, stands alongside the banks of the River Helm. The Regency mansion had been home to several families since the time it was built, around two centuries ago. Descendants of the original owners had been compelled to put the property up for sale following the disastrous Wall Street Crash of 1929, which sent stock markets worldwide into freefall and caused their investments to become scarcely more valuable than the paper used to print the share certificates.

The new proprietors did not enjoy the delights of the building for many years. A tragic misadventure saw them visit London at the start of the Blitz, which claimed thousands of lives, including the owners of Helmwater Hall. With no relatives to inherit the stately home, the house went back on the market, but the sale was delayed until after the end of World War II, as it had been commandeered by the Ministry of War to be used as a training base for new recruits.

Post-war, Helmwater Hall had remained in the same family, and those currently resident were the third generation to call it home. Gary Morton and his wife Rebecca were both sporting and socially minded, so summer was the happiest season of the year for them. With their son and daughter away at university and boarding school respectively, Gary and Rebecca seized the opportunity that freedom from parental responsibility offered by attending events that suited their interests.

Lawn tennis at Wimbledon, test cricket at various grounds, rowing regattas, and horse racing events such as Royal Ascot or the Ebor meeting at York — all fell within the scope of their enjoyment and were essential entries in their crowded calendar.

It was only on their return from a test match that Gary and Rebecca discovered Helmwater Hall had been home to another resident during their absence.

A week after the Wintersett Grange burglary, when Mike Nash walked into the Helmsdale station, he wondered for a moment if he'd accidentally wandered onto the set of *Groundhog Day*. He was greeted with a scowl from the normally cheerful Steve Meadows.

'What is it this time, Steve? There's obviously something wrong.'

'I can see why you're such a good detective, Mike, there isn't much gets past you.' Steve's attempt at humour failed, possibly because of the sour expression on his face. 'We had another bloody hoax call last night. This time, some nutcase made a treble nine call to report a barn fire near Kirk Bolton. They told the operator there had been kids playing around nearby, and one of them was carrying what looked like a petrol can. Given the possibility of it being an arson attack, we sent a couple of patrol cars out, and Doug Curran dispatched a pair of fire engines to the scene. Except, of course, they were unable to find any fire, or any kids messing about. So once again, I'm stuck with the paperwork.'

'Did the call come from a phone box again?'

'No, this time it was from a mobile, which — surprise, surprise — turned out to be a pay-as-you-go. Of course, when we tried to contact the number we got no response. It was either switched off, or the hoaxer ditched the SIM card.'

Nash's notion about *Groundhog Day* intensified an hour later, when he received a phone call from Steve. He listened, made a note on his pad, and went in search of Clara, who was standing alongside the coffee machine in the kitchen. 'No time for that, I'm afraid,' he told her. 'We've been called to an incident. With Viv on a rest day, we'll have to leave Adil in charge of the ship while we're out.'

'Where are we going?'

'Another burglary. Helmwater Hall, far side of Drover's Halt, halfway between there and Winter Bridge. The owners apparently have several large collections of coins, stamps, and timepieces. In addition, the thieves took all the wife's jewellery, plus ten thousand pounds in cash.'

'Why would anyone keep such a large amount of money in their house? It seems like asking for trouble.'

'That thought occurred to me, so perhaps it's one of the first questions we should ask.' Nash glanced down at the notes he'd made. 'Names are Gary and Rebecca Morton.'

The answer, when they met the couple, was simple. 'I was due to travel to Sheffield later this week, to meet a man who has three wristwatches for sale, and would only accept cash for them,' Morton told them. 'They're quite rare, and would add considerably to my collection.' His face clouded over as he added, 'Except that now I no longer have a collection.'

They listened to Mr and Mrs Morton's tale of woe, conducted in the conservatory that overlooked the nearby river. Clara admired the view, with the immaculately trimmed lawns, colourful flower beds, the fringes framed by huge, stately weeping willows. She thought that even though they had suffered substantially due to the robbery, such an outlook would provide enormous consolation.

* * *

There was no chance to inspect the burglars' point of entry, as this was being examined by the CSI team, so Gary Morton explained how they discovered the break-in. 'Rebecca went to put a load of clothes into the washing machine. We've been away for two weeks and had just arrived home. It seemed pointless to lug the cases upstairs, only to have to bring all the clothing back down, so we unpacked the bags in the hallway. The utility room is at the rear of the house, alongside the double garage. I'm afraid when we had the alarms fitted we forgot to include that room in the system. They got in through that door.'

'Have you any idea when the robbery might have taken place?'

Rebecca answered Clara's question immediately. 'It must have been last night, because Mrs Rhodes, who cleans for us, visited the house yesterday. When I spoke to her this morning, she confirmed that she had vacuumed throughout, and mopped the kitchen and utility room floors. There was definitely nothing amiss then.'

Having gleaned the details and value of the collections, they headed back to Helmsdale station. Clara told Nash, 'Before you ask, I've added up the value. It tops the estimate from Wintersett Grange by some twenty thousand pounds.'

As they approached the outskirts of town, Nash gave voice to the strange thought that had occurred to him. 'Both this burglary and the one a week ago took place following a hoax triple nine call about non-existent emergencies, supposedly happening several miles away. What does that remind you of?'

Clara puzzled for a few moments, and it was only as they were entering the police station car park that the answer came to her. 'It's the same MO as the Country House Bandits. But it can't be down to them. All the members of that gang have been murdered, in case you've forgotten.'

Nash smiled, but corrected her. 'Not all. There's Terry Palmer for one. He's still at large, plus the others Corey Davies mentioned, the ones who travelled in the Mercedes. There is one distinct difference, however, but even that might be an indication of a link to the Bandits.'

'What difference? And how is it a link?'

'Looking through the old case files, it was apparent there were more members. We discussed the fact that some of the goods stolen were both bulky and heavy. But in these two robberies, everything taken was light enough to be carried by one person, possibly two. If there weren't enough burglars available to transport the heavier stuff, they'd have to concentrate on smaller items. This wouldn't rule out the remaining gang members.'

* * *

'Am I speaking to Vincent?'

The answer was cautious, but in the affirmative, so the caller continued, 'Vincent, I have a job for you, if you're interested.'

'Who is this?'

'Never mind names, I think you're more interested in money. You come highly recommended — even if your services aren't cheap.'

'How do I know you're genuine? This might be a trap. Just because you've had a recommendation, or so you say, that's not proof you're the real deal.'

'In view of your reputation, I don't think there would be anyone brave enough, or stupid enough, to try and trap you.'

'I still need proof you're on the level, because without it, and I mean solid proof, I'm ending this call now.'

'Don't do that. I was told you'd be suspicious.'

'Really? So what's the code word?'

'*Foxglove.*'

There was a short silence before Vincent asked, 'OK, so what do I call you? And what do you want me to do?'

'If you must, you can call me Keeper. But let's start by talking money. Then I'll explain what I want. It's complicated, so I've accounted for that in the amount I'm prepared to offer.'

The call lasted over twenty minutes, and the final requirement stipulated by the caller had Vincent momentarily baffled.

'Let me explain. I have some items of clothing you must wear as you do the job. I will include a SOCO coverall for you to wear under them. That will stop you from contaminating the clothes. When you've finished, you must return the clothing to a pre-arranged drop-off point and destroy the coverall.'

Vincent smiled. Did this Keeper think he didn't take any precautions? He had a stock of necessary protective gear — coveralls, gloves, overshoes, and masks.

The Keeper continued, 'Sixty per cent of your fee will be paid into a bank account you specify today. The remainder will be paid once I have confirmation that the job has been completed.'

The caller added another proviso. 'One more thing. During your visit to the property, I want you to be careless. The more evidence you can leave behind, the better. I will provide some for you.'

Vincent was still more than a little apprehensive, now he had learned the lengths this man would go to in order to achieve his cold-blooded aim. The caller's final comment left Vincent feeling somewhat reassured. 'If everything goes as planned, I will have further assignments for you in the very near future.'

When the call was over, the Keeper turned to his partner and explained the reasoning behind the phone call. 'You must agree, Wellie has outlived his purpose. He's more of a threat than all the others. Fitting Palmer up for killing him will get rid of the last piece of my excess baggage. Once this is over, we can concentrate on disposing of your unwanted accessory — and a plan is already beginning to form, based on his interest in dangerous pursuits. But that's for the future.'

'What's next on the agenda?'

'We need to change our visitor's diet. Once we've done that, we can treat him to a little luxury.'

'You're going to have to explain that.'

The explanation made sense, and it demonstrated yet again the Keeper's ability to plan every move with meticulous precision.

CHAPTER THIRTY

Something had changed . . . but how, and what was it? The food he had been given on a regular daily basis seemed to have altered in flavour. Was that true, or was it yet another figment of his imagination? His brain was too befuddled to come up with even the simplest of theories.

He was still trying to get his head around this when the nightmares began. Full-on, horrific, graphic nightmares that involved him and his former associates. Out of the darkness they had appeared one by one. First to arrive was Frank Watson, followed a short while later by Joe Lambert. He had been about to greet Joe when Peter Swallow made his presence known.

The three others were imprisoned with him, but this time they were all in the same cell. And now, in his nightmare, for the first time Palmer was able to see their captor. No wonder he had been kept in darkness, for this was a terrifying sight. The grotesque figure seemed to grow in stature with every movement. Far scarier was the disfigurement, one he could never have believed was possible.

Admittedly, Terry Palmer was no anatomical genius, but he felt certain such a creature could not exist naturally. Or so it had seemed, until the fiend appeared before him.

Almost ten feet in height, with four legs, four arms and three heads, each countenance disfigured by criss-cross lines from which blood and other vile-smelling liquids dripped in a continuous stream. Terry wanted to run, screaming in fear as he tried to escape this horrifying spectacle, but was unable to move or speak.

How long these visions continued to torment him, Palmer wasn't sure. It could have been hours, days, or even longer. Then things got worse. One by one, the monster devoured his old associates. First to go was Frank Watson, who had been wrapped round by the monster's tail, which was actually an immense snake. The snake lifted Frank as if he was a tiny infant, before presenting his prisoner to one of the mouths, which totally engulfed poor Frank in one fluid movement, as the orifice widened to become a yawning, bottomless chasm. Soon afterwards, Joe Lambert was also swallowed whole by the ogre in a ghastly repetition of the same manoeuvre.

Terry had been about to ask Joe something, but the chance never arose. What was it he'd wanted Joe to tell him? He hadn't been able to remember, but then Birdie Swallow provided the answer, almost as if he'd become a skilled mind-reader. 'You wanted to ask Joe about Norma, and why she ditched you, but it's too late now. It's too late for Frank, for Joe, and for me.'

Even as Birdie was ending his sentence, he too was swallowed whole. Now, Terry was alone with the monster. As he sought desperately for a way to avoid the dreadful fate his friends had suffered, Palmer was unaware that everything he'd experienced was nothing more than the hallucinogenic effect of the drugs that were coursing relentlessly through his system.

Then, as he tried to prepare for the dreadful ending he knew he'd be unable to escape, everything changed. Somehow, he had escaped the monster's clutches and been transported elsewhere. Had his situation improved, or got suddenly worse? Instead of three-headed monsters, he was in a swamp, surrounded by countless alligators, snakes, sharks, killer whales and piranhas, such as he'd only seen on nature programmes he'd watched while in prison.

Sweat coursed down his face, running as freely as tears, and every pore in his body exuded perspiration. Again, Terry had no idea how long he'd been in that terrible place before he was rescued, pulled clear of those menacing figures by his saviour, who stripped him of his clothing and began to towel him dry.

Was any of this real? Or had he imagined everything, including the final bizarre twist. He'd been given a haircut, by someone with only a rudimentary knowledge of a barber's skills. Such was the lack of proficiency that on occasion several of Terry's hairs had been pulled out by the root.

Still confused as to what was real and what was imaginary, Terry had been almost relieved to discover he'd been returned to his cold, dark cell. Or had he? Or was that merely wishful thinking? Were new terrors lurking in the shadows waiting to pounce? And why was he wearing a jogging suit? Where were his trainers? Any relief he'd felt was short-lived, because shortly after he'd eaten his meal, the worst-case scenario developed when the monster reappeared in his peripheral vision.

As he lay terrified, in another room a question was posed. 'What was the purpose of all that?'

'The sauna made him sweat uncontrollably. Rubbing him dry using his clothing as a towel put large quantities of his DNA onto it. When Vincent goes visiting, he'll be wearing that clothing. He's had strict instructions to ensure there's a liberal transfer onto the corpses, and items at the scene. To supplement those, the hairs removed from Palmer's head will have his DNA in the roots, so those will be scattered on, or close to, the bodies. Now all we have to do is get Vincent to take delivery of the items he needs, and then he can give Wellie the boot.'

* * *

Kirk Bolton Lodge was on the outskirts of the village bearing the same name, and had once been the residence of the local squire. That had been almost three hundred years previously, but time had enhanced the beauty of the stone building, rather than detracting from its appearance. The facade was now covered in ivy, and presented an imposing spectacle, had there been observers to take in the sight.

For most people, the word 'lodge' implied a small adjunct to a larger property, but that was not so in this instance. Surrounded on three sides by woodland, and with the frontage facing the magnificent scenery provided by the mountain slopes of Stark Ghyll, Kirk Bolton Lodge was a truly impressive edifice.

Entrance to the grounds came via a pair of intricately forged wrought-iron gates, which hung from stone gateposts, each surmounted by a lion couchant, a visibly splendid example of the stonemason's craft.

From there, the long driveway was flanked on either side by avenues of tall, graceful poplar trees, before opening out onto the gravel forecourt in front of the house. Although the facade was impressive, few people had occasion to admire it. The occupants, who had lived in the lodge for several years, were known to be reclusive, but little else about them was hard fact, being mostly rumour.

Villages are natural hives of gossip, but in Kirk Bolton, many of the inhabitants weren't even aware of the lodge owners' names. Biographical details were even more scant. In the early days following moving into the property, they had made it abundantly clear, by shutting themselves away, that they valued their privacy above all else, and they would go to great lengths to protect it. *Leave well alone* was the unspoken message.

Rumours did eventually begin to circulate, few of which bore even the slightest resemblance to the truth. One of these, which gained popular acclaim, was that the owner of the lodge was a former pop singer, desperate to avoid the attention of his adoring fans. Extensions to this fantasy included the myth that he was living there with his gay lover, or that he had founded a cult and was surrounded by a collective of nubile young women who had become his sex slaves.

Another, equally unfounded, rumour was of a far graver nature, and told of a much sadder background to the lodge's owner, a history that involved the loss of his wife and family in a devastating fire. This led to a terrible disfigurement, as he tried in vain to save the lives of his loved ones. Recovering from this traumatic incident, he had opted to retire from life, and buried himself away, attended only by one full-time carer.

None of these fantasies bore even the slightest resemblance to the truth, but served to amuse and entertain the gossipmongers as they were downing their pints in the local hostelry.

Unfortunately, recent developments in technology resulted in the lodge's occupants' desire for privacy being less secure than they believed. Fortunately, for their peace of mind, they were blissfully unaware of the trio of devices giving covert surveillance of not only the property and its surroundings but themselves.

* * *

Vincent was ultra-cautious by nature, a facet of his personality he shared with his new client. This trait was part of the reason for his continued success, and had enabled him to remain out of reach for many years. Although there were those, on both sides of the law, who wished to bring him to book for the crimes he had committed, their efforts had always been thwarted.

Police officers in several forces throughout the country were aware the murders they had investigated were professional hits. Identifying the assassin, let alone arresting him and putting him on trial, remained only a dream.

Likewise, relatives, friends, and associates of his victims were also desperately keen to see him suffer for the loss of their nearest and dearest, but their objective was of a far more savage nature. Some had even tried offering incentives to trace the elusive hitman, with rewards reaching five-figure sums, in exchange for information that would lead to his identity being revealed. Despite tempting those with a history of revealing useful facts, or even rumours, Vincent remained untraceable, a shadowy figure of nightmares.

When undertaking a new assignment, Vincent laid down strict rules of engagement for his client to follow. Principal among these was a total embargo on face-to-face meetings. This was accompanied by a request, which was in effect a thinly disguised order, that once the initial contact had been made, all subsequent communications should be via a specific mobile phone number. The mobile in question, a pay-as-you-go model, would be purchased specifically for that customer's transactions. Once the task had been carried out and payment received, Vincent removed the SIM card, cutting it into many pieces before disposing of both card and phone.

Having provisionally accepted a new client's offer, Vincent's next task was always to carry out discreet but thorough background checks, on both the customer and the potential target. Only when he was satisfied on both counts would Vincent confirm the arrangement.

In the present instance, his research into the person he'd been asked to eliminate led him to believe it would be one of his less-taxing assignments. Both the information he'd been given regarding the potential victim, and the remote location where the target was living, were highly advantageous.

When it came to checking out his client, that was a totally different matter. The person who had contacted him seemed to be as shadowy a figure as Vincent himself. Extensive research into the man's background yielded little — or more accurately, nothing.

Despite this minor setback, given the generous, almost lavish reward on offer, plus the promise of further lucrative contracts to follow, Vincent allowed his desire for financial gain to overrule his better judgement.

This was by no means the only difference in the task facing him. Much of Vincent's undoubted success stemmed from his meticulous avoidance of leaving incriminating evidence, at the murder site or elsewhere. In this instance, however, the client's instructions provided for a totally different scenario. In carrying out the task, Vincent was ordered to ensure as much trace as possible should be available to the officers of the law and their forensic counterparts.

This would involve carefully released DNA, plus removal from the crime scene of several items, one of which was a highly traceable asset belonging to the victim. Locating this after the event would also be made easy for the police, and the combined effect of Vincent's efforts would enable them to complete their enquiries and make an arrest quickly. There was a minor snag to this arrangement, one that involved transport, and it took a good deal of thought before Vincent came up with a workable solution.

Having collected the items left for him at the pre-arranged location, Vincent prepared for the task ahead. Late in the evening, as the summer's day yielded to dusk, he set out on his expedition.

CHAPTER THIRTY-ONE

Several miles from his destination, Vincent parked his sports car in a side street, and switched to an older vehicle stolen the previous day, now bearing false number plates. He drove to a large car park, and then changed his mode of transport completely. As he began the third leg of his journey, he smiled slightly. He couldn't imagine there were many instances when such a vehicle had been used for what he had in mind.

He was unaware that his manoeuvre was being observed by the occupants of a van parked discreetly nearby. 'I wondered how he was going to do it. You have to give him full marks for coming up with such an ingenious solution to the problem. I have to admit using a powered bicycle was something I'd never have thought up.'

'Yes, but he's taller than I assumed. His clothing looks a bit tight.'

They both laughed.

It was shortly after eleven o'clock when Vincent reached the property that housed his victims. Having scaled the high stone wall surrounding the grounds, he followed the route he had carefully selected during his earlier observation of the lie of the land. Within five minutes, he reached the rear of the building, from where he planned to enter.

It had been a very hot day, and the residual warmth made the next part of his task easier. As he glanced along the wall, Vincent noticed a ground-floor window had been left open, ideal for him to climb through. It seemed the occupants had been so confident their remote location would render them safe, they had failed to take even the most elementary precautions. That was likely to prove a fatal error.

Wearing the clothing, as instructed, and latex gloves, Vincent scrambled through the aperture and was standing in a large kitchen. Now he would have to make his way along the ground floor, without alerting the residents to their unexpected visitor.

He inched his way slowly down the hallway, taking care to use the extreme edges of the floor where his passage was less likely to cause a betraying creak. His observation of the building, shortly before making his entrance, had revealed two expensive-looking table lamps, illuminating what he assumed was a sitting room. With the curtains wide open, he had been able to see his targets seated inside that room.

As he made his way along, Vincent saw the reflection of light beneath the door.

Seconds later, Vincent burst into the room and immediately sought the light switch. He flicked it, and the effect was dramatic. One of the two occupants screamed, her fear generated by Vincent's dramatic appearance, and by the pistol in his hand. Before either of them could move, there were two bright flashes of light accompanied by loud detonations, and both residents slumped back in their seats. Vincent advanced towards them, watched them fighting for breath, enjoying the terror in their eyes. He watched and waited, as blood began to cover their clothing. 'That should be enough,' he said, as he smiled at his terrified victims.

Two more shots echoed around the room.

Vincent's work at the house was far from over. He located the room he wanted, searched, and found what he needed. The next ten minutes were spent disposing of the documents he'd unearthed.

It took a while before he found the other items he'd been instructed to remove from the property. Leaving the laptop he had collected on the bottom step, he headed upstairs. He then collected several small, but valuable, items of jewellery, leaving the remainder inside an open drawer in the bedroom. Another search didn't take long. He located the keys he would use to leave the house by the rear and make his way to the adjoining garage.

All that had been easy, Vincent thought. His next task had to be one of the most bizarre he'd ever been asked to undertake. He returned to the sitting room. Slowly and carefully, he kneeled in front of each victim in turn, leaned forward, and hugged them to him. This enabled profuse quantities of blood to stain the clothing he'd been provided with. In exchange, a liberal amount of DNA transferred from his apparel to his victims.

From the pocket of the jogging bottoms he was wearing, he took a small plastic bag and distributed the contents, scattering tiny fragments of hair onto the victims, the chair arms, and the Persian rug surrounding them. Vincent left, closing the door, leaving the crime scene brightly illuminated. Every effort had to be made for the victims to be discovered sooner rather than later.

Not too soon, though, because he had more to do.

Inside the garage, Vincent took a bin liner from his pocket, struggled out of the blood-stained layer of clothing, and placed them in the bag. This he placed on the mat inside the footwell of one of the cars. He lowered his protective hood, smiling to himself at the thought of being spotted while driving wearing the hood. Having operated the electrically controlled door, he climbed into the driving seat of the Mercedes and drove away. At the gates, he used the hand-held remote to open them, went through, and stopped. He closed the gates behind him, loaded his electric bicycle into the car boot, and resumed his journey.

Fifteen minutes later, Vincent re-entered the car park. Following his instructions to the letter, he drove the luxury vehicle to the most remote section of the large plot, which was deserted and in total darkness.

Once he'd manoeuvred the Mercedes into the designated position, Vincent climbed out and removed the electric bike from the boot. He crossed the parking area to the old car he'd stolen for the mission, and placed the bike along with his protective suit inside.

An hour later, he drove the old car into an abandoned quarry, removed a petrol can from inside, and doused the car liberally with its contents. He placed the laptop and petrol can on the driver's seat, and removed his latex gloves. Having reached through the open window, he placed these on top of the can, stood well back, struck a match and flicked it inside, turning away instantly to avoid the sudden explosive draught of ignited fuel. When he was satisfied the car was beyond salvage, he walked away, knowing he had a fifteen-minute walk ahead of him before he reached the street where he'd left his sports car.

Within minutes of Vincent leaving the Mercedes, a Ford Transit pulled alongside it and stopped. The occupants opened the back doors of the van and removed a semi-naked, unconscious young man. Having retrieved the blood-stained clothing from the Mercedes' footwell, they dressed their passenger, before manhandling him into the driving seat. After locking the car doors, one of them threw the keys under the vehicle chassis. Five minutes later, they too exited the car park.

'One good thing,' the driver told his companion, 'at least he won't feel uncomfortable when he's locked away again. Being inside a prison cell will be like home from home for him — if he survives.'

* * *

The following morning, the driver of a small car parked up at a discreet distance from Kirk Bolton Lodge and the driveway leading to it. This was far enough away to avoid being observed during the short period of time necessary to complete the task, but close enough for the wireless connection to operate. It was sheer chance this day had been earmarked for a system check, to verify the actions of the residents.

The driver opened a powerful laptop, and began to download images from the night vision cameras that had been placed in the trees to the front of the property. The operation took just minutes. It was only on returning home and after opening the files that the driver discovered the horrific event recorded by the cameras the previous night.

This was a shocking development, one which changed every preconceived idea about what was going on. But what was the significance of this brutal slaughter? One thing for certain, this information would have to be shared, but who could the driver trust with what could be dynamite?

The only illumination in the room was being provided by the laptop screen. The operator sat watching footage from the trio of surveillance cameras. It had taken a long time, and some very detailed planning, to obtain the best available equipment, and to install the units in the most advantageous locations. Places which commanded the best views of the house and the approach to it. Added difficulties were the need to ensure complete secrecy, both during the installation and once the cameras commenced operation. The slightest risk of detection would have ruined the positive outcome the watcher was so desperately keen to achieve.

As the footage played out, that outcome appeared to have been totally destroyed, blown away by the assassin's bullets. Once the watcher recovered from the shocking images on screen, there was much to ponder. How could this have happened? More to the point, who had reason to kill these specific targets in so professional a manner?

Motive might provide the answer, but there were several to choose from. Was the crime due to greed, revenge, or the need for self-preservation? Or could it be a combination of factors that had resulted in these deaths? One thing for certain, the event was a game-changer — big style. The most immediate dilemma faced by the watcher was, what to do with the footage? It was quite a while before a solution came to mind. Even activating that would need careful planning, but that was the watcher's forte.

* * *

The shopkeeper eyed the approaching customer with mild alarm, his attention drawn to the garment shielding all but a fragment of the face, this added to by the dark glasses. Another puzzling anomaly was the shopper's use of latex gloves, a most unusual trait.

Seeing his gaze, and his startled expression, the customer sought to reassure him. 'Don't worry, I have a skin condition, and these are purely a precaution, to prevent me breaking out in a rash.'

The purchases made, the cash handed over, the customer left the store. The hoodie they were wearing protected their features from the CCTV cameras located at various points along the street. Passers-by might have considered it strange for someone to wear such an item of clothing on a bright, hot, sunny day. But this was no more peculiar than donning latex gloves prior to purchasing a micro flash drive and a pack of padded envelopes, plus a roll of sticky labels.

Returning to the darkened room, the hoodie wearer unwrapped the purchases, plugged the flash drive into one of the laptop's USB ports and waited for the devices to synchronize. Once that was achieved, the transfer of the surveillance footage began. After it was complete, the drive could be placed in an envelope, the address typed onto one of the labels and posted to its recipient. Only when all that was achieved could the latex gloves be ditched.

CHAPTER THIRTY-TWO

Helm Dairies took in many of the outlying areas of the dale, including such places as Kirk Bolton. Deliveries to the village and its surrounds took place on the Monday, Wednesday and Friday of each week. One of their regular customers had set up a working arrangement with the dairy. Every other Monday, a small invoice covering the previous two weeks' supply would be left, along with the milk and any other produce that had been ordered. These were placed inside a container, closely resembling a large bird box, secured to the wall alongside the main gate. On the following Friday, the delivery man would collect an envelope from the box in payment for the invoice.

Having completed his round on Friday, the delivery man returned to the depot and headed straight for the manager's office. 'I think there might be a problem at Kirk Bolton Lodge,' he began.

'What sort of a problem?'

'I left the invoice on Monday as usual, so I expected there to be an envelope with the brass in it to collect today. When I got to the Lodge, not only was there no envelope, but the two pints of milk I delivered on Wednesday were still inside the box — and they hadn't left any empties for me to bring back.'

'Didn't you try ringing the doorbell or knocking?'

The delivery man gave him a withering glance. 'It's easy to tell you've never been anywhere near the property. Not only are there electronically controlled gates, but the house is a bloody long way up the drive. All in all, I reckon there's summat amiss.'

'Maybe they've gone away for a few days and forgot to cancel the milk. It's happened before, loads of times.'

'I don't think so. Although I couldn't get to the house, it has big windows and I noticed there was a light shining in one of the downstairs rooms. That in itself was odd, because it was already daytime. It was quite overcast this morning, so it wasn't sunlight being reflected.'

'That does sound a bit weird. Maybe we'd better report it, in case somebody's been taken ill.' The manager didn't add 'or worse', but the delivery man knew exactly what he was implying. The manager picked up the phone and began to dial.

At about the same time, a security guard at the Good Buys supermarket in Helmsdale was talking to the store manager. 'There's a car parked at the far end of the car park. It's been there over twenty-four hours.'

The manager groaned. 'Not another old banger some idiot's dumped rather than taking it to the scrapyard?'

The guard smiled. 'I don't think so. This is a top-of-the-range Mercedes, and judging from the registration plate, it's less than twelve months old. That's not all, though, far from it. The car doors are locked and there's somebody in the driver's seat. He appears to be out of it — or worse. I've tried banging on the window and the car roof to wake him, but he didn't stir. He's either fast asleep, under the influence of drink or drugs — or dead.'

'Whatever's wrong, we'd better get the police involved. I've got the number for Helmsdale station. I don't want to make an emergency call if it turns out to be nothing.'

As the guard was about to leave, the manager called him back. 'Have you got the registration number?'

* * *

Sergeant Steve Meadows' line was engaged, as he was dealing with a request for a welfare check, so the call from Good Buys supermarket diverted to CID, where DC Adil Hassan answered it. Having noted all the details, he began by conducting a DVLA search and scribbling the results on his notepad.

Next, Adil sought advice on how to proceed from Clara. He was in the middle of explaining the problem when Steve Meadows passed by, en route to the kitchen and the coffee machine. 'I checked with DVLA,' Adil told Clara, 'and the registered keeper of the Mercedes is someone by the name of Welham, who lives at Kirk Bolton Lodge.'

'Hang on, Adil,' Meadows interrupted. 'Did you say Kirk Bolton Lodge?'

'Yes, Steve, why? Do you know something about the house?'

'No, but I've just taken a call from Helm Dairies, and I'm in the middle of requesting a welfare check at the property. The milkman reported the recent deliveries haven't been taken in and there's a light on in a downstairs room, even during daylight.'

'Let's get Mike involved,' Clara suggested. She waved through to Nash's office to attract his attention. Nash was seated behind his desk, desperately trying to keep his eyes open. Clara smiled at the others. 'I'll go and get him.'

She entered his office. 'Mike, wouldn't you be better taking the paternity leave?'

'I'm OK. It's just the night-time disturbances — I'll get used to it. Alondra's doing really well trying to make sure I get my sleep. Lisa takes over during the day while she has a rest. I'm coming.' He stood upright, stretched and followed Clara into the general office. Once he'd heard both accounts, he told Meadows, 'Get your guys to do the welfare check and we'll head to Good Buys and try to wake Sleeping Beauty.'

Clara snorted. 'Don't believe the fairy tale, Mike. Nobody would mistake you for Prince Charming.'

Before leaving, Nash made a quick phone call, the gist of which he explained to Clara once they were en route. 'I've asked Jimmy Johnson to join us at the supermarket. If anybody can figure out how to get into a locked car, Jimmy's the man.'

At the car park, the detectives were guided to the location of the Mercedes by the store's security guard. Seconds after arriving alongside the luxury vehicle, a small van bearing the name and logo of JJ Security Systems pulled to a halt behind them. The owner of this company, reformed burglar Jimmy Johnson, stepped out of the van and greeted them in his rich Glaswegian dialect.

Having glanced at the target vehicle, Jimmy shook his head despairingly. He prowled around the Mercedes, inspecting the doors, the bonnet and boot, groping around the wheel arches, and even peering beneath the chassis. Nash assumed he was looking for a hiding place containing an access device for the car, until Johnson turned and addressed them.

'I ken three ways tae get in tae this motor. Ye cud call the supplying dealer for a replacement key, but this chappie here would be cold and stiff afore it arrived. Or ye could smash the window, but that might be a wee bit tricky, as they're probably shatter-proof glass.' He paused for dramatic effect before adding, 'I'd say the best bet would be tae use the key that is lyin' agin the front wheel on the passenger side.'

Jimmy shook his head in mock despair at their bemused expressions. 'Ye polis,' he said, his tone one of disgust, 'I dinna ken how ye've the nerve to call yersen detectives. Wud you tell me why he left the keys under the car, and locked hissen inside?' He grinned, waved cheerily, jumped back into his van, and drove away.

They waited for a member of the supermarket staff to bring a long-handled brush. This item, borrowed from the store cleaner, would be the best tool to effect the retrieval of the car key. As they waited, Nash and Mironova attempted to attract the attention of the car's occupant. Their efforts were hampered by the richly tinted side windows and windscreen. Nash wondered if these were below the minimum safety level prescribed by law. If that was so, they must have been adapted, as the manufacturer would certainly not countenance such mistreatment of their vehicle. Even the bright reflection of the sunlight on the windscreen proved more of a hindrance than a help.

The man inside the car was in the driving seat, but lay face down across the passenger side, rendering his facial features invisible from outside. After prolonged close scrutiny, with his hands cupped around his eyes to shield them from the glare, Nash told Clara, 'I think our man's alive. I can't be certain, but I thought I saw his chest move slightly.'

Clara copied the manoeuvre, and from her slightly different angle, was able to catch a glimpse of the shirt the occupant was wearing. 'Good Lord!' she exclaimed, taking an involuntary step backwards. 'I can't be sure, but I think I know who it is.'

'Who?'

'Terry Palmer.'

'What makes you think that?'

'The shirt looks to be identical to the one Palmer had on when he was released from prison. On the CCTV images, as he was walking away from the prison gates, I spotted the name of the footballer on the back. It made me realize how long Palmer's been out of circulation, because that player retired five or six years ago.'

'I never had you down as a soccer aficionado.'

'I'm not, but David watches it on telly when there's nothing else worthwhile on.'

'That will be almost every night, I reckon. Anyway, here's our man with the broom. We'll soon know if you're right or wrong.' Nash turned to the security guard. 'Did you request an ambulance when you called the emergency operator?'

'I didn't make the call. The store manager handled it.'

As he was speaking, the distant wail of a siren could be heard. Seconds later, as Nash was taking delivery of the newly retrieved car keys, his question was answered. An emergency responder, blue lights flashing and siren blaring, raced through the car park entrance.

'He's likely to cause more casualties driving at that rate,' Clara muttered.

The security guard waved to attract the paramedic's attention, and the luridly painted vehicle pulled up alongside the Mercedes. Within a couple of minutes Mironova's suspicions were proved correct. Once they got a clear view of the occupant's face, they knew it was Terry Palmer.

The paramedic set to work examining him and setting up a drip. He confirmed that Palmer was alive — just. 'His pulse is very slow, his blood pressure is in his boots, and his pupils are extremely dilated. He's unresponsive, even when being manhandled. This man is seriously ill, and my best guess is he's overdosed on something. But one thing for certain, whatever is in his system, he certainly couldn't have driven this car in his present state. I suppose he could have been sedated. But at the moment, there's no way to determine which, if either, of my suppositions is correct, or if there's a totally different reason. We need to get him to hospital as fast as we can. Then we can do some checks and take a blood sample. Without them, anything is pure guesswork. What we need now is an ambulance.'

Nash had turned the paramedic's attention to the blood-stained clothing Palmer was wearing. 'We're going to need those for examination by our forensic people,' he told him. 'The garments must only be handled under sterile conditions, to avoid contamination of potential evidence. To ensure that happens, I'll make arrangements for someone to collect them at Netherdale General.'

The paramedic stared at the shirt and jogging bottoms, both of which were liberally covered in what his expert eye suggested were bloodstains. Despite coming into daily contact with injuries and worse, the health worker shuddered. There could be no innocent explanation for such a large quantity of blood on a person who had no open wounds.

Nash and Mironova watched as Palmer was removed, slowly and carefully, from the Mercedes, placed on a wheeled stretcher, and loaded into the waiting ambulance, which had only just arrived. The three paramedics then began working on their patient.

CHAPTER THIRTY-THREE

Mironova had donned a pair of latex gloves in preparation for an examination of the interior of the car. Having drawn a blank in the footwell of the front and rear seats, she opened the glove compartment and gasped with surprise. She reached into the small compartment, removed a selection of its contents, and spread them out on the front passenger seat for inspection.

Her action was unobserved, as Nash was facing away from the car's interior. He took out his mobile and called Steve Meadows. Having instructed the sergeant to have someone from Netherdale sent round to the general hospital and collect Palmer's clothing, he asked how things were progressing at Kirk Bolton Lodge.

'The guys I sent to carry out the welfare check rang me a couple of minutes ago. They can't get through the gates, which appear to be electronically controlled. They're going to have to try and gain entry to the grounds by climbing an eight-foot-high stone wall with spikes on top.' Meadows chuckled. 'One of them asked if I could send him a cricket box to protect him from damaging his crown jewels on those spikes.'

'You'd better warn them to be extra careful, the ambulance and paramedics are all tied up here. But there's no need for them climbing. We're at the scene involving the occupants' car, and there's a remote on the floor. It was probably used to open the gates. Send a patrol car here to collect it, will you? They can deliver it to the officers at the lodge.'

Nash told Meadows what they'd discovered, and it was only after he'd ended the call that Clara, who had been waiting patiently, was able to attract his attention.

'Mike, come and have a look at what I've found. I think I've an idea as to how Terry Palmer's been whiling away his time since he was released from prison.'

Nash walked round the front of the car and joined her, peering in through the open passenger door. On the seat was an evidence bag containing a small collection of jewellery items, comprising two bracelets, a pair of pendants, some earrings and three wristwatches.

A closer inspection of the watches revealed the makers' names, all of which suggested extremely high quality. The jewels also looked to be far better than costume, with what appeared to be diamonds, rubies, sapphires, and emeralds — their settings gold, silver, or platinum.

'I think we'll find all of these were stolen during the Wintersett Grange and Helmwater Hall burglaries,' Clara said. 'I did the inventories following those robberies, and these pieces seem to correspond with items on those lists.'

'I'd better lock that evidence bag in my glovebox, ensuring they're out of sight. We don't want the local shoplifters thinking it's their birthday and Christmas combined. We'll have to take them back to Helmsdale for a detailed check before handing them over to Forensics. With luck, they'll be plastered with Palmer's prints, so we'll be able to charge him with two counts of burglary, if not worse.'

'Why did you say "if not worse"? Is there something else?'

'There certainly is,' Nash's tone was grim. 'Think about the state of his clothing.'

Hardened though she was, Clara recoiled at the thought of the bloodstains. 'You're right. I don't understand this. There was no violence at either Wintersett Grange or Helmwater Hall. Both those burglaries took place while the residents were away, so where has all that blood come from?'

'That is an extremely good question, Clara, and it makes me wonder exactly what went on at Kirk Bolton Lodge, and what our guys will find there when they eventually manage to access the property.'

* * *

Forty minutes after their initial report to Sergeant Meadows, the officers charged with carrying out the welfare check managed to gain access to the grounds using the remote to open the gates.

It was fortunate, because their concern regarding ascent of the wall were well founded. Had they done so, they realized they would have had to make their way through dense undergrowth, comprising mostly briars and brambles, possibly resulting in several painful scratches.

A few minutes passed in a fruitless attempt to gain the attention of the occupants by banging loudly on the front door, alternating using their fists with wielding the heavy cast-iron knocker in the shape of a ram's head.

The failure of both strategies led one of the officers to switch tactics. He walked briskly towards the corner of the building, to the room where a chandelier and lamps were burning, despite the sun being now at its zenith.

Cupping his hands to shield his eyes from the glare, he peered in through the window, then recoiled in horror. This caused him to trip over a rose bush, which took instant revenge by inflicting several scratches. As he scrambled to his feet, the officer, having released a string of Anglo-Saxon swear words, summoned his colleague and reported what he'd seen. He invited him to take a look to confirm this wasn't a terrible figment of his imagination.

* * *

As the ambulance left, Nash's mobile rang. He listened intently for a short while, before issuing a string of instructions, ending by saying, 'Clara and I will be on our way as soon as we can get away from here.'

Nash signalled for Clara to join him. 'I've instructed Steve Meadows to send one of his men here, to stand guard over the Merc until recovery arrives. I've also told him to detail one of his blokes to remain at Netherdale General to guard Palmer, and if he regains consciousness, to have him manacled to the hospital bed.'

'That seems like an extreme measure. Is it really necessary?'

'I didn't think so, until I got the report on the welfare check at Kirk Bolton Lodge. The officers were unable to rouse the occupants. That's hardly surprising, because Steve told me one of them peered through a ground floor window and saw two people inside, seated in armchairs, their clothing covered in blood. Fortunately, the back door was unlocked, and they were able to gain access and confirm they are both dead, having suffered what they believe are gunshot wounds.'

Nash paused. 'The fact that Terry Palmer was found inside a car belonging to the owner of Kirk Bolton Lodge, and that his clothing was covered in blood, tends to suggest he might have been responsible for a double murder. I also told Steve to call out Mexican Pete and the boffins, and said we'd head for the crime scene as soon as someone arrives here to relieve us.'

* * *

When they reached Kirk Bolton, the detectives found one of the uniformed officers waiting alongside the wrought-iron gates. These were wide open, much to Nash's relief.

'Thanks for sending the remote, sir. I didn't fancy a fight with the undergrowth,' the constable told Nash. 'I knew from Steve there would be a fair amount of traffic heading for the lodge. I'll stop anyone who isn't expected entering. I'm doing the log, if that's OK with you.'

'That's fine, carry on. Where's your colleague?'

'He's guarding the crime scene.' The constable grinned. 'At least that's what he's supposed to be doing, but last time I checked he was busy fertilizing the roses with his full English breakfast.'

'If he's been sick inside the house, we'll need his DNA for elimination purposes.'

'No, he saved his sausage hurling for an outdoor event.' He shook his head. 'It's horrendous in there, sir.'

'I assume you checked the rest of the house over to ensure there were no other victims elsewhere?'

'We did. Thankfully, the rest of the place is clean. Otherwise, my mate would probably have moved on to disposing of last night's dinner.'

'OK, will you direct Professor Ramirez and the boffins, please?'

All humour vanished when the detectives reached the house, where they greeted a very pale-looking constable, before donning protective clothing prior to entering the property.

'Before we start, what do we know about the people who live here — or rather, lived here?' Nash asked.

Clara flipped her notebook open. 'The only information we have comes via DVLA. The registered keeper of the Mercedes is listed as Gabriel Welham of this address. He has a full driving licence, with three penalty points for speeding. I also checked the Electoral Register on the way here, but curiously, there's no listing on it for anyone at Kirk Bolton Lodge.'

'That's a bit odd. I thought it's compulsory to register all occupants of a given address.'

'According to what I read, you can be fined for failing to fill in the Electoral Register, unless you have a valid reason. Acceptable excuses are a prolonged stay in hospital or severe learning difficulties. It seems the inhabitants of Kirk Bolton Lodge chose to ignore such trivialities, and were unfazed by the dire threat of a fine.'

CHAPTER THIRTY-FOUR

The crime scene was as horrific as the officers had reported. When Clara surveyed it, the word 'bloodbath' sprang to mind. Despite the terrible sight, she was about to step forward into the room when Nash put a restraining hand on her arm, asking, 'What do you make of that?'

Clara looked to where he was pointing. The armchairs containing the victims were about four feet apart, separated by a small side table — ideal, Clara guessed, for a mug of coffee or a glass of wine. As she peered at the section of carpet in front of the chairs, as Nash had indicated, Clara could see drops of what appeared to be bloodstains on the textured pile. The area looked scuffed. 'I'm not sure what to make of it, to be honest. What do you think? Perhaps he was injured,' Clara suggested.

'Palmer wasn't injured. The paramedics checked.'

The detectives advanced slowly into the room. They had only taken a couple of paces inside when Nash glanced round, then stopped abruptly, his attention caught by something in the far corner. 'I don't believe it,' he muttered.

'What don't you believe?'

Nash pointed to what he'd seen, and Clara followed the direction of his hand. On a plinth, she could see a very large sculpture, a depiction of a lion, quite unlike anything she'd ever seen before. 'What is it? I mean, I know it's a lion, but why has it got you so agitated?'

'I'm guessing this must be a copy of something quite unique. It's one of the treasures from the Mausoleum of Halicarnassus, now known as Bodrum, in Turkey. The original is kept in the British Museum, and is literally priceless. Even a copy like this would be extremely valuable, probably worth six figures, maybe more.'

Clara was intrigued, 'How on earth did you learn all that? Have you a secret hobby, such as archaeology?'

Nash smiled. 'Speech Day in my final term at school. Every year they get distinguished people to address the pupils, telling them of their achievements. That time, it was an old boy who actually *was* an archaeologist, and he was giving away signed copies of a book he'd written about his adventures. I was interested enough to bag a copy and read it.' He shrugged. 'I don't think he'd have challenged Charles Dickens or Agatha Christie as an author, but parts of the book were quite interesting.' He gestured towards the sculpture. 'I recognized the statue from some of the photos in his memoir.'

'OK, I get all that, but why is finding it here getting you so worked up?'

'A sculpture identical to this one was stolen during a burglary of a stately home in Cheshire around twelve or thirteen years ago. The robbery was one of the earlier escapades of the Country House Bandits. I read the details in the inventory of items which have never been recovered. Given that we've just seen a member of that gang, covered in blood, inside a Mercedes belonging to this house owner, I think the connection is obvious, don't you?'

'In other words, you believe this is a classic case of "when thieves fall out", yes?'

'I certainly don't think Palmer chose this house and these victims at random, especially when you study the artwork.' Nash pointed to the wall opposite them. 'That's an L. S. Lowry painting. I remember the last one at auction sold for around two and a half million. If that's the original, not a print, I expect we'll find it on the Bandits' stolen property list as well.'

The detectives turned their attention to the bodies, albeit observing them from a distance. 'It looks as though they were each shot twice.'

'Let's hope our worthy professor and his scientific sidekicks can provide us with an explanation.'

Never had the expression 'speak of the devil, and he will appear', been more appropriate, Clara thought. Just as Nash was finishing his sentence, a voice from behind startled them both.

'Good morning. I think you should know that almost all my mortuary drawers are full — with bodies you've already provided. You don't have to go out of your way to prevent me from getting bored, because I can assure you, at the pace you discover corpses, that's never going to happen. Tell me, are you working on piece rate? With a productivity bonus, once you've achieved your target?' The pathologist indicated the corpses. 'Is this the full body count? Or are there several others elsewhere in the house?'

'I'm sorry to disappoint you, Professor, but this is the sum total. Our uniform colleagues checked the rest of the building. However, if you're desperate, I can go find some more for you.'

'Don't bother. Two is ample, thank you.'

* * *

As the room began to fill up with the pathologist's assistants and a crew of Forensic officers, Nash and Mironova retreated, informing Ramirez of their intention to search the rest of the property. 'I'm not sure uniform checked the cupboard under the stairs, so there could be a few more corpses hidden inside it,' Nash said, as he turned to leave.

'Is there anything in particular we should be looking for?' Clara asked.

He pondered her question for a moment. 'Yes, we need to find documentary evidence enabling us to identify the victims. We've assumed the male to be Gabriel Welham, but that might not be so. For all we know, Welham could have had this property listed as an Airbnb, and these are simply temporary residents. Therefore, we need to find photo ID, such as passports, driving licences, or something similar.'

'Why is this so important?'

'Because I'm getting more and more convinced that Mr Gabriel Welham is far from being a model citizen, assuming him to be one of the corpses. We need to establish if that's correct, or simply my imagination working overtime.' He grinned. 'I thought I'd say that to save you the trouble.'

'Actually, I don't think that's one of your wilder theories.'

On the opposite side of the ground floor was a small room Clara guessed had once been another lounge but which had been converted for use as an office or study. 'This looks like an excellent place to start,' she told Nash.

It wasn't long before Clara's prediction proved accurate. Their first find was a pair of passports in the names of Gabriel Welham and Thelma Daley. The images on these bore a strong resemblance to the shooting victims, removing any remaining doubts about the dead man's identity and enabling them to put a name to the female victim.

'We need to find out what we can about Thelma Daley,' Clara suggested.

'Phone the station and ask Viv or Adil to get working on it, will you? While you're doing that I'll keep searching. I'm particularly keen to discover anything I can find about Welham's finances. Running a place like this can't be cheap, and as yet we've no idea where his money came from, or what he did for a living, apart from being a suspected serial burglar.'

Their search of the desk yielded disappointingly meagre results. 'I don't get it,' Clara commented. 'There are no bank statements, or ones from credit card companies. Nothing to indicate where Welham's money came from — or where it went, for that matter.'

In frustration, she turned her attention to the almost-full shredder alongside the desk. After sifting through the contents, she told Nash, 'I think I've solved the mystery of the missing statements. There's a heap of shredded documents in here, and from what I can make out, they all contain mostly numbers. I'm not sure if that's a step forward or back.'

Nash was examining a folder he'd removed from the bottom drawer of the desk. 'What do you make of this, Clara?'

He passed her the file. The cover merely contained a set of initials. 'I wonder what CCA stands for? Do you think it could represent someone's name?'

'I've no idea. That's why I asked you.'

She opened it up and found a single sheet of ruled A4 paper inside, neatly divided into vertical columns. The first of these was reserved for what seemed to be specific dates, all in chronological order. The remainder, although containing subject headings, were completely baffling.

She read them aloud. 'IN(B), IN(D), IN(PT), and (TOK). What on earth do those stand for?'

'At a risk of repeating myself, I've absolutely no idea. But clearly they refer to something important. Otherwise, Welham wouldn't have kept this file, when he'd already shredded his bank statements.' He paused. 'If it was Welham who shredded them.'

'Who else could have done it?'

'I'm not sure, Terry Palmer? If he believed the statements contained something incriminating.'

Clara ran her eyes down the columns. 'If this is to do with money, I think you're right about them being important, judging by the figures he's entered here. Did you find anything else in that drawer?'

'Not so far.'

* * *

Eventually, they decided there was nothing else significant in the desk, or the small office as a whole. Before leaving the room, Nash cast a final glance round. 'I'm beginning to wonder if we're looking in the wrong place. It's possible the reason we failed to find anything useful in here is because Welham kept it all elsewhere. Accepting the fact that we suspect the bank and credit card statements have been shredded, we've only found one document holder, no wallet or purse.'

'Hang on a minute,' Clara said. 'Where's the laptop? There's a lead here on the floor, obviously fallen off the desk. So where is it? There wasn't one in the car with Palmer.'

Nash looked at the empty desk. 'No, there wasn't. So what happened to it?'

'Maybe he put it in the boot.'

'For someone the paramedic said was in no fit state to drive, Palmer did very well, didn't he?'

It was only when they moved to the first floor and entered what was clearly the master bedroom that they discovered something else of interest. One of the drawers to the dressing table had been left open, and Clara headed straight for it.

She peered at the drawer's contents for several seconds, before giving a gasp of surprise. 'Mike, come and take a look at what I've found. Somebody's going to be really happy — a couple of local landowners, to be precise, together with their insurance companies.'

'And you accuse me of saying things nobody else can understand,' he grumbled.

'It's known as payback, Mike.'

He inspected the items that had attracted her attention. 'I wonder why these items weren't kept in the jewellery box on top, along with the other stuff.'

'Probably because it doesn't belong in this house. These items were also on the inventories I did at Wintersett Grange and Helmwater Hall. We found part of the haul in the Mercedes along with Terry Palmer, but unless I'm very much mistaken, the remaining proceeds from those robberies appear to be sitting in this drawer.'

'This is getting weirder and weirder. We had Palmer earmarked for those burglaries, but maybe that's no longer feasible. Even if he didn't do those thefts, why remove only some of the goods and leave the rest?'

'I think I can provide answers to both those questions, Mike. I believe the goods were in this house because either Gabriel Welham or Thelma Daley, or both of them, committed those burglaries or were responsible for receiving stolen property. As to why Palmer only nicked a few of the items from in here, I'd say he chose what would be easily sellable, and less likely to cause potential buyers to ask awkward questions. We put out a list of the stolen goods following the robberies, and sent them to jewellers, pawnbrokers, and the like. The stuff in this drawer is all easily identifiable, and Palmer, with his record of stealing precious goods, must have realized it was too risky trying to dispose of them.'

'That all sounds completely logical,' Nash agreed. 'Leaving two outstanding questions. Which of our two victims is the cat burglar, Gabriel or Thelma? Or were they merely acting as fences?'

The answer came when Nash's mobile rang. 'Yes, Adil, what have you got?' Nash listened for a while. 'That is extremely interesting, and it bears out something we've just found. Will you print it off and leave it on either my desk or Clara's?'

Nash paused for a second then asked, 'Do me a favour? Phone the Mercedes dealers in Netherdale and ask them about Welham's car. This is what I need to know . . .'

He turned to Clara. 'Adil's been researching Thelma Daley, and he's come up with some interesting background. Apparently, Thelma has been imprisoned twice, both times for burglary. She's also got convictions for prostitution, affray, and shoplifting, but those were non-custodial.'

'She sounds like a nice girl,' Clara muttered. 'Why did you ask Adil to phone the Merc dealers?'

'I want to know how long Welham's been a customer of theirs.'

'Why is that important?'

'If he's been buying high-end cars for the past fifteen years, I think he could have been the driver of the vehicle Corey

Davies saw at one of the gang's robberies. If that's so, my theory about photophobia could be a non-starter. However, there could be a completely different reason the passenger in the Mercedes wore sunglasses, even in the dead of night.'

'What reason is that?'

'It could be he was afraid of being recognized. But there again, that's only a theory.'

'As if there weren't enough of those lying around,' Clara muttered.

A few minutes later, Hassan called back with an update. After ending the call, Nash told Clara, 'Apparently Welham has been a customer of the Mercedes dealership for over fifteen years, and during that time he's changed vehicles four times. I think that makes my latest theory far more likely, don't you?'

Having visited every part of the house without finding anything else relevant to their investigation, Nash suggested they leave the Forensic team to continue their work and return to Helmsdale. 'Apart from anything else, I'm beginning to get withdrawal symptoms due to lack of caffeine.'

CHAPTER THIRTY-FIVE

Later that afternoon, the detectives received a preliminary report on Palmer's condition via one of the medical team at Netherdale General. By then, Nash and Mironova had brought Pearce and Hassan up to speed with developments at Kirk Bolton Lodge.

Nash listened as the doctor told him, 'In the circumstances, I don't believe what I'm about to tell you contravenes patient confidentiality. The patient is heavily sedated. Whether that's self-induced or he's been fed the drugs is impossible to tell. I've tried the usual antidote for street drugs such as heroin, to bring him down, but it hasn't worked. Given the state he was in, and the amount that he must have taken to end up that way, he's lucky to be alive. It's as well he was found, otherwise you would have a completely different situation on your hands. From examination of his flesh, I can confirm that the sedative was ingested rather than injected. He's beginning to regain consciousness, but it's a very slow process and he's far from being lucid.'

The medic paused, before adding another twist in the tale of Terry Palmer. 'There is one other complication you should be aware of. We can't be sure about this, so please don't take it as gospel — only the results of the blood tests will prove whether we're right or wrong. Given the bizarre nature of his ramblings during his brief moments of consciousness, we're beginning to wonder if there might be more than one substance in his system. There is a possibility, and I believe it's quite a strong one, that Mr Palmer could also be under the influence of a strong hallucinogenic. If that proves to be the case, once again we can't determine if that's by choice or otherwise. We'll keep you updated on his condition, and also share the results of those blood tests with you. But until we can be absolutely certain he's totally free from any potentially harmful chemical influences, it looks as if he'll be with us for some while.'

* * *

Two days later, the Helmsdale team received further news from both the doctors and Forensics. Pearce had volunteered to collect sandwiches for the team, while Nash was on his landline, so Clara and Adil took the calls.

Clara began, telling the others, 'Netherdale General rang while you were busy. They've received the results of Palmer's blood test.' She glanced down at the notes she'd made and grimaced. 'Part of what the doctor told me was in English, but the names of the drugs they discovered certainly weren't. When I asked for a translation, he said the test confirmed Palmer had been sedated, but also he'd ingested some weird amphetamine-based substance that is known to cause severe hallucinations. They were surprised Palmer survived, given his less than sturdy physique. When they knew what he'd taken, they checked him over again and were also mildly surprised there was no evidence he'd been self-harming, which is apparently one of the more common side-effects of that drug.'

'That's interesting, but we still have no idea if Palmer took those drugs of his own accord or whether he was force-fed them.'

'One thing the medic told me that might give a clue in that respect is the hallucinogenic drug is extremely expensive. Unless you're prepared to pay street corner prices, you'd need a prescription to obtain them.'

Nash could tell Hassan was eager to speak. 'What news have you got, Adil?'

'While Clara was on with the hospital, I fielded a call from Forensics. They've also got some interesting news, though it's pretty much what we expected to hear. They've run tests on the blood-stained clothing Palmer was wearing. There's a complete match to both victims at Kirk Bolton Lodge. Their crime scene findings will take a bit longer, but they did tell me they were able to retrieve hair samples from near the bodies which are not the same colour as Welham's or his girlfriend, but which do look similar to Palmer's.'

'Clara, you three will have to deal with anything that comes in tomorrow,' Nash said. 'I got a call from the chief constable. Jackie and I have been summoned to attend a meeting in Birmingham with officers from narcotics squads nationwide. As a result of the information Corey Davies supplied, there have already been several arrests, and further operations will be planned based on what we now know.'

During Nash's absence, the day passed without incident until Clara, who was the last to leave the CID suite, was about to pick up her car keys. It was quite late, and she was surprised when the phone rang, more so when she realized the caller was also working after normal office hours. She listened to the report from the head of Forensics with growing interest, which turned to shock at his final revelation.

Having ended the call, Clara sank back into her chair and stared at the folder on her desk, into which she'd just scribbled a note. As she mulled over the new twist to what was an already complicated investigation, she pondered what to do with the information she had just received. She tried Nash's mobile, but it went straight to voicemail. Eventually, unwilling to disturb him if he was already at home with Alondra and the baby, she decided to send him a text. The message read, '*Meet me at Kirk Bolton Lodge tomorrow morning — urgent!*'

Only then did she pick up her car keys — and the folder.

* * *

It was shortly after eight o'clock the next morning that Clara watched Nash's Range Rover drive slowly along the avenue of poplar trees leading to Kirk Bolton Lodge. She walked across the portico sheltering the open front door to greet him.

'OK, I'm here. What's the panic?' Nash asked, after telling Clara about the previous day's meeting.

'I got a call from Forensics yesterday evening. It was much as expected, with one notable exception. They matched the DNA from the crime scene to that of Palmer. There were traces on both victims, via transfer of sweat probably, plus some of the hairs found on the carpet and the side table near the bodies had sufficient roots to provide a match.'

'That sounds like game, set and match to me, so what's the urgency?'

'Because they also found another match. When they ran Gabriel Welham's DNA through the system, they discovered it was already on file. Welham's DNA corresponds exactly with that taken off the gun you retrieved from the Hand of Glory lead mine.'

Nash stared at Clara for several seconds in complete disbelief, before managing to ask, 'Are you trying to tell me Gabriel Welham is responsible for those four murders?'

'Not exactly. I believe Gabriel Welham has committed six murders. When the boffin told me about the mine, it set me thinking. I sent you that text in the hope I'd be proved right, and I think I have been. Come inside and let me show you what I've just found.'

Clara led the way into the large hall and headed for the umbrella stand in one corner. 'I checked the stand when we were here, but didn't give this a thought.'

As she picked up one item from within, Nash noticed she was wearing protective gloves. She held up a walking cane, and with a deft twist removed the ornate silver mount on the top and slid it away from the body of the stick. The light reflected from the steel of the lethal sword that formed the interior.

Clara pointed to several places along the blade where the metal was discoloured by what appeared to be bloodstains. 'I believe this is the weapon used to kill Joe Lambert and Peter Swallow.'

'I'm willing to bet you're right, Clara, and that's an outstanding piece of detective work. I suggest we take some photos of this in situ, showing both the stick complete, and also with the blade revealed. Then we place it in an evidence bag and take it to Forensics. This is far too important an item to be left to chance.'

* * *

Back at Helmsdale, Nash told Viv and Adil of Clara's discovery. Then he had an idea. 'It's a shame we don't have his laptop, although Clara and I are sure he had one, but what about his phone?' Turning to Clara, he said, 'There's something we failed to check out at Kirk Bolton. At the time, it didn't seem important because we were convinced we'd got Palmer bang to rights.'

'What did we miss?'

'There was no sign of either Welham, or his mistress, having a mobile phone, which seems odd. We ought to at least check the landline and get a record of all incoming and outgoing calls. Adil, contact potential service providers, will you?'

Hassan was lucky, in that the first provider he contacted confirmed they had the account for Welham. Once he informed them of the reason for his question, they were only too happy to cooperate.

Twenty-four hours later, he was able to hand the call record to Nash, who examined it with Clara. There were numerous calls to and from the same mobile, but the note Adil had put alongside provided more frustration. '*This is a pay-as-you-go mobile*,' he'd written.

The other number that appeared on the record regularly was equally frustrating, but for a different reason. Hassan had identified the number as belonging to a Netherdale company named Dale Investments Ltd, but research showed the company had been liquidated several months earlier.

CHAPTER THIRTY-SIX

Later that day, Nash was notified that Palmer had been cleared for release from hospital. He told Clara the news and added, 'I'm going to ask Jackie Fleming to arrange for him to be taken to HQ. I'm also going to tell her about the development at Kirk Bolton Lodge — and about your superb piece of deduction re the swordstick. If all goes to plan, I vote we travel through to Netherdale and interview Palmer. Now that he's been discharged by the medics, we can get the final piece of the jigsaw in place.'

On the drive over to headquarters, conscious they only had twenty-four hours, Nash and Clara discussed tactics for the upcoming encounter. They shared their plan with Jackie Fleming, who told them she was going to watch the interview on CCTV.

Having made the opening announcement, Clara stared at their prime suspect, as Nash asked if he required legal representation. Anyone less like a ruthless double murderer would be hard to imagine, she thought. Palmer was small in stature and slender in build, but that wouldn't have prevented him from pulling the trigger of the handgun used to kill Welham and his mistress. Palmer's expression was one of apprehension, mingled with what she thought was sadness. Was that because he knew what was to come?

Palmer declined the offer of a solicitor, and Clara recited the formal caution. In her role as observer, she continued to watch Palmer, who appeared to be totally confused by what Nash was saying, probably due to the after-effects of the drugs he'd ingested.

'OK, Terry,' Nash began, his tone warm and friendly, 'would you care to tell us where you've been recently, and what you've been up to?'

'I've been in my cell.'

'No, I'm not talking about your time in prison. I'm referring to your whereabouts following your release.'

Palmer frowned. 'I was in my cell, then I was in hospital, then they brought me here.'

'Are you claiming you don't remember anything from the moment you were released from prison, until you came round from the drugs you'd been taking before you were admitted to hospital?'

Palmer remained silent for quite a while. Was that silence a tacit admission of guilt? Clara was unsure, because their suspect still seemed confused by Nash's questions. Had the hospital discharge been premature, perhaps?

Eventually, Palmer spoke, but what he said seemed to make little or no sense. 'When I came out, I went for a pint — well, a few pints, actually. I do remember that, or the first bit at least. Then I was put back inside, but this time it was a different cell.' He shuddered. 'This one was awful, far worse than the one I'd got used to. I was alone almost all of the time.' Suddenly, he looked panic-stricken. 'Please don't send me back to that one,' he pleaded.

It was the detectives' turn to look confused, because little of what Palmer had told them related to any of the facts at their disposal. If they thought what he'd said so far was strange, his replies to Nash's further questions seemed outlandish.

'You claim you were in your cell, but we know for a fact you had been released long before the couple at Kirk Bolton Lodge were murdered.'

Another puzzled frown crossed Palmer's face.

Either he doesn't remember or he's a damned good actor, Clara thought.

'Kirk Bolton Lodge? Where's that?'

'You know where that is, Terry. You've been there,' Nash said.

'No, I haven't.' Terry shook his head and stared at Nash. 'Who was murdered?'

'Oh, come off it, Terry. You know perfectly well the Lodge is at the edge of Kirk Bolton village. Are you trying to fool us by pretending you don't know who lived there? Are you claiming you don't know Gabriel Welham?'

'Gabriel who?'

'Gabriel Welham, the man you shot inside Kirk Bolton Lodge, along with his girlfriend, Thelma Daley.'

'I've no idea what you're talking about. I don't know who these people are. I haven't killed anybody. How could I? I was in my cell.' He began to tremble.

'Of course you don't know them, and we know you've never done anything wrong.'

Nash turned to Clara and lowered his voice, as if confiding in her. 'I'll let you into a closely guarded secret, Sergeant Mironova. As long as you give me your solemn promise not to divulge it. Everyone in prison is innocent. They're all victims of a fiendish plot. At least, that's what they'd like us to think. It's a shame we're not taken in by their lies.'

Turning back to Palmer, Nash said, 'Cut the nonsense, Terry, because we don't believe you. The rubbish you've spouted so far is as unbelievable as the little fairy tale I've just told Sergeant Mironova. That being so, why not admit you murdered Gabriel Welham and Thelma Daley, shooting them in cold blood as they sat watching telly.'

'I've told you before, I don't know who these people are.'

'It should be "were", not "are", because they're both dead — dead, because you killed them. One more question for you, Terry, or rather two questions. Where did you get hold of the handgun you used to shoot them? And what was your motive? Was it money you were after, money he refused to give you? Money you thought was due to you from the Country House Bandit robberies? Or was it revenge, for what he did to Joe Lambert and Peter Swallow?'

Nash's last question provoked an instant reaction from Palmer, but Clara reckoned she couldn't have predicted what he was about to say, even if she'd been given a hundred years to guess.

'I know Joe and Birdie are dead, Frank's dead too, because I saw them die. They were all in the cell with me, but then the monster came.' Palmer shuddered, and Clara saw an expression of abject fear on his face. 'It was a terrible thing. Massive, with three heads, four arms, four legs, an enormous mouth.' He leaned forward as if passing a confidence. 'It had a tail, but that was really a snake. That mouth was so big it swallowed them up whole, one by one. First it was Frank, then Joe, and then Birdie.' His eyes were now wide — he looked terrified. 'It was coming after me next, but someone dragged me out of that awful place just in time. I don't know how, but I ended up in a tropical swamp. That was almost as bad as being in the cell. It was unbearably hot, and there were alligators, sharks, and piranha fish, and other deadly creatures.' He began hyperventilating. 'Please, please, don't send me back. Not to either of those places.'

'Right, I've heard enough. Interview suspended.' Nash signalled to Clara to make the closing announcement, before telling Palmer, 'We'll resume this when you're in a fit state to tell us the truth, rather than that nonsensical rigmarole you've just been spouting.'

* * *

On leaving the room, the detectives met up with Jackie Fleming. 'What do you make of that?' she asked.

'I don't know what to make of it. Clara, go and ask the custody sergeant to get the nurse to have a look at him, will you? My first job is to have a word with the doctor who authorized Palmer's release. They might think they've shifted the hallucinogenic drugs from his system, but by what I've just heard, I reckon he's still away with the fairies.'

Nash's conversation with the medic gave little enlightenment, although the doctor did relay one snippet of information, albeit accidentally, that later proved highly pertinent. In answer to Nash's question, which amounted almost to an accusation, the doctor assured him, 'Before we discharged him, we conducted blood tests which showed Mr Palmer's system was completely free from all drugs. Why do you ask? Is he behaving strangely?'

'You can say that again, without fear of exaggeration. He's been rambling on about monsters and strange creatures. Which, in the circumstances, we found highly suspicious.'

'Don't tell me, let me guess, was it about a three-headed monster that swallowed people whole? Or did he ask if you'd found the goat?'

Nash wondered briefly if the doctor had been helping himself to some of Palmer's medication. 'No, he never mentioned a goat. What made you think he'd ask about one?'

'When he was in hospital, he kept asking if we'd found the goat. We assumed it was merely part of his hallucination, but with the far more terrifying nightmares he's had to endure, we thought a relatively harmless creature like a goat was of little consequence, so we ignored it. There was far worse than a goat wandering through his disturbed mind.'

Nash thanked the doctor, before telling Jackie, 'I think we should delay resuming the interview until tomorrow, when hopefully Palmer will be a little more lucid and rational.'

CHAPTER THIRTY-SEVEN

At eight o' clock the next morning, Clara dismissed all thoughts of déjà vu, as she intoned the opening announcement prior to the continuance of the Palmer interview. Once again, the suspect refused the offer of legal representation, leaving Nash free to begin searching for answers he hoped, this time, would contain some semblance of normality.

A few hours rest had, it seemed, enabled Palmer's memory to return, if only in part. Initially, however, the detectives wondered if this was merely another example of how Palmer's deranged mind worked. Or if someone had sneaked into Netherdale police station overnight and topped up his drug intake.

'Yesterday, you told us you went for a few pints following your release from prison,' Nash began. 'Can you tell us the location of the pub you visited?'

Palmer thought for a few moments, then looked up, his expression clear evidence that he recalled something, even before he spoke. 'I'm not sure. I can't remember the pub's name, but I think it was quite close to the prison. Your officers should be able to tell you, though. I'm sure they'll remember me.'

'What officers are you talking about?'

'They found me in the street. After going ten years without, I wasn't used to beer. I got legless and started throwing up. One of them got a bit peeved because I was sick all over his boots. They carted me off to a cell until I'd sobered up.'

'Was this the cell where you met up with the man-eating monster?'

The confident expression on Palmer's face vanished instantly, as he began to tremble with fear. For long enough, the detectives thought he was either unwilling or unable to reply. Eventually, after a long struggle, he managed to say, 'No, I don't think so. I think that was later, but I'm a bit confused.'

You and me both, Clara thought. She listened as Nash continued.

'There was a lady in the van. I got a lift. I think she was going near to Leeds. Can you ask her?'

Nash smiled at him. 'You think we can do that? Find the lady and ask her?'

Palmer nodded.

'You are confused, aren't you?'

Palmer nodded again, as if he believed they were making headway at last.

'Are you claiming you were kept in another prison, possibly in Leeds, following your release? Or is that prison only inside your mind, a product of your distorted imagination? That would hardly be surprising, would it, given the quantity of hallucinogenic drugs the doctors found in your system.'

Palmer stared at Nash, as if insulted. 'I don't take drugs. I never have done.'

The denial was astounding, and Nash weighed up his next question carefully. 'I'm surprised you're able to be so confident in that denial. In fact, given the huge quantities of sedatives and other substances the doctors found in your system, I'm astonished you can remember anything.' He paused briefly before adding, 'Even your graphic description of the monster that swallowed your fellow gang members whole must have been hard to recall. One other thing that puzzles me is how you paid for such expensive substances, and who you obtained them from. Was it the same dealer who supplied you with the handgun?'

'I didn't take any sedatives, or any drugs. I told you so. Why don't you believe . . . ?' Palmer's voice trailed off, as he grasped the significance of Nash's final question. 'Handgun? What handgun are you on about?'

'Surely you can recall our conversation yesterday. I'm talking about the gun you used to shoot Gabriel Welham and his girlfriend Thelma Daley.'

Palmer frowned. 'Didn't you mention those people yesterday? I seem to recall hearing those names.'

'That's right, Terry. And the good news is, it shows part of your memory is returning. Let's see if we can help it along, shall we? We believe Gabriel Welham was the leader of the Country House Bandits. We found one extremely distinctive sculpture in his house, plus an oil painting, that match items stolen years ago from a stately home in Cheshire. We also know Welham owned several Mercedes cars, similar to the one used by the gang leader, and also the one you stole after you killed him.'

Palmer's face was a study, Clara thought, as he grasped the significance of Nash's opening remarks. He looked even more puzzled as the questioning continued remorselessly.

'Now we've established the connection, all we need to tie up the last threads is the motive. Was it greed, recompense for your years inside, or revenge for the death of Frank Watson, Joe Lambert, and Birdie Swallow? They were all stabbed to death, in two cases by Welham in person. Oh, and would you mind telling us where you disposed of the gun you used to shoot Welham and his girlfriend?'

'They're all dead? Frank, Joe, and Birdie? Just like I said yesterday? I don't think you're right, though. This man Welham couldn't have killed them. It was the monster that devoured them. I was there. I saw it happen.'

'Oh yes, I'd forgotten about the monster. Just refresh my memory, will you? Was it three heads or four the monster had?'

'Three.' Palmer's tone was surly. Clearly he'd recognized the disbelief in Nash's voice.

Everything changed, however, at Nash's next question. 'When did this happen? Was it while you were looking for the goat?'

Palmer had been staring morosely at the table, but at the mention of the word 'goat' his head jerked up, as if controlled by an invisible puppeteer. 'How did you know about the goat? Did they tell you? Have you found it? They must have it back.'

'Who must have it back?'

'The people who put me in the cell. I heard them talking, and that was the reason they needed me there, because the goat had escaped.'

Nash sighed wearily and signalled for Clara to make the closing announcement. 'I've heard enough of your nonsense, Terry, so we're going to proceed with the formalities, which means you will be charged with the murders of Gabriel Welham and Thelma Daley.'

Having completed the process by handing Palmer over to the care of the custody sergeant, Nash and Mironova reconvened with Superintendent Fleming.

'We're getting nowhere questioning Palmer, and I'm not sure it matters whether we continue or not. We've enough evidence to put to CPS and charge him,' Nash began. 'I'm beginning to wonder if he hopes to put us off the scent with the drivel he's spouting, or whether he's criminally insane, but either way, it's immaterial. We now have clear evidence of his guilt — the Mercedes where he was found, the stolen items of jewellery in his possession, and above all, the bloodstains on his clothing. Add to that his DNA found at the crime scene, and the only thing we're short of is the murder weapon. But I think we've more than enough to proceed without that.'

'Where are you with regard to motive?' Jackie asked.

'That's where it gets a bit tricky. It could be one of two reasons. It's possible Palmer confronted Welham, who we believe was one of the leading lights in the Country House Bandits, and demanded his share of the loot in return for being locked away for ten years. Alternatively, he might have learned that Lambert and Swallow had been murdered and decided to take his revenge. That puzzles me, though, because it came as a heck of a surprise to me when we discovered Welham was responsible for the Hand of Glory murders, and when our tame genius, Clara, found the swordstick we believe was used to stab Lambert and Swallow. How Palmer could have found out Welham had killed them is beyond me.'

* * *

Nash reviewed the evidence from Kirk Bolton Lodge. After examining the strange file retrieved from the study, he called for Clara to join him. 'Remember we were puzzled by that document with all the initials on it?' He held up the sheet of paper as he spoke.

'Yes, what of it?'

'Now we know Welham was one of the leaders of the Country House Bandits, isn't it likely he was involved with the Keeper in the other criminal activities?'

'That sounds logical, but where are you going with this?'

'I believe this —' Nash held up the paper — 'is an income and expenditure summary. If my guess is correct, those headings could represent the sources. IN(B) could stand for "Income (burglary)", IN(D) is "Income (drugs)", IN(PT) is "Income (people trafficking)", and (TOK) on the opposite side is "(To Keeper)".'

Everything Nash said made sense, and it was the following day when they received a shock of such seismic proportions it turned the whole case on its head.

CHAPTER THIRTY-EIGHT

Nash was first to arrive at the station, closely followed by the other members of the team. As he was passing through reception, Steve Meadows told him, 'There's an item of post addressed for your attention. I've put it on your desk.'

When he reached his office, Nash found a small padded envelope bearing his name on the address label. He opened the package, his curiosity roused. Seconds later, he examined the contents, and then called Viv Pearce to join him.

He handed Pearce a flash drive. 'Viv, this has just arrived in the post, addressed to me. Will you check it over to ensure it doesn't contain a virus that will send all our computers into orbit, or whatever happens when they get infected? After you've done that, we can see what it's about.'

Having given Pearce the drive, Nash placed the envelope on top of his in tray. Fifteen minutes later, Pearce called him through to inspect the contents of the flash drive.

Flanked by Clara and Adil, Nash watched as Pearce pressed the start button. The first image was a note of instructions, telling the viewer there was a point when it was necessary to fast-forward the following, and giving the times.

'What's that about?' Clara asked.

'Just watch,' Viv replied. 'I've only skimmed through.'

The video clearly showed the facade of a building, one Clara and Nash recognized immediately.

'That's Kirk Bolton Lodge,' Clara exclaimed.

'Yes, but keep watching. This next bit is where it gets really interesting.'

The scene changed to a darker one — obviously the camera had the facility to operate after nightfall. Soon, the detectives noticed a shadowy figure approaching the front of the property. Then Clara noticed something else. 'There's a light on in one of the downstairs rooms. Hang on, isn't that the room where the bodies were found?'

'Yes, but watch carefully, because it's all about to change,' Pearce told her.

Another five minutes passed, which seemed far longer to the detectives viewing the video for the first time. During this time, the sender had zoomed the footage. Suddenly another, far stronger, light blazed out through that room's window. The added illumination clearly displayed two figures seated in armchairs.

The detectives watched in surprise as another figure entered the room and confronted the occupants. Within seconds, there followed two bright flashes.

As the killer passed the window, Clara exclaimed, 'That's Terry Palmer's shirt!'

The victims were still alive. The intruder stood, as if waiting. After a few moments, he fired twice more.

The killer turned and headed out of the room, and the hall light was now visible. Across the other side of the house frontage, another light was switched on.

'That's the office,' Clara told the others.

Ten minutes passed before the light was off, and lights upstairs were being turned on, and then off, in various rooms.

'He's looking for something,' Adil said.

'Yes, the jewellery. He knows exactly what he's doing,' Nash commented.

Eventually, the lights were extinguished, and the killer returned to the sitting room.

What followed next almost defied belief. He walked across to the woman's chair, crouched in front of her, pulled her forward as if to hug her, then sat her back. He shuffled across on his knees to the man, and repeated the process.

'What the hell is he doing?' Clara asked.

'Making sure he has blood from both victims on his clothing. That's why he didn't kill them straight away. Had he done so, their hearts would have stopped pumping, and there wouldn't be sufficient blood for his needs. I could also suggest he's ensuring he leaves his DNA.'

They expected the drama to end there, but the assassin then appeared to sprinkle something near his victims, before finally leaving the scene of his crime. They thought there was nothing more to reveal, but after Pearce fast-forwarded the footage for what seemed an age, the detectives saw the Mercedes driving slowly along the tree-lined drive towards the gates.

Something in the footage concerned Nash, so he asked, 'Viv, can you rewind to where the killer is standing with his back to the camera, shortly after he shot the couple the first time?'

Clara noticed that Nash's voice was tense as he asked the question, and wondered why. The answer came soon afterwards. Pearce did as requested, and Nash then asked, 'Can you zoom in more on that frame, Viv?'

'I can do, to an extent, Mike. Hang on — he's wearing a hood. Like the type on a protective suit. But it's under his clothes. Why would he do that?'

They looked at the screen. 'You're right, Viv, he has. Well spotted.' He then asked his colleagues, 'How tall do you reckon that person is?'

The camera angle showed part of the room, which gave Clara some help in framing her answer. 'It's difficult to be completely accurate, because the windowsill cuts off the lower part of his legs. Judging by the Adams fireplace alongside him — they're about four feet high, which barely comes above his waist — I'd guess he must be at least six feet tall, possibly even more.'

'Why is that important, Mike?' Adil asked.

'Because if Clara's estimate is anywhere near correct, which I believe it is, Terry Palmer could not have murdered Gabriel Welham and Thelma Daley. Going from his prison record sheet, and having interviewed Palmer twice, I can say for definite that he's only five feet, four inches tall.'

* * *

Their viewing was interrupted at that point when Nash's phone rang. He moved into his office to take the call from Chief Constable Ruth Edwards.

'I've been away dealing with the drugs case,' she reminded him. 'I just wanted to phone and say well done to you and the team. Jackie's just brought me up to speed, and told me you have the Kirk Bolton case wrapped up and the killer in custody. Despite there being other murders being unsolved, I guess that means you can relax a bit.'

Nash couldn't resist the temptation to tease her. 'Yes, Ruth, we've been doing that by watching a film.' He laughed.

'I gather you are alone?'

'Yes, you know I am. Otherwise I would have called you ma'am. But what you said is wrong. We have also identified the killer responsible for the Hand of Glory mine murders, and the stabbings of the two Country House Bandits. That's down to Forensics, plus Clara's brilliant deduction. However, the action movie we've just seen proves we've got the wrong suspect in custody for the Kirk Bolton Lodge killings.'

'You're going to have to explain that one, Mike.'

Having told her about the DNA, plus the swordstick Clara found, he went on to explain, 'We were convinced Terry Palmer killed the couple at the Lodge, but I'm now certain he was the subject of an extremely clever frame-up. This conclusion isn't the result of any brilliant detective work, more down to sheer chance, plus the real killer being unaware he was being filmed when he shot Gabriel Welham and Thelma Daley.'

'Tell me more, please.'

'When I arrived this morning, someone had sent me a flash drive, anonymously. Viv loaded it onto his computer, and we've just watched the footage. It was obviously taken from covert surveillance cameras, sited in front of Kirk Bolton Lodge. This clearly shows the murders taking place, with the killer wearing a shirt identical to that belonging to Terry Palmer. The murderer's actions ensured Palmer's DNA was left at the crime scene, and his clothing was liberally covered in blood. However, the assassin couldn't have been aware of the camera, which clearly shows the person responsible for the murders. Unless Palmer donned a pair of stilts, he couldn't have killed that couple, because the footage proves the man responsible was almost a foot taller than Palmer.'

'That is bad news, but at least you've solved the other murders, or so you suggested. Who was responsible for all those killings?'

'That's where it gets really interesting. We're still waiting final confirmation, via DNA from the swordstick, but we believe Gabriel Welham was the person responsible for them all. His DNA was on the gun retrieved from the mine, and the presence of the swordstick in the umbrella stand at Kirk Bolton Lodge goes a long way to proving he murdered Lambert and Swallow.'

There was a pause as the chief took everything Nash had told her on board. 'There's another mystery here, one you've barely touched on.'

'What's that?'

'You haven't mentioned it, but it could be significant. Who had Kirk Bolton Lodge under covert surveillance, and was concerned enough to send you the flash drive proving Palmer's innocence? I think Jackie and I should visit Helmsdale this afternoon and watch that movie. Will you ensure you have some popcorn ready?'

Nash returned to the general office, and Clara summed up the new situation concisely. 'So, now we have to discover who positioned those surveillance cameras at Kirk Bolton

Lodge. Plus who framed Palmer for the murders, having first doped him with hallucinogenic drugs, sufficient to have him talking about three-headed monsters, dangerous crocodiles, and missing goats.'

There was a pause before Nash started to laugh.

'What's so funny, Mike?' Viv asked.

'Something Palmer told us during interview. He said, when he was put in a cell, he heard two of his captors talking. He thought one of them said they'd brought him there because they were looking for an escaped goat.'

'I still don't understand. Why is that funny?'

'I think Palmer either misheard — or didn't twig — what they were talking about. I believe what the man actually said was, "We've brought Palmer here, because we're looking for a scapegoat."'

CHAPTER THIRTY-NINE

It was to be a day of surprises, the second of these coming when Nash received the forensic report on the bloodstained swordstick. The head of the scientific team phoned the results in shortly after lunchtime, the call coinciding with the arrival of the chief constable, accompanied by Superintendent Fleming.

Nash listened to what the Forensic officer had to reveal with interest, thanked him, and after ending the call, went into the outer office to deliver the news. He waited until the visitors had watched the video from the flash drive, with Pearce acting as projectionist, and was pleased their opinion matched that of the other detectives.

'We'll have to put the wheels in motion for Palmer to be released,' Ruth Edwards told them. 'Is there any specific way you think we should handle it?'

'I think it should be done with as little publicity as possible,' Nash replied. 'We still don't know who committed the murders, and as things stand, they believe their plan to fit Palmer up has succeeded. I reckon they intended for him to have died before he was discovered in the car park. It would be useful if they were to remain ignorant of the fact that we believe him to have been framed, and in particular, for them not to learn how we realized he wasn't the killer. Given what has happened to Palmer's associates, he could now be in danger when he's released. We should provide some sort of protection.'

'I take your point. See to that would you, Jackie? Is there anything else we should know, Mike?'

'Yes, another interesting fact has just emerged. When you arrived, I was on the phone with the head of Forensics. He told me the swordstick has been tested, and the recent bloodstains are those of Joe Lambert and Birdie Swallow. I think that is absolute proof Gabriel Welham killed them. However, our boffins succeeded in finding another, older and quite minute specimen between the blade and the hilt. Obviously Welham missed it when he cleaned the sword.'

'Do they know who the blood belongs to?' Pearce and Hassan asked the question in chorus.

'They do indeed. And, to my mind, it removes the last remaining doubt regarding Welham's involvement with the Country House Bandits, and the motive for at least seven murders he committed. The DNA from the older blood matches that of Arthur Fawcett.'

'Who is Arthur Fawcett?' the chief constable asked.

'Arthur Fawcett, aka "Artful Artie", was a skilled burglar with convictions for safecracking. Apparently, there were few locks he couldn't bypass. Corey Davies told us Artful Artie was the technician who performed a key role in the Country House Bandits' operations back in the day.' Nash paused. 'Fawcett was murdered in Harrogate seven years ago. Having received deep penetrating stab wounds, such as might be delivered by a sword.'

'As you say, that seems to wrap the case up nicely, with the exception of the Kirk Bolton Lodge murders, which still remain a mystery,' Jackie Fleming remarked. 'Finding the person responsible for that crime has to be our priority.'

'Jackie's right,' the chief said. 'And I think you should look back in pride at what you've achieved over the past few weeks. In addition to getting a shoplifting gang and a couple of serial farm burglars behind bars, you've identified a murderer who has slaughtered seven victims. You've also recovered some very expensive stolen property, including a Lowry painting worth millions. That has to be an outstanding result.'

'That might be true,' Nash agreed. 'But there's one major outstanding problem. We still haven't identified the head of the organization.'

'I thought this Welham character was the gang leader?'

'No, there has to be someone else, someone even higher up the food chain than Welham.'

'What makes you think that?'

'When Corey Davies was removed from the Country House Bandits because he smashed a valuable piece of porcelain, someone blackmailed him into working for the drug-running operation. The person who did that was obviously part of the robbery gang, but was also involved in drugs, human trafficking, prostitution, and money laundering. We have found no concrete evidence yet to suggest Welham participated in those crimes. We believe he acted as second-in-command of the Country House Bandits. He was the cleaner — the hitman who disposed of those who became a threat or a liability. But in doing so, he became the biggest liability of all, because he was the only person privy to a closely guarded secret — the identity of the head honcho. So, the cleaner had to be disposed of as well.'

'That suggests we're still a long way from putting a lid on this appalling series of events.'

'I'm afraid that is absolutely correct.'

* * *

During the journey home that evening, Nash reflected on the day's revelations, focusing on Fleming's remarks and the chief constable's praise. It was all very well getting results on the major crimes they'd had to deal with, but there remained several unanswered questions, plus two unsolved killings. At present, they had no clue as to the identity of the man who had murdered Gabriel Welham and Thelma Daley. Even the motive they believed was behind the killings was only speculation.

There was also the perplexing aspect of how the Kirk Bolton Lodge case had been resolved, proving Palmer's innocence. Who had installed surveillance cameras in the grounds of the lodge? And what was their motive in keeping watch on Gabriel Welham? It was obviously not the work of the killer. The camera footage negated the murderer's elaborate and carefully planned frame-up of Terry Palmer. Sending that flash drive to the police would have been the last thing the killer wanted to happen.

Nash was driving past the end of Hillside Crescent, where Corey Davies lived, as he pondered the unknown person who had conducted the Kirk Bolton Lodge surveillance. Now they knew both Corey Davies and Gabriel Welham had been involved with the Country House Bandits, Nash wondered if these two events were in some way connected. An intruder had broken into Davies' house without stealing anything. Could there have been a totally different reason for this unusual intrusion? Had someone actually been monitoring the activities of anyone associated with the Bandits? Could they have entered Davies' house to remove some surveillance or recording device? If so, who was this mysterious person, and what was their objective?

Dwelling on the events at the Lodge provoked another memory, of that mysterious folder in Welham's desk and the conclusion he and Clara had drawn from the paperwork.

As to the day's other revelation, this threw up another mystery. After learning of the DNA on the swordstick, Nash had revisited the file covering the murder of Arthur 'Artful Artie' Fawcett. The most telling piece of information within the folder was the note, penned by DC Hassan, after researching Fawcett's background. Seven years down the line from Fawcett's murder, there was still no trace of his daughter. Joanne Fawcett had vanished only weeks after her father's death, and there was every reason to believe she had done so deliberately. Why was that? Had she been afraid for her life, or was there another, unconnected reason?

He had reached the outskirts of Helmsdale, and was pondering the other unsolved mystery, the identity of the head of the Country House Bandits, the one known only as 'The Keeper'. Who was he? And what was the significance of that nickname, if any?

He glanced sideways, noticing a group of boys playing soccer on the recreation ground to his left. As he passed, Nash remembered that several of the Bandits' burglary targets had been connected with professional football, in various ways. One had been an international player, another was a Premier League manager, and two others were directors of major clubs. Could that be the connection? If so, how were they linked?

These questions were sidelines to the main issue, which had been resolved via the team's excellent detective work. They had identified a killer who had ruthlessly murdered four gang members and four of their associates. It was an outstanding result, leaving only the deaths of the assassin and his mistress yet to be solved.

He arrived home and was, as usual, greeted by Teal. He patted her on the head, and she led him into the lounge. There he smiled at the sight. Alondra, the wife he thought he would never be able to marry, was seated on the sofa nursing their new daughter. Alongside her was Daniel, the son Mike hadn't known existed until the boy was six years old, who was stroking Lucy's fingers, tenderly. This scene was one Mike had never expected to experience.

He took his mobile from his pocket and quickly snapped the family, his family.

'That's one for the album,' he said.

THE END

ACKNOWLEDGEMENTS

It is unusual for an author to thank their ancestors, but on this occasion I feel I must. My great-grandmother Mary was one of the Green family of Greenhow, a village atop Greenhow Hill, a small hamlet of lead miners above Pateley Bridge in North Yorkshire. It was researching my past that led to the basic idea for *Death Sentence*.

Of course, I always thank my in-house editor, my wife, who keeps me on track, and my reader, Wendy McPhee, who tells me if everything makes sense — and where it doesn't.

And thanks to the staff at Joffe Books, too numerous to mention, other than Emma, Steph, Jodi, and Matthew, who work to ensure my work is available for my readers.

THE JOFFE BOOKS STORY

We began in 2014 when Jasper agreed to publish his mum's much-rejected romance novel and it became a bestseller.

Since then we've grown into the largest independent publisher in the UK. We're extremely proud to publish some of the very best writers in the world, including Joy Ellis, Faith Martin, Caro Ramsay, Helen Forrester, Simon Brett and Robert Goddard. Everyone at Joffe Books loves reading and we never forget that it all begins with the magic of an author telling a story.

We are proud to publish talented first-time authors, as well as established writers whose books we love introducing to a new generation of readers.

We won Trade Publisher of the Year at the Independent Publishing Awards in 2023. We have been shortlisted for Independent Publisher of the Year at the British Book Awards for the last four years, and were shortlisted for the Diversity and Inclusivity Award at the 2022 Independent Publishing Awards. In 2023 we were shortlisted for Publisher of the Year at the RNA Industry Awards.

We built this company with your help, and we love to hear from you, so please email us about absolutely anything bookish at feedback@joffebooks.com

If you want to receive free books every Friday and hear about all our new releases, join our mailing list: www.joffebooks.com/contact

And when you tell your friends about us, just remember: it's pronounced Joffe as in coffee or toffee!